TRICK PLAY

FAKE BOYFRIEND BOOK 2

EDEN FINLEY

TRICK PLAY

DISCLAIMER/TRIGGER WARNINGS

Please note that these characters have strong opinions on things. These are their own opinions and not that of the author. Just because Matt thinks cats are assholes, that doesn't mean Eden thinks that. Although, her cat can be an asshole at times.

She's also an Australian girl, so please excuse her serious lack of knowledge when it comes to American sports. She grew up on soccer, cricket, and rugby.

Matt was technically not eligible to be drafted when he was. Shhh, we're putting that down to editing error. Or we could use the argument that the NFL in these books in no way represent the real NFL. Yup, that works too.

(In other words, authors are humans and we make mistakes no matter how much research we put into our books. Apologies in advance.)

TRADEMARKS USED IN TRICK PLAY.

This is a work of fiction. As such, team names—like the Bulldogs, Warriors, and Cougars—are completely made up. The views in this book in no way reflect the views and principles of the NFL or any of their real teams.

Names of some colleges have been fabricated so not to misrepresent their policies and values, curriculum, or facilities.

Names, characters, businesses, places, events and incidents are either the products of the author's imagination or used in a fictitious manner. Any resemblance to actual persons, living or dead, or actual events is purely coincidental.

CHAPTER ONE

MATT

It was the punk-ass cocky smile on his face that did me in, but the five drinks on an empty stomach didn't help. I was usually more careful. With the bass thrumming through me, a buzz in my veins, and a sea of available hookups dancing and grinding in front of me, I dropped my guard.

A loss always made me needy, even more so when it blew our chances to go to the Super Bowl. Our season was done, and this random guy, with his dark hair and bright eyes, made me forget all that. It wasn't a common thing—hooking up in a club— but it wasn't the first time I'd done it. Had no delusion it would be the last either.

I wasn't the type of closet case to put on a show by parading women around. No, I was the type who kept to myself, put my head down, and stayed out of trouble. But on nights where I just ... *needed*, I couldn't stop myself. I needed an adrenaline fix—a high—even if it was in the form of meaningless sex. I needed a sense of accomplishment. It wasn't like a win on the field, but it was the closest thing to it.

No words were spoken. There was no need for any. I lost myself in the random stranger and didn't even flinch when he took my cap off—my safety net. Or when he kissed me. I was too far gone to notice the assholes with cell phones who'd recognized me. And even when the flashes went off, I was too distracted by a hot, wet mouth making me moan.

That was the last time I'd ever be known as Matt Jackson, tight end for the Bulldogs. From that moment, I was Matt Jackson, that gay football player who got caught with his pants down.

"Matt," a deep voice says.

I'm brought out of the memory of that night and thrust into the seriousness of my present. My knee bounces as the two suits behind the desk explain how they're going to *fix* me. No, not me, my *image*. Apparently the two things are separate, but I ain't so sure. I'm as broken as my image is.

"The photos of you in the nightclub make you look sleazy and predatory," the old dude says.

I glare at Damon, my actual agent, but because he's a noob, the other guy is here to oversee everything and make sure Damon doesn't screw it up. I'm his first official client. The gay ex-baseball player representing a recently outed football megastar? The media is going ape-shit over us.

I should count myself lucky. When my scandal hit, my previous representation dropped me. My endorsements left. My contract with the Pennsylvania Bulldogs was up, and surprise, surprise, they weren't interested in renewing. My career was dead. If it wasn't for my ex-roommate and regular hookup from college, Maddox, introducing me to his boyfriend, Damon, I never would've signed with OnTrack Sports.

"Predatory is the wrong word," Damon says before I can put the old guy in his place. "But the pictures don't work in your favor."

"And how do you propose we fix it?" I ask. "Those photos are out there forever. There's nothing we can do about that."

"Instead of hiding, we throw you into the public more," Damon says.

I groan. "No football team wants to invite the circus to town. I just want to play."

"And to play football, you have to look like you're not hoping a teammate drops the soap," the old dude says. I should learn his name so I'll know who to add to my ever-growing shit list.

Even Damon cringes at him this time, but he can't say anything—the asshole is his boss.

"I'm not into straight guys, thanks," I say.

"You need to appear taken and not interested," Damon says, more diplomatically. "The photos were taken months ago, right? We address the issue by saying it's a non-issue anymore. Since then, you've met someone, fallen in love, and are in a committed and serious relationship. You won't be hooking up with randoms in bars, you won't be getting arrested for DUIs, you won't—"

"I ain't ever been arrested for a DUI. I've never been arrested, period."

"We know that, but you think the media cares?" Damon says. "They'll pin anything they can on you. You're in the spotlight now whether you like it or not, and it's your job to appear employable by a team. *Any* team. Because right now, you're in limbo. We've got two months before training camp to get you a contract."

"So, I have to find a boyfriend. That's what you're sayin'?"

"We found you one already," Damon says.

"What?"

"My friend Noah. You met him at his place where Maddox introduced us."

I barely remember anything that's happened since the photos were released, so I only have a vague memory of that night. I never understood the phrase "on autopilot" until my world fell into an unknown abyss. All conversations from the last few weeks are a blur.

"Noah's cool," Damon says. "Can be a dick at times, but it's a front. I called in a favor and already got him to agree to this."

"So, just like that, you're pimpin' me out, huh?" I'm not trying to be a surly asshole, but this is my *life*. I also hate that my accent, which I've trained myself to get rid of, seeps into my words the more agitated I get.

"This is a business arrangement," Damon says. "We're setting up some PR events for you two to attend together, and we're going to announce your relationship after the cruise we've booked for you to get to know each other. Seven nights round trip to Bermuda. Maddy and I are coming too."

"Shouldn't you be here trying to find me a contract instead of going on a cruise? Shouldn't I be doing something else? Somethin' football related?"

"Matt." Great, even Damon's getting over my attitude. "Your main focus should be on fixing your image, because without doing that, you won't see a contract."

"Aren't there rules in the league about anti-discrimination?"

"I have another meeting," the old guy says and turns to Damon. "You can handle it from here."

When he leaves, Damon sighs. "Look, if we could take the discrimination road, we would, but it won't achieve what we want. If you were happy to retire from football with a nice lump sum payout, we could maybe fight this. But the truth is, we'll probably lose."

"Why? Contract negotiations were going fine until I was outed."

"All sports contracts include a morality clause. Even if those photos had been of you with a woman, the Bulldogs would've had the right to dump your contract. Would they have if it'd been a woman? Probably not. But we can't prove that. They *can* prove your morality is questionable after getting freaky in a club with a random guy. Again, if it'd been a woman, you might be facing the same scrutiny."

"That's bullshit, and you know it. There have been rape allegations around some players, and they never got fired."

"Well, fuck, Matt." Professional Damon is replaced with friend Damon. I reckon I like him better than the suit he hides behind. "What do you want to do about it? You can fight for your reputation and try to win back your spot in the NFL or ride the rainbow train into court and possibly lose everything. In a perfect world, this would all blow over, but we both know that's not how *our* world works. When I played baseball and there were rumors of me being the number one draft pick, the pressure was doubled because I was an openly gay player. The media jumps on this shit because people think they have a right to know everything about everyone's business—especially athletes and famous people—because it bumps up their ratings. With any luck, another football scandal will break before training camp and you'll be pushed out of the spotlight. But until that happens, you're it, and we need to do everything to make sure the rest of the articles posted about you are positive."

"Nice pep talk," I grumble. "When's the cruise?"

"Two weeks."

I fake a smile. "Can't wait."

The plan is to leave checking in to the last possible moment, but two hours before I'm set to leave the hotel Damon's agency put me up in last night, there's a knock on my door, and standing behind it is the guy hired to be my boyfriend for a few months.

Noah Huntington III. I had to Google him. As soon as his picture popped up on my screen, I recognized him from that night I met Damon. Of course, of all the people I met that night, Noah had to be the hottest one there. Only problem with that is he knew it too. His mansion didn't impress me, but his piercing blue-green eyes that somehow held both arrogance and charm had me wishing Maddox hadn't left me alone to do God knows what to Damon in the spare bedroom of Noah's house.

And now I'm going to be stuck with him for months. Great.

His father is the former governor of New York and is now a democratic senator. He's an old white dude, and his mother is African-American. Toss in a gay son, and they're the picture-perfect family for a utopian world where it doesn't matter what race, religion, or orientation you are.

I understand why Damon chose Noah to be my boyfriend, but I worry it's too gimmicky—too *let's shove our point down people's throats*. It feels *fake*.

That's because it is, dumbass.

Those annoyingly hypnotic blue-green eyes stare back at

me, and a smirk plays on Noah's lips. Dark skin and toned muscles, all wrapped up in the confidence of a rich trust-fund kid. I hate to admit it, but it makes me dislike him already because I *envy* him.

I also can't call him a kid when he's three years older than me.

The only time I've ever exuded Noah's type of confidence is on the field. Football has been my escape from everything. It's been my savior. My focus. Now I'm being forced to show off the side of me I've been hiding forever.

Hiding wasn't by choice; it was a necessity. There have only been a handful of gay players in NFL history, but the ones who have come out publicly have all done so after retirement or got cut during preseason.

"Matt?" Noah brings me out of yet another inner freak out about my career falling apart. He reaches for my shoulder and squeezes. It's supposed to be a reassuring gesture, but all it does is make me keenly aware that a hot guy is touching me. We won't be crossing those lines—this is business and nothing else— so I flinch away from him.

His brow furrows. "You okay? You're not stroking out on me, are you?"

"Sorry." I step aside to let him in.

When he brushes past me, he meets my eyes and smiles. He has an athletic build like a basketball player—all arms and legs— and is almost my height, but he's skinny. Then again, it's probably unfair to compare him to my two-hundred-thirty-pound frame.

Noah wheels his suitcase in behind him.

"I thought we were meeting on the ship," I say.

"Damon told me to get down here so we can arrive together.

OTS either has a leak or maybe the cruise ship company has talkative staff. There's paparazzi set up at the terminal. We're supposed to act coy as if we don't know they're going to be at the docks."

"Goddamn it. This is already turning into a shit show." How much longer will this be a story? "Make yourself at home. I'll pack."

"You're not packed?" Noah asks.

"I planned on going last minute."

"Good idea. Keep them waiting."

"Right." Like I planned this.

All I need to do is shove my toothbrush and shaving kit in my bag, even though I didn't end up using the razor this morning. I haven't shaved in weeks. My beard is impressive, and I can't be bothered getting rid of it.

It takes all of two minutes to pack my stuff, while Noah sits on my hotel bed, tapping away on his phone.

Trading my Bulldogs cap for an old Yankees one, I pull it on and a pair of aviators that cover half my face.

"You think changing your hat will make you more inconspicuous?" Noah asks, phone still in hand.

I hate those things. Never used to. Now when I see them, I'm paranoid someone's taking a photo of me. And mine? It goes off every two minutes and has for the past several weeks. The off button is my only savior.

"Matt?" Noah asks. "Are you always this spacey?"

"Are you always this nosy?"

Noah throws his hands up in surrender. "No need to bite my head off. But seriously, don't let Damon see you in that ball cap. He'll probably drop you as a client."

"Mets fan?"

"The biggest. Like psycho about it."

"The other hat I have is my Bulldogs one."

"Here, we'll swap." Noah throws his Mets cap at me.

"Won't Damon be pissed at you for the Yankees hat?"

Noah grins. "It'll be a good way to mess with him."

"Sounds like a healthy friendship." I slip his hat on and pull it down low.

I double-check I haven't forgotten anything while Noah waits for me in the hallway.

When we head for the elevators to go down to the garage, I avoid eye contact and don't bother saying anything either. Like Damon said, this is a business arrangement. Pure and simple. I don't need to be friends with the guy to make it look like we're together or whatever.

Personally, I don't think this charade will work in getting me a contract or fixing my image. I don't see how it could work. If I do get on another team, having a boyfriend won't mean shit in the locker room. I'll still get the stare downs, the slurs, the threats ... The world may be more tolerant now, but we're far from acceptance. Especially in the sporting world where closet doors have only recently started to creak open.

Noah taps away on his phone through the halls of the hotel and in the elevator. The tap, tap, tapping noise has me gritting my teeth. I want to throw his phone at the wall.

"You okay?" Noah asks, his eyes not even on me but on his screen.

"I'm fine."

"Yeah, seems it."

"How would you even know? Your eyes are glued to that thing." I tip my head in the direction of his phone.

Noah shoves it in his pocket. "There. Gone. Now what's up?"

"You mean apart from the obvious? My career's in the toilet and my representation thinks I'm so desperate they have to find a boyfriend for me? Yeah, my life's fucking grand right now."

He averts his gaze as he mutters, "What did Damon sign me up for?"

CHAPTER TWO

NOAH

Free cruise, he said. Pretend to be Matt Jackson's boyfriend, he said. It'll be fun, he said. You know what Damon didn't say? That Matt Jackson is a miserable asshole.

A *hot*, miserable asshole with his muscles, tanned skin, and tattoo sleeve. Don't even get me started on the beard he's growing out. But all of that aside, he's still miserable.

Damon owes me big time. I'd text him and complain, but apparently my phone is evil—if the way Matt glares at it is any indication.

These next few months are going to be fun. Why did I agree to this again?

Oh, right. I want to take my father's *Don't do anything to ruin my political image* warning and shove it up his—

The elevator opens to the glass alcove of the basement garage. "Fuck a duck," Matt says out of nowhere.

"What?"

He tips his head in the direction of the doors. There await two paparazzi for him to make his exit.

"How did they get in the garage?" I ask.

"Who knows." Matt hangs his head. "How they knew I was at this hotel is the bigger question." He stares at my pocket where my phone is as if that holds an answer.

"Paranoid much? I didn't rat you out. This fake relationship thing is going to get plenty of publicity without me adding to it." Talk about trust issues.

His eyes dart to the guys outside the door and back to me. "Let's get this over with." Matt grabs my hand and pulls me through the garage. His grip is deathly and not at all loving or romantic-looking. It looks like we're trying too hard.

"Ease up, would you?" I make sure the reporters can't hear. "They'll think you're kidnapping me or forcing me if you hold on any tighter."

Matt's hold on me loosens but not by much. I fix it by prying my hand free and throwing my arm around him casually. His stiff shoulders give me nothing to work with, and my arm slides right off. Forcing it to stay on his shoulder would photograph even more awkward than the death grip he had on my hand. Improvising, I pretend I'm trying to shield him from the cameras as we rush to the car.

"Give me the keys and you get in the passenger side," I say.

"Nobody drives my Lambo but me."

Great, a car nut. "Fine. Get in the driver's seat but pop the trunk for me."

Quicker than humanly possible, I put my suitcase and his duffel bag in the trunk and climb in the passenger seat.

The two photographers shove their cameras in my face, and if they're good at their jobs, I'll be identified before we get to the docks. The story will hit the media sites before the ship departs, which means I'll be in cell range when Dad finds out. His people no doubt have a Google alert set up for me.

I was hoping to be halfway to Bermuda before he found out. The fallout will be so much more spectacular if he can't get a hold of me for seven days.

Matt's hesitant on the accelerator.

"Just run them over," I say.

"Yeah, that'll clean up my image. I can see the headlines now. *Matt Jackson in Altercation with Paparazzi.*"

Damn it. Something in my gut churns. I think it might be sympathy, but that can't be right. It has to be hard being Matt Jackson, but Noah Huntington usually doesn't care about other people's lives.

Maybe it's empathy. Being the son of a prominent senator who's got *future presidential candidate* written all over him, I've had my share of being in the media, so I've had a taste of what he's going through. When I was a teenager, papers liked to print lame stories about the mayor's son being caught at an illegal, underage bonfire in the Hamptons and other harmless articles that weren't seen as reckless to anyone but my father and his precious image. But this? This is a bloodbath.

Matt's been dubbed the bad boy of football—gay edition. Random hookups in nightclubs, drunken antics, and a drug problem probably. Damon tells me the drug addiction is fabricated, but the media doesn't care about facts.

"You know where you're going?" I ask when we finally crawl out of the underground garage.

"No idea."

"There's a reason OTS booked you a room here. The cruise terminal is a few blocks that way." I point.

I get a nod in response. Why do I get the feeling this is what I'm going to have to endure for the foreseeable future?

I take out my phone, much to Matt's disgust.

"Can't you go two minutes without that thing?" he asks. If he's going to give me attitude, I'll give it right back.

"Nope."

NOAH: *YOU OWE ME. I THOUGHT I WAS A FAKE BOYFRIEND. NOT A FAKE HUSBAND.*

DAMON: *FAKE HUSBAND?*

NOAH: *WE'RE ALREADY ACTING LIKE A MARRIED COUPLE. IS HE ALWAYS THIS CRANKY?*

DAMON: *OH. UMM … MADDOX SAYS HE'S NOT, BUT I'VE ONLY KNOWN HIM TO BE SURLY.*

NOAH: *SOMETHING YOU CONVENIENTLY LEFT OUT WHEN YOU ASKED ME TO DO THIS THING.*

He responds with the angel emoji. Asshole.

"Where to now?" Matt asks.

With my instructions, we pull up to the terminal and drop the car off in long-term parking. Matt scoffs at my six-thousand-dollar Gucci suitcase as he pulls his no-name-brand duffel bag out of the trunk.

"Okay, what's wrong with my luggage?" I ask.

He shakes his head as if the answer is obvious and stalks off.

Yup, Damon definitely owes me.

We follow the path like the rest of the cruise guests being herded toward the ship, but when I catch sight of the paparazzi lining the entrance, I freeze. We were told there'd be media, but it must be a slow news day, because this is insane. I count at least fifteen people holding obnoxiously large cameras.

Matt stops in his tracks. "I-I can't ... I can't do this," he says quietly.

People bump past us and glare for holding them up.

I've seen the articles online and, well, everywhere, but it's not until I'm staring down the lens of a million cameras all wanting a photo of us that I realize it's not just a matter of a photo. It's the need for a story. The more scandalous the better. And right now, there is no bigger scandal than Matt.

I pretend I'm unaffected, but the truth is, it's a whole lot more daunting being on this side of it.

"It's easy. We walk through the crowd, say *no comment* every five seconds, and ignore everything else."

Matt's feet lock to the ground, his skin pales, and it looks like he could vomit. "I ..."

"Matt," I murmur. "We need to move. We're standing in the middle of the walkway, and you can't afford to freeze up right now."

The media spots us, and they begin converging.

"Babe, I left something in the car," I say loud enough for them to hear. I turn back and head toward the parking lot, weaving my way through a few more people heading for the terminal. I practically have to drag Matt who's in shutdown mode.

A parking attendant stands by the boom gate of the garage, and I wave him over. "Is there anything you can do about the photographers over there?"

The dude's eyes flit from Matt to me and back again. "Umm ... I ... I'm sorry, but are you Matt Jackson?"

"Yes. He is. So, can you see why we wouldn't mind bypassing the swarming vultures?"

"Right. But, uh, there's only one way onto that ship, so no matter what, you're going to have to get past them."

"Thanks for nothing," I mumble and continue to drag Matt back to his car.

A quick look over my shoulder shows one or two ambitious assholes with cameras coming our way.

I pin Matt up against his car and lean in, speaking low. "Okay, you're going to have to snap out of whatever panic attack you're having, because we're thirty seconds away from being photographed again, and you look like you're about to shit a brick."

Matt manages a nod, but I'm not convinced he's not going to freak out again as soon as flashes start going off in his face.

But the photographers are on us, and I do the only thing I can think of to snap him out of his trance. I cradle his head and bring my mouth to his, all the while hoping his eyes haven't grown to the size of saucers. That wouldn't make for a great photo.

Matt tenses, his mouth not responding to mine. My lips are soft against the steel bars that have taken residence on his face. His overgrown facial hair has gotten past the scruffy stage and is soft against my smooth skin.

"Better do a better job than that," I whisper against his lips so the paparazzi can't hear.

"If it weren't for the photographers, I'd kick your ass right now, Huntington."

"Let's not play the last name game, *Jackson*. I'm *helping* you here."

"Seems like you're tryin' to get your time in the spotlight."

I pull back but stay close. "Let's have this conversation somewhere else. You ready to face them?"

"No."

"Need me to kiss you again?"

He frowns. "Fine. Let's go."

Huh. He'd rather deal with the media than kiss me. Someone get me a crash cart, because my ego just flatlined.

Suddenly Matt has no issues with walking through a crowd full of photographers. It's slow going, and I make sure to keep my face neutral as the flashes go off in my eyes.

Damon told me I'm supposed to sell this lie, but I'll bet if I were to reach out and grab Matt's hand, he'd swat it away. Or try to break my bones.

When we make it through the throng of media and into the terminal building, Matt doesn't relax at all. Lines of people fill the space, and there's not much room to move.

Matt doesn't stop glancing around as if looking for an emergency exit.

When we finally get to the front of our line and check in our baggage, we're given our room keys but told the rooms aren't open yet.

Matt tries to hide it, but he tenses, and his eyes practically bug out of his head. He needs to get away from the crowds before he freezes up again or, even worse, loses it in front of everyone.

I lean in and lower my voice as I ask the check-in lady, "Is that really true or is it more convenient if we're not in the rooms?" I tip my head in Matt's direction. "You know who that is? Think we can catch a break here?"

The woman looks Matt up and down, and her eyes light up in recognition. "I'll have a look for you, sir." She types something into her computer. "Housekeeping has your room all set, so you're free to go there. I'll put a push on getting your luggage to you immediately."

"Thank you."

The plan is to take Matt straight to the room until he chills the fuck out, but as soon as we clear the gangway and reach the welcoming lounge, we both stop short at a woman wearing a towel and hissing at Damon and Maddox.

"Who the hell is that?" Matt asks.

I recognize her when she flips her wet, blonde hair. "That's Stacy. Damon's sister. Looks like he's in trouble."

"Should we—"

I put my hand on his chest to prevent him from going over there. "Don't. You don't want to see Stacy pissed. And considering she's only wearing a towel and yelling? No one on this ship is safe."

We leave Maddox and Damon to their tongue lashing and try to find our room. The halls of the ship are so narrow they barely fit Matt's wide frame. When we weave our way past guests and finally find our room, we can't get inside fast enough. Matt leans against the door and breathes a huge sigh of relief.

OTS must be cheap-asses to put us up in a regular stateroom instead of a suite, but I won't voice that aloud. Everyone already sees me as the spoiled rich guy, and at least we have a balcony.

"What the fuck was that?" Matt asks.

"Stacy yelling at Damon or—"

"The kiss."

"Oh, we're still on that, are we?"

"That's not ... we're not ... we need some ground rules."

God, this guy is unbelievable. "Dunno if you know this, but boyfriends kiss, and the vultures on your ass think we're together. Also, you were about to flip your shit at them. You didn't give me much option."

"This is a business arrangement, and I don't know what your game is yet, but I ain't gonna let you use me to get famous or land a reality show or whatever you're here for."

"There goes my dream of becoming a regular on *Keeping Up with the Kardashians*," I say dryly. "Are you seriously this pessimistic?"

"Well, you cain't be here for the money. You're loaded." The angrier he gets, the more drawled his words become, and I hate that it's adorable.

"I'm not even getting paid. I'm here as a favor, you jackass."

Wow, about an hour into our relationship, we're already fighting. This is only one of the reasons I don't do real relationships. What was I thinking saying yes to this?

You know why, my conscience reminds me.

"Are you really standing there telling me there's nothin' in this for you? Why would you agree to this?" Matt asks.

"Because Damon's probably the closest person to me in this world, and he asked me to do it. Maybe, I'm a decent guy." *Underneath all the bullshit.*

Matt stares at me as if he doesn't believe me.

I roll my eyes. "Believe what you want, but trust me when I say I don't have to play tricks or manipulate you to get my face in the media. I've already got it by standing next to you. You're everywhere."

"I don't want to be everywhere," he yells. "I just wanna play football. It's all I fucking have." Matt sits on the bed and runs his hands through his wild hair. "*Had.*"

I grit my teeth and squeeze his shoulder in a reassuring gesture, even if he is being an ass. "And I'm here to help you get football back." *Annoying my dad in the process is just a bonus.* "How about we go find Damon and see what's on our agenda?"

"We have an agenda?"

"He told me about some magazine shoot and interview, but I don't know when that is."

"W-what?" Matt pales. "I'm not doing interviews."

I throw my hands up. "Don't shoot the messenger."

"Fuck this." Matt stomps his way to the door but turns at the last second. "You comin'?"

Has it been a few months yet?

"Where's your boyfriend?" Matt barks at Maddox when we find him in the bar area.

"Headache. He's napping."

"Why was Stacy yelling at you earlier?" I ask.

A redheaded guy I've never seen before comes to Maddox's side.

"Holy shit, you're Matt Jackson," he blurts out.

Just what we need—random people approaching Matt. I'm about to tell him to fuck off, but in a nice way, when Maddox says, "Aaand this is my very uncool friend, Jared. He's the reason Stacy was naked and yelling at us earlier. She didn't know he'd be here."

Matt hesitantly holds out his hand for Jared to shake. "Just Matt is fine. You don't need to use my last name. Especially so loud." He glances around the small bar.

"I'm Noah," I say and lift my chin in greeting.

"When will Damon finish napping?" Matt asks. "He's supposed to talk to us about what exactly we're doing here."

"We're about to leave port," Maddox says, "so why don't you go up to the main deck and wave at all the paparazzi back on land. Maybe give one of them the finger while you're at it."

"Yeah, Damon would have my balls if I do that," Matt says.

"I don't think you have a future in PR," I add.

Maddox shrugs. "Fine. Do what you want. I'm going to drink."

Jared points at Maddox. "*That* is a great idea. I'm in."

"I read they have an onboard gym, so guess I'll be there if you need me." Matt stalks off, and his strides are long and fast as if he can't get away fast enough.

"Great. You guys set me up with a gym rat," I say.

"He plays for the NFL. That's a given," Maddox points out.

"Guess I'm going to the gym then," I say. "Damon told me not to leave Matt's side this whole week, but he's not giving me much to work with. Is he always this standoffish?"

"He's been through a lot," Maddox says. "Cut him some slack."

"Fine," I say. "But I'm playing nice, and he keeps rebuffing me. He knows I'm doing him a favor by going along with this, right?"

"It's not like you have anything better to do. You just can't handle that Matt doesn't want you," Maddox says. "Does your poor ego need stroking?"

"You going to do it?"

"Pass."

"What did they teach you guys at Olmstead University? You both obviously can't see quality when you find it." It's no secret I hit on Maddox when I first met him. Damon needed some healthy competition to get him to admit he had a thing for Maddox.

I give Maddox and his friend a wave and chase after Matt. He's not in the room, and I assume he went straight to the gym seeing as he was already wearing sweatpants. I change out of my jeans and into my gym shorts, put on my sneakers, and then make my way to the onboard gym.

I find Matt on a machine in the corner. His long, powerful legs carry him on a treadmill. His tight ass, strong body ... It's a shame he's an asshole because we so could've turned this game into a few months of sweaty fun.

My cock likes that idea.

No, I say to him. *We're not allowed to like that guy, so down, boy.*

When I jump on the machine next to him, he leaves and goes to the weights section.

Okay, I guess that's how it's going to be.

Half an hour goes by and then an hour. I think he's done when he goes to fill up his water bottle, but nope. He chugs it back and then heads to another machine.

By hour two of nonstop working out, I'm fairly certain I'm dying. I wobble my way on shaky legs over to Matt who's now on a rowing machine. "Are you done yet?"

He shakes his head and breathes hard. "Another hour."

"Well, I'm heading back to the room. If I can make it that far." I can't be sure, but as I slip away, I swear he chuckles. But Matt laughing? So far that seems impossible, so I assure myself I'm hearing things.

After a long and hot shower to loosen my muscles, I check my phone, which I purposefully left in the room while working out. As expected, there are voicemails from my mom and dad. We're too far out at sea now, so I can't call my service to see what they say, but I'm certain I already know.

"What are you doing in the tabloids with that football player? Do you know how this looks? Break it off. Immediately." And Mom's would be *"Why do you have to upset your father?"*

When I see there's five text messages from Aron, my stomach rolls. I don't know if I can deal with him yet, although I thought this reaction might've been coming. Maybe I should've warned him, but I haven't spoken to him for a month, so I thought it'd be too weird to message him and be all *"Heads-up, I'm dating Matt Jackson now, so I'm going to be everywhere for a while."*

Aron and I went through all of college and three years of friendship without hooking up. For some reason, this past year, we thought it was a good idea to start sleeping together. It's the dumbest thing I've ever done, because while I like the guy, I knew I would never fall for him. I was clear from the beginning it was going to be casual, and he agreed at first. Then a few months ago, he wanted the real deal, so I broke it off, but he'd still come back for more and promise he could keep it casual. I'm an idiot for going there in the first place. Fuck buddies never work. Someone always gets hurt in the end, and part of me wishes it was me this time, because besides Damon, Aron's the closest thing I have to a real friend. Or, at least he was until I screwed it up.

I bypass the messages from Aron and check the one from Damon which was sent two hours ago. It says Matt and I have dinner reservations at one of the fancy-ass restaurants onboard, so I dress in a gray Gucci suit and wait for Matt.

Another two hours pass before he enters the room, drenched in sweat.

"Seriously?" I say. "Four hours of training?"

"You think I have these muscles from sitting on my ass?" He

takes his shirt off and points to his abs, and my breath catches in my throat. "It's my job to stay fit."

Taut muscles and tattoos. All the things on a guy that moms don't want their kids to bring home for family dinners. My eyes lock on his shoulder tatt and its intricate design that makes his biceps look even more impressive.

Matt heads for the bathroom and breaks my gaze away.

"Good luck in there. If I struggled to fit in the shower, you have no hope. Also, we have dinner reservations in fifteen minutes, so you have to hurry up."

I get a grunt in response.

It's official. I'm dating a caveman. Fake dating, but still.

If only he talked like a caveman and produced a few syllables all the time, I might actually like the guy. I thought I was capable of being an asshole, but Matt has that act down in spades.

CHAPTER THREE

Noah reaches for my hand on top of the candlelit table. My back stiffens and the urge to pull away is too much. As casually as I can, I slide my hand from beneath his and put it in my lap.

"Okay, what's up with that?" Noah asks.

"What's up with what?"

He glances around the restaurant. We're one of only a few couples in here, and I assume it's because it's one of the restaurants you have to pay extra for.

Moving closer, Noah speaks low. "Is it a PDA thing? Because I'm pretty sure the whole point of us being here is to show off how much we're in love, and that's not going to happen if these people see you pull away from me. We'll need to work out a way we can look like we're in love that doesn't interfere with whatever weird touching thing you're against."

"I'm not against PDA," I snap. "I'm just ... not used to it." The only time I allowed myself to touch another man was in those clubs—when I pretended I was someone else.

Noah leans back in his seat. "How many people knew you were gay before the tabloids outed you?"

I breathe in deep and reach for the glass of wine Noah ordered as soon as we walked into this stupid restaurant.

"Matt ..."

"None, okay."

"None? But you hooked up with Maddox in college."

I shrug. "Doesn't mean I told him I was gay. We had a mutual understanding that it was fooling around. We both claimed to be straight even when we were ... doing not so straight things."

Noah smiles. "You're trying really hard to be vague right now, aren't you?"

I lean in. "I'm scared if I talk about Maddox too loudly it'll somehow magically summon Damon and he'll kick my ass for even remembering I've seen Maddox naked."

Noah lifts his hand. "Whoa, whoa, whoa, let's pause there for a second. You made a joke? An honest to God joke?"

I take a deep breath. "Contrary to my behavior today, I'm not an asshole all the time. This"—I wave my hand between us —"this whole thing stresses me out. I don't know how to be a couple in public because I've never been a couple in public. I've never been a couple, period."

"*Never?*"

"I couldn't afford for it to get out. I didn't want to force someone to live in the closet for God knew how long, and I've never trusted anyone enough to keep my secret."

"How'd that work out for ya?" Noah gestures to where we are and why we're here.

"Turns out anonymous hookups in clubs aren't so trust-worthy either."

"You don't say."

"You try being celibate and see how long you last before you're scoping for BJs in a seedy nightclub."

"Thanks to you, I guess I'm going to be celibate for however long you need me to be your boyfriend."

I hadn't even thought of that. Since the scandal, I've had no desire to get back out there again, but it didn't occur to me that Noah offering to do this means he's been put in the exact same situation I'm in.

"I'm sorry."

Noah smiles. "This just became my favorite place on the ship. A joke and an apology within minutes of each other? Is this place magical?"

I sigh. Loudly.

"Oh wait, he's back. Never mind."

"Why do I have the feeling you get your ass kicked a lot?"

Noah smirks. "If my big, bad daddy didn't have a list of lawyers longer than the Kardashian's family tree, I'm sure I would've been beaten up a lot more."

"Look, I know I've been an ass, and I want to thank you for what you did today—getting me out of the parking lot and away from the reporters as fast as you could. I'll try not to be ornery, but—"

"You're going through a lot. Don't worry about me having to be celibate or needing to sell this lie. I knew what I signed up for."

"Why *did* you agree to this?"

Noah's excuse that he's doing it for Damon doesn't make a whole lot of sense to me.

"I have my reasons just like you do." Noah sips his wine before adding, "I did think you'd be more thankful, though."

"I am. Thankful, I mean. I may not understand how this is going to work or how it'll help me get a contract, but Maddox says I can trust Damon, so I'm going with it. I don't mean to be an ass, but I'm gambling my entire livelihood on this working."

Noah nods. "It's a lot of pressure."

Now that we're in the middle of the ocean and away from stupid photographers, it's the first time I've been able to breathe since my news broke.

"So, truce?" I ask. "Can we start this thing over again?"

He stares at me without answering a little too long, and it makes me shift in my seat. Noah holds up his glass of wine for a toast. "Truce."

The truce lasts all of dinner before everything goes to shit. As soon as we get back to the room, Noah hands me a beer from the minibar, and I start to go out onto the small balcony, but Noah pulls me back.

"Maybe we should talk in here. I was out there earlier, and I could hear people talking a few cabins down."

With a nod, I plant my ass on the small sofa in the room, and then Noah takes the seat next to me.

The sound of water crashing over the bow still reaches the room from the black abyss that is the Atlantic Ocean. It's peaceful until Noah opens his mouth again.

"We should make out."

I choke and splutter on my beer. "Why in the hell should we do that?"

"I'm not hitting on you, you jackass."

"Pretty sure askin' me to kiss you contradicts that statement."

"Hear me out. You're uncomfortable in public, and we don't know each other. The way to make it look natural is if we *are* natural. Therefore, if we make out, you'll loosen up."

I hate that he has a point, but we can't cross those lines. "We should make this a purely platonic arrangement so there's no confusion."

"There will be no confusion on my part. I understand why you'd be hesitant, because, well, look at me. You're worried about liking it too much." Noah gestures to himself, and I force myself not to look.

"Yeah, you're lucky I haven't jumped you already." Even though he does have a great body. Damn him.

"I could goad you into doing it, but I don't think I have to. You know this is a good idea."

"It's really not."

"Scared you're going to fall for me?" he taunts. "All the boys do."

"Fall for your wallet, maybe," I mumble.

His eyes turn a stormy gray as they narrow, and if looks could kill—

"Fall for you after one kiss?" I scoff. "Not possible." It's not possible after multiple kisses. I reckon I'm incapable of love, because I don't know what the fuck it is.

Noah moves closer.

"Noah ..." I shift on the seat.

"You're way too uptight. I promise I'm not trying to fuck you. Although, that could definitely be fun."

A tentative hand skims up my side and around my back.

My body freezes, and if Noah thought I was uptight thirty seconds ago, it's nothing compared to how tense I am right now.

"We have a photoshoot in two days." His breath tickles my cheek. "You're going to have to be relaxed and pretend that you like me."

"So, we can do this then." My voice cracks and I clear my throat. "I don't understand the point of it now."

"You look about as comfortable as I did when my housekeeper walked in on me balls deep inside my boyfriend senior year of high school. That was a fun way to come out to the parents."

"You ... wha ... *how?*"

If he said that as a distraction, it's working.

"Breathe," Noah says. "And just let me kiss you."

This is a stupid idea. Really stupid. Even so, there's a part of me that not only wants it but hopes he has a point, because there's no way I can pretend to be in love with a guy I don't know and am nervous around.

"Fine." I lean forward and put my beer on the coffee table in front of us.

He stares at me dumbfounded, as if he wasn't expecting me to give in. Maybe this is a game to him. If it is, he's winning.

That doesn't stop either of us from moving closer to one another.

My lips inch toward his but before I kiss him, I add in a low voice, "This is an experiment only. A one-time thing."

"Matt—"

"This isn't going to work, and when it doesn't, I will gladly rub it in your face every day we have to play this stupid charade."

Noah laughs, as if he knows I'm trying to convince myself

and not him, but I cut him off with my lips on his. Unlike earlier today where I didn't react—didn't do anything—this time, I take charge. My tongue pushes past his lips, and I refuse to let out the groan that tries to escape when it meets his. Two seconds into the kiss, I know this is a huge mistake.

I ignore the tightening in my pants and the shiver that runs through me as his hands trail down my spine. Then, suddenly, I'm on my back as he pins me to the sofa that's way too small to fit both of us.

That doesn't stop us, though.

His cock lines up with mine, and even through two layers of suit pants, I know he's long and thick.

Shit, don't think about his dick.

Noah's lips break away from mine and skim my bearded cheek. "Thought you said you weren't going to enjoy this," he says in my ear.

"I'm not." Hmm, probably would've been more convincing if my voice didn't crack like a twelve-year-old seeing his first dirty magazine ... or in my case a football magazine. Boys in tight pants and pads? It's no wonder I loved the sport when Dad first forced me to play.

Noah rotates his hips slowly, grinding his hard body against my even harder cock. "Pretty sure this says otherwise."

"I'm a gay man with a hot guy's tongue down my throat. It's simple chemistry. It doesn't mean anything."

"You're wrong. This is anything but simple." Noah's mouth comes back down on mine again, and this time, I can't hold back the moan.

I'm no longer on the ship. I've fallen overboard and am drowning in Noah, and I don't want to come up for air.

"Matt," he murmurs against my mouth, and his voice may as well have been a bucket of ice.

I push him off me and sit up, straightening my shirt in the process. "See. Didn't work."

I reach for my beer to wash the taste of Noah down.

He wipes his mouth and breaks into a cocky-ass smile. "So, you felt nothing, huh?"

"Right." More beer goes down my throat.

"Keep telling yourself that." He stands and makes his way out on to the balcony. I'm left with uncomfortably tight pants and more confusion than following a trick play on the field.

I've never been kissed like that before. Ever. Not that I have a long list of guys I've kissed. A lot of hookups were quick BJs and not much else. I didn't even exchange names with most of them let alone saliva.

Noah kisses like he lives—with assured confidence. He tastes like money and privilege. Somehow.

I have no right to judge him for being rich. Hell, he's probably not that much richer than I am. The thing is, I know what it's like to be poor, but Noah's sheltered life means he knows nothing about the real world and struggling.

I need to keep my head on straight. I can't start getting distracted by Noah purely for the fact he can kiss and has a big dick.

But it felt good being that close to him. Then again, it'd probably feel good to be close to anyone right now.

I don't want to admit to myself what I've been trying to deny for four years—ever since being drafted to the NFL. I'm so tired of being alone.

CHAPTER FOUR

NOAH

I'm pretty sure there's something fundamentally wrong with me. On what planet was it a good idea to make out with Matt?

I expected it to be like this afternoon—like kissing a dead fish. I never expected to *like* it.

Hey, hot asshole guy, stick your tongue in my mouth because it'll make us more comfortable.

Matt's right. I'm an idiot. Wait ... I don't think he's called me that. At least, not to my face. But it's true.

Always thinking with my dick, even when I don't mean to. I honestly thought kissing would take away that tension and awkwardness between us. I was wrong. So very wrong. Because now all I want to do is do it again. And again. And then maybe head south.

Stop. It.

When I've calmed down enough to go back inside, I flop down on the bed—the only bed in our room—and cover my eyes with my arm. Didn't think of the sleeping arrangement until now.

We have to have a shared bed or the housekeeping staff could leak that we were sleeping in separate rooms, letting the world know our whole relationship is a sham. The bed's not exactly wide, and when Matt's as tall and wide as he is, it's going to be a tight fit.

"I'm heading back to the gym," Matt says and starts rummaging through his clothes.

"Again?"

"Running clears my head."

"Thought there'd be nothing to clear seeing as the kiss didn't do anything for you?" I'm proud normal Noah comes out and I can act like that kiss didn't rattle me. "I'd join you, but my legs are still jelly from this afternoon's session."

"I don't need a babysitter."

"Right. That's why Damon hired me to watch over you and pretend to be your boyfriend. Yup."

Matt huffs and starts stripping.

I suck in a breath and hold it, because I don't think I can survive another viewing. The guy's body is insane. Instead of ogling his tattoos this time, my eyes go to his strong muscles, thick and powerful thighs, and the large bulge in his boxer briefs.

Instinctively, my tongue darts out.

What have I started?

Before I'm ready to stop looking at him, he's dressed and heading for the door. "I'll be back later."

My cock pulses as he disappears into the hallway. Good. I can take care of my predicament, hopefully pass out, and then forget my failed attempt at making our situation somewhat bearable. I don't know why I thought my dick would be immune to him just because he's surly. It basically doesn't discriminate against anyone. Well, apart from women.

I stare down at my cock. Still hard. Damn it. Usually thoughts of having sex with women makes it deflate pretty fast.

With no other option, I go to the bathroom and jerk off. All it takes is thinking about Matt's mouth, his thick beard, and that impressive cock that was pressed against me when we kissed. But coming only takes the edge off. One single thought of Matt's tongue and I get hard again.

A second time helps exhaust me but in no way satisfies my need. I fall into bed in my boxer briefs and beg for sleep to consume me.

Unfortunately for me, Matt returns at that moment.

"You weren't gone for long," I say.

"Just needed a quick run."

I snigger. "I bet."

I refuse to look at him because of his sweaty abs, tight pecs ... damn, jerking off twice wasn't enough. The shower starts in the bathroom and the temptation to rub another one out is overwhelming, but having already come twice, I don't think I'll have time.

Lucky too, because Matt only takes two minutes. He would've walked out and found me with my hand on my dick. If that's not the definition of creepy, I don't know what is.

The bed dips behind me. "They couldn't have gotten us a suite with two beds?" he grumbles. His arm is flush against my back, and the heat radiating off him has me burning up. Jesus H. Christ, he's barely touching me, but it makes me edgy.

I'm starting to think Damon's set me up as some sort of

payback for something I did to him. This could very well be seven nights of torture.

Then I remember I've signed on to do this until preseason, if not longer.

Maybe the anguish I'll cause Dad isn't worth the effort needed to achieve it.

"Mmm," I complain, "Fuck off, Aron."

Aron is a damn snuggler. I hate cuddling. He knew that when I started up with him. At first, he was cool with it and left as soon as we were done, but then he asked to stay one night. And then the next. Big red flags right there, but I didn't end it. I should have, because then I wouldn't be here ... wait.

His heavier than normal weight doesn't budge when I try to shove him, and that's when I snap into focus and remember where I am.

"Who's Aron?" the weight on top of me asks.

Matt rolls onto his back, finally freeing me from the confines of uninvited intimacy.

I reach above my head and stretch my back out. "No one."

"I'm calling bullshit."

"I'm calling none of your business." I sit up and throw my legs over the edge of the bed.

"It is my business if it's going to be a problem. Do you already have a boyfriend? Last thing I need is another scandal where I'm a homewrecker, and—"

"He's an ex, okay? No, not even that. He's a guy I fooled around with for about twelve months."

"A *year?* You slept with someone for an entire year and didn't consider him your boyfriend?"

Yeah, hard to miss the condescension there, Matt.

"We were casual," I say. "We both dated other guys in between."

Although, the last few months, Aron kept dropping hints about not doing that anymore. He wanted to come out of the relationship closet and tell our friends we were fooling around, so if we wanted to go home together one night, they wouldn't bat an eye. God, I was so blind to not see he wanted more than what we'd promised each other.

"I'm going to the gym," Matt says and starts rummaging through his suitcase.

Holy mother of Jesus. "Again? There is such a thing as burn out, you know. No team will want you if you're injured."

"I'm at the peak of my game. I've never been fitter."

"Then why wasn't your contract renewed well before the scandal?"

Hurt flashes across his face before he schools it. "A few months before everything happened, I had a talk with the offensive coach. He said there was obvious distrust on the field and all signs pointed to me being the instigator. I didn't play well with others, apparently."

"You? An asshole to people? I'm shocked."

He cracks a small smile. "The team wanted me to go to strip clubs and out after games and be friends with them all. I wanted to play football and then run home and lock the closet door. The less I hung out with them, the less chance of being caught out."

I purse my lips. "Okay, that's what I don't get. How did you let someone photograph you in that club?"

"What, you think I handed someone the camera and said *please, ruin my life?*"

"You were a hardass about it—not even getting close to your teammates—and then you go and throw it all away for a blowjob?"

"Moment of weakness. I rarely hit those clubs. The first year in the NFL, I never touched another guy. Hence the tattoos." Matt rubs his forearm.

"Right. Because celibacy equals tattoos?"

"I needed *something*. Adrenaline, pain ..."

"I don't get it."

Matt sighs. "The first time I hooked up during my second year, it was after a loss. I fumbled the ball on a play that could've put us on top. Losses happen, and everyone makes mistakes, but it was the first real fuckup I'd had where the loss could've been blamed solely on me. So, I scoped out a club, took a random guy into the bathroom, and then blew him. Then I could claim to be good at something, right?"

"I wouldn't know. I haven't had the pleasure." And there goes my mouth again.

"And you never will," Matt says and heads to the tiny bathroom to change into gym gear.

I stare down at my hard cock. All Matt has to do now is mention giving a BJ and my dick wants in on the action. If I hadn't already realized it, it's abundantly clear that the stupidest thing I've done all year wasn't hurting Aron. It was kissing Matt.

After meeting up with the others for breakfast, they decide to spend the day doing some ropes course on one of the outer decks, but I need space from Matt.

I also need to find an internet kiosk. This morning when Matt went back to the gym, I caved and checked my messages from Aron. They all consisted of a different version of *please tell me this is a joke.*

Telling him the truth is tempting, but I signed a non-disclosure agreement. There's only a select few who know Matt and I are in a sham relationship. Plus, I'm hoping it'll help Aron move on if he thinks I'm with someone else.

Signing into the ship's computer, I open my email and stare at the cursor blinking at me. It's mocking me, I know it is. I fight the urge to flip it off.

If the last month has taught me anything, it's that I have to get straight to the point with Aron. Any pussyfooting about and he worms his way back in. So, I go for the gut punch and hate myself for doing it.

I'M SORRY. I MET MATT AND IT JUST HAPPENED. I DIDN'T EXPECT TO FALL SO FAST, BUT I HAVE.

My eyes close as I hit send. No matter what my friends believe or think of me, I don't *like* being an asshole. I hate that I hurt Aron.

A chat bubble pops up.

Shit.

ARON: *WHAT ARE YOU PLAYING AT? YOU DON'T FALL FOR PEOPLE. THAT'S WHAT YOU'VE REPEATEDLY TOLD ME FOR A YEAR.*

NOAH: *I DON'T. USUALLY. MATT'S DIFFERENT.*

ARON: *IS THIS YOUR WAY OF GETTING ME TO BACK OFF? I TOLD YOU I WAS OKAY WITH GOING BACK TO BEING CASUAL.*

NOAH: *I CAN'T TALK RIGHT NOW. I'M ON A SHIP IN THE MIDDLE OF THE ATLANTIC. WITH MATT. MY BOYFRIEND. THE CASUAL THING WASN'T WORKING, AND WE BOTH KNOW IT. I'VE MOVED ON AND SO SHOULD YOU.*

I hold my breath until the green light around Aron's name disappears. Before I log off, I open up a new chat window with our friend Wyatt. He's probably the most nurturing of the guys in our group. Actually, he'd be more nurturing than our friends Skylar and Rebecca too. Those girls can be ruthless, and they're going to have my balls when they find out I screwed Aron over.

NOAH: *CAN YOU CHECK ON ARON IN A FEW DAYS? TAKE HIM OUT. HE NEEDS TO GET LAID.*

The response comes immediately.

WYATT: *HAVE FUN WITH YOUR FOOTBALL PLAYER WHILE IT LASTS. TRY NOT TO SHIT ALL OVER HIS HEART TOO.*

Along with his nurturing nature, Wyatt also has a flair for the dramatic, and it figures he'd take Aron's side. He should. He's not saying anything I don't already know, but it sits wrong in my gut. If I didn't have the NDA, I'd reassure Wyatt that no hearts were on the line when it came to Matt and me. He's surly and I'm ... I don't know exactly what his problem is with me, but it's obvious he has one.

One night down. Countless more to go.

CHAPTER FIVE

MATT

When I arrive at our room in the afternoon, Noah's on the balcony. He sits with his feet up on the railing which looks too high to be comfortable, but he looks good doing it.

He lifts his hand and swigs a sip of his beer. His fifth by the look of the empties on the small round table out there.

Wouldn't be the first man I've driven to the bottle. *Right, Dad?*

My father always blamed us kids for his urge to drink. I wonder if he's been sober at all since I was outed. I want to call my siblings and ask how everything is back home since my secret went public, but I don't have their numbers anymore. My parents have gone to extreme lengths to keep me from my brothers and sisters. I'm blocked on all social media, and when I try to reach their cell phones, I'm told the number I'm trying no longer exists.

"I can feel you staring at me," Noah calls out and then stands.

I grab my own beer out of the minibar as he joins me in the cabin.

"Bit early in the afternoon to be drinking, isn't it?" I ask.

Noah raises a dark eyebrow at me and pierces me with his aqua eyes. They're more blue than green reflecting off the ocean. Why the fuck am I thinking about the color of his eyes?

"Says the guy holding a beer." He takes another gulp.

"Misery loves company, and apparently I'm doing a great job of bringing you down with me."

"Don't flatter yourself. This"—Noah lifts his bottle—"has nothing to do with you."

"Did your obnoxious attitude annoy one of the staff and they pissed in your lunch?"

He snorts. "Hey, I'm a lovable guy. You just don't see it."

No, I could see it. I could see how his laid-back attitude, sense of humor, and all-round arrogant charm could suck someone in, but I'm not here for that.

"Uh, Damon finally gave me our schedule." I reach into my pocket and give Noah the folded sheet of paper.

"Get to know each other," Noah says and then laughs. "Without killing each other. Good luck with that one, am I right?"

"It's a tall order."

"Wait, full spread magazine shoot and interview with *Out and Proud Magazine* when we get to Bermuda?"

I take a large sip of beer. "Yup."

"Are you going to have a panic attack again?"

"Not gonna lie, there's a good chance."

"Just think, any time you start to panic, my lips will be there for you. It says here, it's a joint interview."

When I groan, Noah laughs. "You like seeing me squirm, don't you?" I ask.

"It's so easy." Noah stares at the sheet of paper. "After that, it looks like you go home to PA for a few weeks until a charity benefit thing for ... really? LGBTQ Alliance Ball? They're really shoving the gay thing down people's throats, huh?"

I choke on my beer. "Thank you. That's what I've been trying to say."

"They need to see us doing normal shit too. Maybe we can talk to them about having a day where we get papped grocery shopping. Being with me wouldn't be all fancy cruises and benefits."

"Isn't that all you do?" I ask. "Rich trust fund guy, no job—"

"I have a job. I just never go to it. They don't pay me, so why should I go?"

"Employee of the year, right here."

"You want to know what my 'job' is?" he asks, using air quotes. "I work on my dad's campaigns. My official title is strategist, but all that means is I sit in a room with a bunch of stuffy people who claim to know the world, yet they go home and sit in their cushy mansions with their lots of money and ignore the homeless on the streets as they walk by. Anytime I come up with ideas, I'm shut down because I'm the boss's son with a polisci degree and no experience." His eyes hold helplessness, and it's the first time I've seen any humbleness from him.

"You want to be a politician?" I ask.

"Something like that." There's something in his voice that makes me think he's lying, or he at least doesn't care if he ends up in the White House. "It was the original plan. Not so much anymore."

"That's all you're going to give me?"

"It's not all sunshine and rainbows over here on the trust fund train," Noah mutters. It's the first time I've seen any real vulnerability from him, and it makes me uncomfortable. I don't know how to respond to it.

"I'd still prefer that to a trailer trash family from Tennessee with six kids to feed and no food." *That's not probably how, moron.*

Noah's arrogant smile returns. "You're from Tennessee? So that's where your accent when you're pissed off comes from."

"Taught mah-self real good-like to talk all educated and shit." I accentuate every word as I would if I were home.

"Why? Southern accents are hot. Better than New York." His forced accent on New York sounds more from the Bronx than Manhattan.

"I guess I associate my accent with the rednecks I grew up with."

Noah leans against the sliding door to the balcony. "Okay, this is good. We're getting to know each other. What was it like growing up with five ... brothers and sisters? Or ...?"

"Two brothers, three sisters. Charlene is twenty-one, Jethro's nineteen, Daisy's sixteen, Fern is fourteen, and Wade is twelve."

Noah whistles. "Haven't your parents heard of birth control?"

I can't hold in the laugh. "Do you say every single thing that pops into your head?"

"Uh, yeah. Sorry."

"Don't be sorry. You have a point. Mom and Dad should've stopped after me. You know how there are people who shouldn't reproduce? My parents would be on that list. Maybe not at the top—they didn't beat us, they kept us clothed and fed, and they weren't monsters—but they just weren't ... there. Football was the only thing Dad and I ever talked about."

"Did they know you were gay before you were outed?"

I don't exactly know what the answer to that is. "There was this guy in high school who I used to fool around with. We thought we were careful, but the more time that's passed, the more I reckon Mom and Dad knew the whole time. When I left for college, they said in no uncertain terms that I didn't have to return. Like ever. I had a full ride to Olmstead and got a summer job to pay for housing so I didn't have to go home over the break. Then I was drafted sophomore year."

"When was the last time you saw your family?"

"That day. When I left for New York. I haven't been back, and they can't afford to visit. I used to speak to my siblings on the phone whenever I'd call, but I've been told to stop calling now too. I guess it was one thing to know I was gay and ignore it, but it's a whole other issue when photos of me are plastered all over the news and internet."

"That's not cool," Noah says quietly.

"It's what I was born into." I'm playing it off like it's not a big deal, but for so long I tried to get Dad to say he was proud of me. Cliché, maybe, but I lived and breathed football because I thought it was what I needed to do to get my parents to accept me.

There were times I wondered if I even liked playing, but then when I went to OU and the pressure from my parents wasn't there anymore, I realized I couldn't live without it. It was in my blood. From that moment, I played for me and me alone.

Noah pushes off the door and slides past me in the small space to get to the minibar. "I'm getting another beer. You want one?"

"Uh, about that. I kinda told the guys we'd go to the cigar bar with them."

He stops mid-reach for a new bottle. "Cigars and scotch. Even better."

Damon huffs in frustration. After drinks at the cigar bar, he follows us back to our cabin to make sure we're prepared for our interview tomorrow as soon as we hit land, but it's not going well thanks to an overconfident smartass who can't take anything seriously.

We've got basics, like where we met, what we studied in college, but Noah must have ADD or something because getting him to concentrate now is like trying to teach a cat how to stop being an asshole.

"Okay, let's try an easy one," Damon says. "What does Matt like to do in his spare time?"

Noah grunts. "I'm guessing getting blowjobs in nightclubs is the incorrect answer?"

I groan and flop backward on the bed. "I give up. Is he always like this?" Don't know why I'm asking when I know the answer will be yes.

"Spend time with you, you dumbass," Damon says to Noah, ignoring me. "You know, when normal couples love each other, they want to spend every waking hour with each other. Athletes get hardly any time off, so the answer is *spend time with you*."

"But that's so ... cheesy," Noah says.

"We need to sell cheese." Damon's trying to keep his voice calm, but it ain't working.

"Cheddar or Swiss?"

Damon stands. "From my experience, there's no point even trying with Noah right now. Sorry, Matt. I tried."

"Fuck you very much," I call after him as he leaves the cabin.

"How unprofessional," Noah says. "But at least it worked. What do you want to do now? Go for a drink? Snack? I think they have one of those lame-ass magician shows ..."

I sit up and stare at him incredulously. "You said all those things just to get out of answering annoying questions?"

He smiles. "You're welcome."

"We need to know this stuff."

"No, we don't. We can wing it, and it's all basic anyway."

"And when we're caught in a lie or we don't know something about the other person?"

"We're supposed to be a newly in love couple," Noah says. "We're not trying to sell that we're soul mates and always have been. It's perfectly natural we don't know every little detail."

"What if they ask about your family?"

Emptiness replaces his normally vibrant eyes. "I'll handle any political questions. I've been trained for it my whole life."

"But I haven't. What if I mess it up?"

"Then you'll be finding the nearest unemployment line." He's joking, but I'm seriously not in the mood. Noah must pick up on it, because he immediately apologizes. "You have nothing to worry about. It's one interview in one magazine that hardly anyone will read anyway."

I scoff. "That's bullshit, and we both know it. One photo ruined my career, but it's going to take a shit ton of positive press to fix it."

With the largest sigh known to man, Noah moves to the minibar and grabs out another beer. It's like the never-ending, bottomless pit of fridges. The housekeeping staff on the boat are like ninjas and restock the second anyone leaves the rooms.

"Fine," he says, his tone defeated. "Let's bore each other to tears with as much information as we can cram in, but if we're going to do this, we should at least make it fun."

"Is it impossible for you to be in the same room as me without a drink in your hand?"

"Not impossible, but it makes it more tolerable."

"Gee, thanks," I mumble. "Note to self: what does Noah like to do in his spare time? *Drink*."

Noah leans against the wall of the small cabin and takes a long pull of beer. "I can think of another way to make this more fun, but you'll hate that one even more."

I don't even need to ask what it is, because his hungry gaze traveling over me gives it all away, and I'm not even going to dignify his innuendo with a response.

Instead, I stand, because suddenly being on a bed is too tempting. I want to kiss that mouth again, press myself against him, and— "I think you're right. This isn't going to achieve anything. We'll go catch that show."

Noah's smugness isn't lost on me, and I realize I've played right into his hands. He didn't want to do this stupid question prep, and he pushed all the right buttons to get both Damon and me to back down.

I don't know whether to be pissed off or impressed.

CHAPTER SIX

NOAH

For the second day in a row, I wake up being spooned by a giant. Matt's body heat makes my back sweaty, but I can't help enjoying the warmth and sense of ease before I snap out of whatever temporary craziness it's causing. I can't like cuddling. Nope. No way.

I push him off me. "For someone who's never had a boyfriend, you sure do like to cuddle."

"It's my body's fault," Matt says through a yawn. "I'm not in control of it when I'm asleep." He rolls over and stretches that long torso of his as the sheet drops to his narrow waist.

"What time's the photoshoot?" I ask.

"As soon as we dock."

I amble out to the balcony. We're still moving, but if I stick my head out as far as I can lean over without falling, there's land visible in the distance.

"I'm going to shower," I say. "Rub one out while I'm at it. Unless ..." I drop my boxers to the floor and my cock juts out, pointing toward my stomach. "You want to join me?"

I have absolutely no idea what I'm doing. Do I want him to say yes, or am I messing with him? I don't know. Knowing me, I'm trying to fuck with him, but I can't be sure I'd admit to joking if he accepted the offer.

"I'm good. Thanks."

Huh. Didn't even get a rise out of him. My eyes travel down his hard stomach to the tent in the sheet. Okay, so I got a rise out of him physically, but he's not biting.

"Fine, but it might be an idea for you to do it too. Just saying, we'll most likely be hanging around in our underwear all day. Oiled up, rubbing against each other. Do you want a hard-on in a magazine?"

"You still don't affect me, so I'll manage."

I cough in between saying "Bullshit."

"Still chemical. Your mouth ruins it for me." He smirks but tries to hide it.

"I could totally show you how good my mouth can be."

For the tiniest, miniscule second, I swear interest flickers across his face, but then he schools his features and it's gone. "Still pass."

"Suit yourself."

A quick shower later—all I had to do was think about waking up next to Matt and I came within thirty seconds of touching myself—I find Matt dressed in board shorts and a black sleeveless shirt.

"Should've jerked it," I sing at him.

"How do you know I didn't?"

I'm hardening again. This guy drives me crazy. "We should fuck."

Matt sighs. "Here we go again. Why, exactly?"

"Hear me out. We're in this relationship until you get a

contract, and after that, you might need me to make appearances so your teammates don't think you're hitting on them or whatever. Because everyone knows all us gay boys want to do in life is hit on straight guys."

Matt laughs. "Right? Not to mention football players are head cases. No way would I go for one."

"You realize you're calling yourself a head case?"

He lets out a humorless huff. "You haven't been paying attention, have you? I'm fucked up."

"Aren't we all?"

"Look, it's not happening. We proved crossing that line makes things weirder, not better like you said it would."

"True, but now it's super weird. There's no going back. All you have to do to get me hard is ... well, breathe. Even your shitty attitude is starting to turn me on."

"Way to get me into bed," Matt says.

"You want candlelight and flowers?"

"Fuck off."

"We don't have to like each other to make each other come."

"I bet you say that to all the guys."

He's frustrating me to no end.

"It was just an idea," I say. "We both get off, your fake relationship becomes semi-real so we're not entirely lying, and we both know it's temporary. We won't fall when we can't stand each other."

Matt stares at me, his expression a mixture of confusion and concern. "Do you really think I don't like you? I'm pissed at the situation, not at you, but it's better if we keep this professional."

"*Why?*"

"I need this strategy to work, and it's not going to if ... sex gets involved. I haven't gone there with other guys, so I won't—"

His mouth slams shut, and he winces as if he's said something wrong.

I run his words over in my head and step closer. "Are you saying what I think you're saying?"

"Nope. Never mind. Never said nothin'." Is that why his accent is reappearing?

"Matt, how many guys have you been with?"

The tips of his ears turn red. "Heaps."

My mouth quirks on one side. "You top or bottom? I assumed Mr. Asshole was a top, but now I'm not so sure you're either."

Matt cracks his neck. "We should go get somethin' to eat before we're due at the shoot." He tries to walk away but I grab his arm. Damn his tattooed biceps being all hard and mouthwatering under my hand.

"Are you a virgin?" I ask, my voice gruff.

"No." He averts his gaze. Matt's so a virgin. "I've done plenty of … stuff. It counts."

"No, it doesn't. Have you ever had anal? Given or received."

"That's not the defining criteria for sex, you know."

"That doesn't answer my question."

"What's it to you?" he snaps.

"Well, before when I said we should fuck, it was only an idea. Now I really think we should."

Matt throws his head back and looks at the roof. "I swear if you don't drop this, the next headline will read *Matt Jackson Murders Boyfriend.*"

"Catchy. But someone as hot—and as old—as you shouldn't be a virgin. We need to rectify that immediately."

Matt grits his teeth. "I'll see you out there. I need some food to stomach your bullshit."

He leaves before I can take the time to realize I've messed up by running my mouth as usual. Only, this time I didn't mean to do it. The foot lodged between my teeth won't budge an inch.

In my defense, how the hell is someone like Matt a virgin? If he could pull off blowjobs in nightclubs when he was closeted, he could've easily taken someone home—or back to the guy's place for complete anonymity. I've even seen guys having sex in clubs like the one he was caught in.

But if I were a twenty-three-year-old virgin, I probably wouldn't want that rubbed in my face.

Wow, I really am an asshole. I need to go apologize. I hope he has a recording device, because Noah Huntington doesn't apologize. Normally.

Matt's not in any of the billions of onboard restaurants when I go looking for him, and after I've checked every one, it's time for the photoshoot.

I hope to find Matt when I go back to the room, but instead, our keeper is there.

Damon follows me into the cabin. "What did you do to him?"

"Tattle on me, did he?"

"He's refusing to do the shoot."

"Ah, I don't think that has anything to do with me. It's a stupid shoot."

"I thought you'd be sympathetic. You know what it's like to have paparazzi follow you."

"I *am* sympathetic. That's why I think a shoot with *Out and Proud Magazine* is a dumb idea. Yes, he should embrace the fact he's gay and not hide it, but flaunting it isn't going to work either. You should've booked *Sports Illustrated* or *Football is Life* for his big, gay interview."

Damon laughs. "*Football is Life?* That's not a magazine."

"Do I look like the type of guy who knows titles of sports magazines? I just mean any interviews he does should be about football, not his sexuality."

"Did you go out and get a PR degree while I wasn't paying attention? And you still haven't told me what you did to piss him off."

"I'll fix it," I say. "I may have accidentally antagonized him. I'll get him to the shoot. I know we can't get out of it, but you might want to re-evaluate the schedule once we're back home. Have us doing normal stuff and quit with the LGBTQ poster boy routine. Had Matt come out on his own, it'd be different, but the world knows he was forced out of the closet, so now it looks like he's trying too hard."

Damon smiles.

"What?" I ask.

"You like him."

"He's a cranky asshole."

"You *really* like him."

"Are we in high school? I'd fuck him, for sure, but we all know I'd fuck anyone with a dick and a pulse."

Damon cocks his head to the side. "Don't do that."

"Don't do what?"

His teasing strikes a chord, and I'm getting defensive. I've known Matt for three days, and he's been angry for most of it. I don't like him. I don't.

"Don't be self-deprecating to cover up how you feel," Damon says.

"Get a psych degree while I wasn't paying attention?" I throw his own words back at him. "I'll get dressed and go apologize and we can get this show on the road. The sooner it's done,

the sooner Matt and I can go to our separate corners of
the ship."

I've known Damon for eight years. He's the closest thing to
a brother I have. That means, when he nods once with a smug
smile, I can practically hear his thoughts.

"I don't have a thing for Matt," I argue.

"Mmhmm."

Jackass.

When we get to Damon's room, Maddox and Matt are nowhere
to be seen.

"You better hope Maddox knocked some sense into him and
they're already onshore at the photoshoot site," Damon says.

"Or what, you'll fire me? Not pay me? Oh wait, you're not
doing that in the first place."

Damon pinches the bridge of his nose. "I have a headache."

"From your concussion?"

"From *you.*"

"Oh. Well, in that case, you're welcome. Come on, I'm going
to fix this."

Damon narrows his eyes. "What exactly did you do to
antagonize him?"

Yeah, not going to tell Damon about Matt's virgin status. I'm
not that much of a dick. "I told him we should fuck."

"You're unbelievable."

"Thanks."

"Not a compliment."

"The way I figure it, we're stuck with each other for the next
few months. May as well get some while we're at it."

"And you say you don't like him," Damon scoffs.

"My cock likes him."

"Yes, well, we all know your dick's not discriminatory."

"Oh, so you can make jokes about me, but when I do it it's self-deprecating?"

"Yup. Pretty much the definition of self-deprecating. Need me to buy you a dictionary? I thought you graduated from college."

We go through the ship checkpoints, scanning our room keys that keep track of who's onboard or not when we're at port.

"Where's the shoot?" I ask.

"Half a mile up the beach. There's a private residence the magazine has rented."

I follow him down the docks and onto the sand. The sun seems hotter in this part of the world, and I break out into an immediate sweat. The humidity doesn't help.

My shirt sticks to my back immediately, so I take it off and tuck it into my waistband.

"Thirty whole seconds before you took your damn shirt off," Damon grumbles.

"I need to give these people some sort of gift." I point to my abs.

"I'd ask for a refund if I were them."

I shove him. "It's hot as balls out here."

We walk past families and couples spending their day at the beach, and I wish for Matt's sake that he could join them instead of endure this interview.

"Would they have really gone without you?" I ask Damon. Maybe Matt made an escape.

"I texted Maddox the address and told him to get Matt there if he could."

"Our phones work again?" Mine is still off and in the cabin somewhere. *Sorry, Dad, still can't return your calls.*

"Yup." As if on cue, Damon's phone buzzes. "Heads up. Paparazzi are lining the property."

I shake my head. "This is getting out of hand. They followed him to Bermuda?"

We round a corner and paparazzi crowd outside a gated beach bungalow.

"Actually, I think these guys are here for you," Damon says. "We probably should've considered your dad's political position when we matched you up with Matt."

I did. "Yeah. That might've been an idea."

Damon's smirk matches my own. "You said yes to piss your old man off, didn't you?"

"Me?" I mock gasp. "I would never do such a thing."

"Liar. Well here you go. Here's your spotlight."

Now that I'm getting what I originally set out to do, it doesn't boost me up as I was expecting. It makes me feel cheaper than a rentboy in one of the seedy nightclubs Matt got caught in. My attention-seeking actions against my father seem childish compared to what Matt's going through.

"You okay? You look ... nervous, but that can't be right. You're Noah Huntington the fucking Third."

"I'm fine. I just didn't expect them to follow us here. I didn't realize the extent in which these people will go to make Matt's life a living hell."

Damon does that smug thing again.

"Shut up," I grumble and push on ahead.

"I didn't say anything," he says, his ex-baseball playing legs keeping up with me easily. "I definitely didn't mention the whole having a thing for Matt again."

Kill me now.

We walk through the throng of media, and my ears prick up at Damon's name being called out too. These guys have done their homework. Damon was almost famous once—before he blew out his shoulder.

In the safety of the property, I turn to him. "They must be desperate if they're recognizing your washed-up has-been ass."

"There's the Noah I love to hate. Or is it hate to love? One or the other. Missed you for a minute there while you were pining over Matt."

"Fuck you."

"I have Maddox for that. Thanks for the offer though."

Damon knocks on the door that's on the side of the house, and some PA lets us in.

"Ah, good, the other one is here," she says and runs off.

"Go find Matt and grovel," Damon says. I go to take a step when he pulls me back. "And don't apologize by offering to blow him. That's why he's pissed off at you in the first place." Not quite, but Damon can believe whatever he wants. "And"— he stops me again—"I don't need to remind you this is your first test. If you guys fail this, we may as well have not bothered at all." He lowers his voice. "Everyone has to believe you're a couple."

"No pressure."

The PA woman appears again, just as flighty and flustered as before. "Here." She hands me a pair of swimming trunks, and not the long boardshorts kind. "Wardrobe is this way."

I mouth "You owe me" to Damon as the little woman drags me away.

He gives me a thumbs-up. Why am I friends with him

again? Oh, right, he's one of the few people who puts up with my bullshit.

Matt avoids eye contact with me as he stands with his arms and legs spread out in the middle of a bedroom while some woman rubs him down with oil. As hard as I try to drag my eyes away from his bubble butt in his tight, really small Speedos, I can't. At least I'm not alone in the attire we have to wear, but keeping my dick contained could be a challenge.

Matt still refuses to look at me.

"Can we have a minute?" I ask the two assistants.

They glance at each other, then at Matt, and then back at me before shuffling out the door.

"M—"

"Not here, Noah." His eyes dart behind me where the girls left. I guess anyone could be listening.

I step closer until I'm pressed against his back. "I'm sorry."

"Okay."

"I mean it. I truly am sorry. If you haven't figured out by now, my mouth likes to speak without my brain's permission."

"Let's just get this done."

"Are we cool?" I ask.

His eyes in the mirror in front of us flick toward the door and then meet mine. "All good. *Babe.*" Leaning back, he kisses my cheek, and for a moment I'm lost—too busy enjoying being this close with his warm lips on me and his beard scraping my skin—but then I realize there's someone standing at the door waiting for us to finish whatever we were doing. Or maybe they're trying to get a scoop.

I step away and beckon her in. "We're ready to go."

Twenty minutes later, we're both oiled up, practically naked, and being ushered out the side of the house. Wooden decking surrounds a tropical pool, with a rock waterfall and bamboo lounger chairs lining the edge.

A small blonde woman with permanent resting bitch face glares at us. "It's so nice to meet you both. We were hoping to do this on the beach, but you boys are causing a stir, so we'll use the pool instead." Maybe she's had so much Botox her face literally can't move anymore. Her words are kind, but her face is frozen. "I'm Callie, I'll be interviewing you while Lars takes photos."

Lars, a hot nerd type, stands behind a camera and tampers with the settings as he gives us a quick wave with his free hand.

"Hope everything's okay?" Callie asks. "One of the PAs said you were bickering and you arrived separately."

Matt glances around, looking for Damon. He's supposed to step in when questions that are off-limits are brought up. She hasn't said the interview has started yet, but that doesn't matter with most journalists. If you don't say something is off the record, it's safe to assume anything you say can and will be held against you in magazine land. I don't suspect she knows we're faking it; I get the feeling she wants gossip to post all over the internet.

"Hate to disappoint," I say, "I was late because Matty made me clean up our room. I'm a slob, and he hates that, even if I did try to get out of it by claiming we're on vacation."

"Trouble in paradise?" Callie asks.

I laugh and wrap my arm around Matt's waist. "Not even close. Just usual couple stuff."

Matt releases a relieved breath, and Callie taps away on her tablet. It won't be usable. No one wants to hear about couples arguing over dirty laundry on the floor. Dirty laundry in their relationship however ...

"Noah, we'll have you on the far lounger, lying down," Lars

says from behind his camera. "Matt, you can sit on the front one and face Callie while she asks you questions."

"Ooh, I get the hard job of sunbaking," I say.

Lars approaches as I lie down, his eyes raking over me. His thick-rimmed glasses slide down his face, bringing my attention to his full lips, and there's no mistaking the interest shimmering in his eyes. Normally, I'd be all over that, but that would be a very shitty thing for a boyfriend to do. So, instead of winking at him or asking how he wants me, I cock my eyebrow at him.

"Lift your arm and put it behind your head to rest on." His voice is gruff. I go to raise my arm when he stops me. "Uh, other arm, the one furthest from the camera. Here, I'll show you."

I bet he will.

While Lars maneuvers me into the position he wants, Damon comes out to join us, and Callie starts firing off questions. She doesn't mind going for the gut punch either.

"So, Matt, how does it feel to be retired?"

Matt tenses but lifts his head toward Damon, who gives Matt a small nod. "Not retired yet," he says easily. I can't see his face, but I can imagine a forced smile. "I'm a free agent and looking for offers."

"There's controversy surrounding your swift exit from the Bulldogs and rumors about them discriminating against you because you're gay."

Not all was lost with Damon's coaching last night. Matt's now able to bullshit his way through this question and others like it.

"That had nothing to do with it at all. I was put on warning a month before they decided not to renew my contract. Because I had to hide a big part of me, I wasn't as open or trusting with my teammates as I should have been. The whole team suffered because of it, and there was no one else to blame but myself. The Bulldogs is a family-oriented team, and they all see the players as their family. I never let them in, and in the end, it meant they wanted more of a team player. Now I don't have to worry about people finding out, I'm ready to be part of a team again, and I won't make the same mistakes by keeping secrets."

"But you had some of the best tight end stats last year."

I'm surprised they've even done their football research.

"That's not everything," Matt says. "Football is a team sport."

"And you evidently played for the *wrong* team."

I glance at the woman out the corner of my eye. You'd think someone who worked for a pro-LGBTQ magazine would have more ... empathy? It feels like she's trying to get a rise out of Matt.

Matt doesn't take the bait, though. Maybe there's hope we can pull this off.

"How do you feel being the first openly gay player in the NFL?" she asks.

"I believe Michael Sam owns that title," Matt says. I have no idea who Michael Sam is.

"Technically, he was the first drafted," she corrects. "Until he was cut during preseason."

Ah, I guess that's why I don't know who he is.

"Well, if we're getting technical, there's Kopay, Smith, McDonald, Simmons, and a handful others who came out after retiring, and I wasn't openly gay while playing for the Bulldogs. So, unless I'm signed to a new team, the title is still up for grabs. To answer your question, I don't think I should feel anything about being an openly gay player. I'm still a player. Gay or straight doesn't have anything to do with it. I deserve to be on that field as much as any of the other guys. I train hard to be the best. All I want to do is play football."

Callie taps away on her tablet furiously, and that there will be the title. *Matt Jackson Just Wants to Play Football.*

Ugh.

"What I do off the field hasn't interfered with my career yet, and I don't intend to let it in the future."

"But it has interfered with your career. You said you never let yourself get close to your teammates, which cost you your contract."

Matt doesn't answer for longer than one would consider normal, as if he's struggling to find the correct answer.

"Can I grab some water?" I complain. "It's exhausting looking this good."

My trick has the desired effect. I don't know where the assistants have run off to, but Camera Boy scurries away to get me a bottle of water while Matt and Callie laugh at me.

"How did you and Noah Huntington meet?" Callie asks Matt.

"My new agent—Damon King at OnTrack Sports—went to college with Noah. I met them both at a party."

"Thanks for the plug," Damon says from the sidelines.

"Best agent I've had."

Lars comes back with my water, and I sip it quickly while he gets back behind the camera. He doesn't take his eyes off me as I swallow the water down. I think someone likes me.

"Was it love at first sight?" Callie asks.

"Yes," I answer at the same time Matt says, "No."

Callie loves our answer; her entire face lights up like she just scored a scoop.

"He definitely made me work for it," I say and force playfulness into my tone. "The first three days, it felt like I was running after him the whole time."

Matt's shoulders bounce, and I think he's trying to hide the fact he's laughing, because what I said isn't a lie. All I've done since we got on the damn ship is proposition him, only to get shut down.

"What will happen if you get an offer from a team on the West Coast?" Callie asks. "Noah's in New York, running his father's campaign."

Running. Pfft. Whenever I'm in the office, I'm treated like a child. Pretty sure I'm not even allowed to hold a pair of scissors.

"We'll cross that bridge if and when we come to it," Matt says. "During the season, my main focus would be football, so even if he was with me, we'd face what every other football couple faces."

Lars cuts in. "Okay, I have enough photos of this concept. Now, Noah, if you could slide onto Matt's chair, and Matt, you lie back with Noah between your legs."

Well, now that sounds fun.

"Uh, with his back to your front," Lars clarifies with a cute blush.

I try to keep from salivating as Matt spreads his legs enough for me to slide in. His cock twitches and digs into my back as I try to get comfortable on top of him. His hand goes to my hip, and suddenly I wish I was the one in Matt's position, because he can hide his hard-on.

Callie's phone starts ringing, and she excuses herself for a moment.

"Told you to jerk it," I say quietly out the side of my mouth. I shift my weight, my back rubbing against him, and he lets out a tiny groan.

"I fucking hate you," he whispers in my ear.

"Somehow I doubt that."

"Matt," Lars says, "Put your head back and close your eyes. Noah, shuffle down so you're using Matt's chest as a pillow and turn your head toward me."

Matt's grip on me hardens to the point of pain as I slide down him. If I hadn't already messed up today by running my mouth, he would hear endless teasing about being unable to say he doesn't want me. He's so hard I'm pretty sure if I wiggled enough, I could make him come.

My cock goes from a semi to an iron spike at the thought of Matt losing it and coming all over me.

Lars clears his throat, and I stare down at my cock which is trying to break free. Won't have to work hard for it in these trunks.

In true Noah fashion, I don't let it faze me. "Sorry. We're still in the honeymoon phase. All I have to do is get near Matt." Totally not lying. I reach down and try to adjust myself. Unsuccessfully.

"No problem," Lars says. "I'll, uh, take photos from the torso up."

"Good idea. I'm guessing you're not allowed to give us privacy for a few minutes." I'm an evil bastard because I love that I'm making the photographer uncomfortable.

His face turns redder than a tomato, and he glances around to make sure no one can hear when he says, "I could get everyone else to leave ..."

The image of me and Matt getting off in front of the hot nerdy guy is way too much overstimulation for my little brain, but then I picture Lars watching Matt, and I'm not liking that idea just as fast. I go to open my mouth to shut him down, but

Damon knows me too well and thinks I'm about to encourage the photographer's behavior.

"Noah, behave," Damon orders.

"Wasn't going to say anything other than no one gets to see Matt naked except me." The sincerity in my words is involuntary, but it entertains Damon all the same. I swear he's two seconds away from making teasing kissy faces like a twelve-year-old girl.

Matt sighs behind me, and I'm starting to think he might be getting used to my antics.

"Where's your better half?" I ask Damon.

"He's gone to check out the island with Stacy and Jared."

"What did I miss?" Callie asks, rejoining us.

"Nothing," Lars says quickly, his face still red. And yep, still love that I rattled him. It's an ego boost. Although, arguably, others would say my ego doesn't need to get any bigger, but it feels good after being rejected by Matt these last few days. I don't know whether to be insulted or flattered. He claims he doesn't hate me—that he's stressed—but he refuses to fool around even though I turn him on. I don't think I've met anyone harder to figure out.

When Callie gets back into interview mode, Matt's cock deflates pretty fast when she asks about his family.

"That's not on the approved list of discussion points," Damon says. "Try again."

Callie huffs. "Okay, who would you say is your biggest supporter?" She's working for her paycheck, that's for sure.

"That would be me. Duh," I say.

"And what about your family, Noah? Are they happy to see you in love with the bad boy of football?"

Hell no. "Honestly, Matt and I are still pretty new, and

there hasn't been a gap in my father's schedule for them to meet yet, but it will happen eventually. They'll love Matt because I love Matt. My parents have always maintained they only want me to be happy." *You know, so long as it's on their terms.*

Damon gives an approving nod, happy with my answer, but it leaves a bitter taste in my mouth. As always, I've acted before I've thought my actions through. Matt is dealing with enough without having to put up with my father's shit too. I'm supposedly here doing Matt a favor, and even if he doesn't realize it, tying his life to mine in any capacity is a good way to get screwed. It's why I haven't had a proper relationship since freshman year of college. Learning my boyfriend was paid off by my parents to break up with me because he wasn't the right image for my dad is the one lesson I will carry with me always. Everyone has a price, and everyone wants something from me.

My dad wants me to be the golden child with the impeccable political career ahead of me.

Hookups have wanted either my money or my connections.

Aron wanted my love—something I don't give to anyone. Granted, I'm the asshole in that situation, but it's still more people asking things of me I can't give.

If I give pieces of me to people who come and go into my life, I'll be left bare and exposed with nothing left of me except bitterness and money I didn't earn.

"Noah?" Matt asks, and I snap out of my trance.

"Huh?"

"You can sit up now. Side by side," Lars says.

"Oh." I sit up and run a hand over my closely shaved head.

Callie fires more questions off at Matt, and he answers them like a pro. I'm too busy wondering if this whole thing is a mistake. My mind goes to the paparazzi waiting for us outside and the ones back on the docks at home. Not to mention the ones at Matt's hotel.

"Damon, can I have a word?" I ask.

He stares between Matt and Callie and hesitates.

"I'm about done with the questions anyway," Callie says. "Lars will want some shots of Matt alone, so they can get started on that."

I go to stand, but Matt pulls me back down. "What's up?" he asks. His eyes hold fear and suspicion.

"Nothing. It's all good. I just have an idea."

His eyes widen. "That doesn't reassure me any."

I wrap my arm around his neck and bring him in close. My lips find the side of his head. "If you're super nice, I'll tell you later."

When I get up and walk away, he's smiling at me. That's better than being pissed.

Damon follows me into the spare room and closes the door behind us for privacy.

"You okay?" Damon asks.

"Yeah, but I want something."

"Uh-oh."

I slump. "I may not act like it, but my brain works ... sometimes. So, this is our only thing on the schedule while we're on this cruise, right? No other commitments other than to get to know each other?"

"Right."

"Matt's never going to relax when he knows if he steps off that ship, the cameras will be there, and when he's onboard, people are snapping photos of him with their cellphones."

"What do you suggest?"

"I have a private plane. I'm taking Matt back to New York

tonight. The paparazzi think he's away for four more days. That's four days where he can be a normal human."

Damon shakes his head. "Boat security. They'll know if you guys leave the boat and don't get back on. All they need is one person to talk."

"Can we give you guys our keycards? Tell the ship crew that Maddox O'Shay and Damon King are leaving the cruise early and then use our room instead of yours. All we have to do is somehow sneak away from the ship without the photographers following."

He rubs his cheek. "If it's what Matt wants to do, we'll make it work."

"Trust me. He'll jump at the chance to have separate beds."

Damon cocks his eyebrow. "I feel like there's a story there, but I'm not sure I want to know it."

"You're probably right about that."

He gives me a nod. "Call your jet."

CHAPTER SEVEN

MATT

"That was more exhausting than a day of sled drills," I say when we get back to the cabin.

"Yeah, I don't know what they are," Noah says, "but I feel way too much like a stripper with all this oily shit on me."

I can't help laughing, because he's right. My skin is gritty, slippery, and smells like coconut. I reckon it'll take industrial strength soap to get it off. "I would make a joke about being lubed up, but you'll probably take it as an opening."

Noah does a double take. "First of all, I can't believe you'd say lube and opening in the same sentence and expect me not to react, and second, I think I like joking Matt."

I try to hide my smile. I don't know what changed during that interview, but with the way he intercepted questions and answered how we wanted him to last night while we were practicing, part of the wall I built when I met Noah to keep our professional distance crumbled, and I'm beginning to see him in a new light.

His arrogant act isn't who he really is. He uses his wiseass attitude to piss people off and get what he wants, but underneath all that, he's not so selfish.

He sat there today and made sure I stayed calm. Well, when he wasn't rubbing against me and getting me hard, anyway. But even that worked as a distraction from the frustrating situation. He didn't need to do that. It's his job to make this look real, not coddle me.

I go to say thank you for what he did today, but he cuts me off.

"I'm gonna grab a shower while you pack," he says. He turns on his heel and heads toward the bathroom, and I can't drag my eyes away from his ass—the ass that looked amazing in his tiny Speedo.

The voice that should be telling me to quit checking him out is drowned out by his words repeating in my head.

"Wait. Pack?" I ask.

Noah's smile, blinding and cocky, sends warmth to my gut, and when the words "I got permission from Damon to take you back to New York early" fall out his mouth, I want to swallow concrete to keep my feet planted to the spot. Otherwise, I run the serious risk of crossing the room and kissing the fuck out of him.

"You ... what?"

He has to say it again or I might not believe it. "You're welcome."

"Why? I mean, why did you do that?"

Noah shrugs. "Well, shit, if you want to stay and endure more of being trapped in this room and trying to ignore the assholes with cellphones taking photos of you on the ship like they did at the cigar bar last night, by all means, we can stay."

"No," I say quickly. "I want to go. I just ... I—"

His grin widens. "You suck at saying thank you. Just so you know. But hey, if you can't find the words, I can think of other ways you can thank me."

And there he goes bringing out the wiseass again. Only, this time, I'm *this* close to taking him up on the offer. "Thank you," I grumble.

"There, that wasn't so hard, was it? Bad news is I did promise Damon we'll still get to know each other. So, you're stuck with me, but it'll be in my four-bedroom townhouse where you can have your own bed."

"I can totally deal with that."

He continues his way to the bathroom, and I start and finish packing before Noah even finishes his quick shower. I've probably put some of his stuff in my bag, but I'm too eager to get outta here and I don't care. We can sort it back in Manhattan.

When Noah emerges wearing only a towel, I audibly gulp. Before I was immune to his body. Okay, not quite immune, but immune enough. Now? How does one afternoon make him so much more attractive?

"You want the shower?" Noah asks, his toned arm lifting to run a hand over his head.

"Umm—"

"Wait, did you pack all my shit too?"

"I just kinda threw everything in a bag."

"If you wanted me to walk around naked, you could have just said so."

Damn his stupid smile and his stupid attitude that's stupid. That's a whole lot of stupidness for one person.

Stupidness that I'm starting to find charming.

What the hell?

"I'm going to shower," I blurt out.

Noah's brow turns into a frown. "O ... kay."

I tip my head, because let's just make this more awkward, and charge past him into the bathroom. As soon as the door is shut, I lean against it and breathe deep. All I have to do is make it until we get back to New York, and then we'll have separate rooms and some space.

I can do that. It's only like a two-hour flight.

I've got this.

I so don't got this.

"You a nervous flyer?" Noah asks next to me.

I startle. "What?"

"Your leg hasn't stopped bouncing since we took off."

"Oh. Umm, right." Yes, let's pretend flying is my issue.

He reaches for my hand. "I know this won't ease your mind, but you're more likely to die in a car crash."

"Yeah, but if a car crashes, you have a chance. A plane goes down? It's all over."

I'd like this to be all over, because as his thumb makes circles on my hand, I'm pretty sure I'm a few seconds away from jumping into his lap.

"I need to take a leak." I unclip my seat belt, and my feet push me toward the back of the plane.

"Thanks for the announcement," he quips.

I'm not going to survive this. I can't keep running to the bathroom every time I need to get away from him.

Although, this bathroom sobers me a little. The fancy-ass private plane has a fancy-ass bathroom with marble tiling, gold trimming, and a giant shower. I don't bother to contemplate how a fully-functional bathroom on a plane works with weight distribution and fuel consumption and just wonder how rich this guy is instead.

I splash my face with water and take a moment to compose myself. When I go back out to Noah, I focus on the one thing that will keep me from being tempted.

"The bathroom is bigger than the bedroom I shared with my two brothers growing up," I say as my ass sinks into the soft leather and I re-buckle my seatbelt. "How rich are you? I mean, I know your family's well off, but private plane? Manhattan townhouse?"

Noah gives me the side-eye, as if assessing how much to say. Or maybe he's wondering where I got the balls to ask him about finances. That's probably not proper etiquette or something. I think. Who the fuck knows.

"My father comes from old money," Noah says. "Like, really old money."

I haven't known Noah long, but there's something about the way he talks about his family that makes me wonder if he's ashamed of them or something.

Then his last name clicks ...

"You're one of *those* Huntingtons? Oil, stocks, real estate, all those other things where you need money to make money?"

"Yup. We're part of all that. My uncle is the one you see in the news for saying idiot-like things. And my cousins are his idiot-like children who are going to run the world one day. My uncle is the head of the Huntington fortune, but Dad's still very much involved. Just, on the downlow."

"Because your dad's in politics," I say.

"Exactly. I'm convinced he did it to give their developer

buddies tax cuts." He flinches when he realizes he said something wrong. "Please don't repeat that."

"We should fuck," I blurt out. Okay, even I know that came out of nowhere, and it was from *my* mouth, but since the interview earlier, I can't stop thinking about it.

Dang it to hell.

Noah stares blankly at me. "Hello, complete randomness. Not that I don't appreciate the abrupt subject change—or the words you just said—but, umm, did I somehow project myself into your brain and make you say that?"

I laugh, but I see his point. "Never mind. Forget it."

His hand goes to my forearm. "No way."

I sigh. "You want to know why I haven't been with anyone ... in that way?"

"Yes," he says a little too quickly. "I couldn't figure it out, and after I pissed you off, I figured it best not to bring it up again, but I'm dying to know."

"My entire life, I've followed a playbook. I know how to act, what to do, and I follow the rules. I told myself I could go to those clubs, get off, and then leave that part of me in the club. Taking guys home, or even going to their place, was a huge risk. The longer I spent with a guy, the more chance of him recognizing me, so I never risked it. I've been thinking that now that's not an issue. I'm out and you're my 'boyfriend.' And while your mouth annoys the heck outta me, I ... I like you."

"Ergo, you're suddenly doing a one-eighty, and we should fuck?"

"Right." I swallow hard. "With you, there is no playbook to live by. I have no idea what I'm doing, and every time you suggest hooking up, a little bit more of me starts to think it's a good idea."

"Score one for wearing you down. And people say persistence is annoying."

I groan. "See? That line last night would've pissed me off. Now I have to bite back from offering to shut you up a different way."

"In my defense, I didn't think you'd ever agree to it."

"So, you're just messin' with me? Because now I feel like a moron."

"No. I mean, I hoped you would agree, but I didn't think it was a possibility. Now that it's happening, I'm having a bout of moral consciousness."

"You have a conscience?"

Noah stares at me confused, as if trying to work out if I'm being an asshole or not.

"That was a joke, by the way. After what you've done for me today ..."

"After this afternoon, I don't think it'll be a good idea."

Confusing much? "Okay, how did we just switch places? Did we fly through the Bermuda Triangle and some weird *Freaky Friday* shit is happening?" I now want to do this, but he's changed his mind?

What kind of fuckery is this?

"I didn't realize how much is at stake for you until we had that interview," Noah says. His tone is sympathetic and genuine, yet another reminder that his outside persona is a front. "What if we cross that line you said you don't want to, one of us fucks up, and it affects your career even more? That's a lot of pressure."

"It's just fucking, Noah."

"In my experience, fucking always leads to someone getting hurt."

"How rough do you like it?" I joke.

Noah cracks up laughing, but it dies as fast as it comes. "You know how I told you about Aron?"

"The kinda ex but not?"

"He, umm, wanted more in the end, and I just couldn't give it to him. I don't like hurting people, but I do it anyway. It's like, I can't help it. I screw up everything good before it can go bad. I don't want to do that to you. You've got enough on your plate without adding my assholiness to it too. It also makes me nervous you changed your mind so quickly."

"You know what I realized during that interview today?"

"That Speedos do absolutely nothing to hide hard-ons?"

I chuckle. "Apart from that—and that you like to play dirty by rubbing all over me—I've followed a certain set of rules since before I hit puberty. When I was younger, if I did anything slightly effeminate, I'd get in trouble and told real men don't act like that. So, I made sure not to. Dad put it in my head that men are supposed to be tough, they're not into other men, they play sports, and act like cavemen. I had to set rules for myself before I even knew what being gay meant and had to hide that I had a crush on boys in my class. And now, even though I hate the way it all came out and I was robbed of being the one to choose how and when I smashed through that closet door, I realize I'm free. For the first time in my life, I can kiss a guy if I want to, be with a guy, hold hands in public with a guy. Unfortunately for you, you've signed on to be my boyfriend, so that guy is you."

"That's how you think you're going to get me into bed? You're contractually not allowed to touch other guys, so you may as well touch the guy you rented to be your boyfriend? I'm feeling the love here. I mean, it has nothing to do with my piercing blue-green eyes that don't belong on a mocha body? My toned muscles, tight ass, and—if I do say so myself—my awesomely sculptured abs?"

"Not to mention your humbling personality," I say. I don't understand his hesitance or what's changed since this morning. "And FYI, it's not renting you if I'm not paying you. Also, I don't need to tell you you're gorgeous. You're well aware of that fact. And so is everyone else with eyes. Lars was disappointed when he asked if we were completely monogamous and I shut him down."

Noah grins. "I knew that dude was into us. That could've been fun."

"A-are you serious? Like ... all of us? Do you have three-somes often?"

"Never. The idea of it is pretty hot though. I'd never be able to pull something like that off."

When I look at him questioningly, he clarifies.

"Campaign trail. Maybe after eight years in the White House, I'll be free of having to worry about what I do in the public eye all the time. It's nowhere near as bad as you, but it's still pretty exhausting."

"See? We're perfect for each other."

Noah stiffens.

"Calm down, I don't mean in a 'let's do this for real' type thing. I just want sex."

"Aaaand I'm back to feeling like a rentboy."

I shrug. "Whatever gets you off."

"I can't decide if I like this Matt. He's definitely better than cranky Matt, but more intense than joking Matt. Did someone slip you some drugs? If so, where are mine?"

"You want me to go back to being pissy? Because I'm pretty sure if you keep talking, it'll happen."

Noah's knee bounces. It's obvious what he wants to do, but for some reason, my agreeing to it has made him pause. Maybe he thinks I can't handle it, or maybe he's worried I'll turn out to be like his ex. "This is a colossal mistake. You know that, right?"

"As big a mistake as getting caught in a gay club?"

"Exactly. Your career is already fucked. I don't want to fuck with your head too."

"Trust me, it's not my head urging me to do this." Now I'm the nervous one, and my leg matches his fidgeting.

His gaze flicks from my eyes to my lips, and then his tongue darts out, but he's tense with reluctance.

"If you're worried I'm going to fall for you, don't be," I say. "I don't belong in your world, and you don't belong in mine. Could you imagine taking me home to meet your family? My family is so poor ... well, there are a million jokes I could finish that sentence with, and they'd all be true. The only reason they ain't livin' in a trailer now is 'cause I paid off their house with my first NFL check. I wasn't brought up to be like you, and the money I've made from playing football doesn't change that. I come from nothing. I've always been trash, and I always will be. I have tabloid photos to prove it."

"Matt—" Noah's tone holds pity, and that's not what I want.

"I'm not looking for sympathy. I'm simply saying we both know this will be over as soon as it needs to be. There's no reason either of us will become attached. You don't do attachments for some reason, and I've never even tried. What I do know is, you drive me so crazy I don't know whether to push you down and fuck you or shut you up by shoving my cock down your throat."

Noah's eyes widen. "Okay, I take it back. I could definitely get used to this Matt."

Rare moments in time slow to the point where you don't know if it's stopped completely, but as we stare each other down, neither of us moving, I begin to wonder if it's happening right now.

Without any warning, he leans across our seats, and I meet him halfway. It's not slow; it's instant. One minute we're apart, and the next we're going at it. He seals his lips over mine, and I try to suck in a breath, but that invites his tongue into my mouth. It sends a jolt down my spine. A masculine moan echoes through the cabin of the small plane, but I don't know who it comes from.

A large hand cups the back of my head, and Noah didn't shave this morning, so his stubble breaks through my soft beard and scrapes my face.

Fingers trail down my neck, tentative and softer than I'm expecting, but Noah's tenderness doesn't last long. His hand drops to my cock and strokes me through my jeans. My balls draw up tight, and I shudder.

My head falls back against the seat, breaking our mouths apart. "Fuck," I hiss.

"Can I?" Noah asks.

Hesitance seeps in as my eyes find the cockpit door where Noah banished the flight attendant upon takeoff. "Uh, when I said we should fuck, I didn't mean it had to be right here and now."

"Don't worry about them." He nods behind him. "They're under strict instructions not to come back in here until we land. Keep your eyes on me. I want you in my mouth." His seat belt loosening rings in my ears, and blue-green eyes fuse me to the seat when he sinks to his knees.

I'm helpless to do anything but watch as Noah undoes my

seatbelt, followed by popping the button on my jeans and then pulling down my zipper, but he doesn't take my cock out.

Bastard.

My hands tremble, so I grip my armrests. Noah's masculine and expensive-smelling cologne blankets me. This is unlike any hookup I've had. The way his hands move over me, the way he stares up at me with those stupid eyes that are unnaturally aqua. Even though this is about getting off, there's no rush as his hand goes under my shirt and over my hard abs and pecs. He hasn't even touched my cock yet, but I'm ready to come.

His mouth quirks. He knows what he's doing to me.

"Are you always this torturous?" I ask.

His smile widens. "You think *this* is torturous?" He pinches my nipple, and pins and needles erupt down my body. "I can do torturous."

"Wanna come," I complain.

"This isn't one of your cheap hookups. I'm going to show you sex is more than a quick BJ in a nightclub."

I squirm in my seat. I ain't used to this level of ... intensity. Get in, get off, disappear. That's what I know.

"Stop freaking out," Noah says. "It's still just sex, but it doesn't have to be quick and meaningless." He stretches up and kisses me again. Slowly this time. It calms my racing heart but does nothing for my hard-on. If anything, it makes it harder.

Noah reaches between us, gripping me through my boxers.

"Oh my God, just pull it out already," I complain.

"For that"—Noah stands—"you need a time out."

Time out? What the fuck? "It's official. You're as annoying in bed as you are out of it."

He unbuttons his light-blue shirt. Agonizingly slow. It takes everything in me not to chant that I hate him over and over again.

His shirt falls off his dark, toned shoulders, and I tell myself not to groan. Don't move. Don't even breathe.

When he reaches for his jeans, I white-knuckle my armrests. Noah's smile simultaneously pisses me off and turns me on. Somehow.

His pants drop to the floor, and I'm not surprised he's going commando—like he knew this would happen. Damn it. His cock is long and hard and—

"I think you're drooling," he says and wraps his fingers around his shaft.

"Gurnnngh."

"Is that English?"

"You're drivin' me crazy." Gah, stupid accent.

"Mmm, speak Southern to me." He strokes his cock, and I've never seen anything more mouthwatering. I want to lean in and take him in my mouth, but I'm sure that will result in a longer time out. Doesn't stop me from licking my lips as he swipes precum from the tip. "You want this?"

All I can manage is a small nod.

He takes one step forward, my anticipation builds, and then the asshole sinks to his knees again.

I groan.

"No complaining."

The second he pulls my cock out of my boxer briefs, tension builds in my gut, and I almost come. "I ain't gonna last long."

Noah chuckles. "*Ain't*. So cute." His head dips and his tongue swipes over my slit, and then he sucks me into his mouth.

"Holy fuck."

I try to grip his hair, but his closely shaved head doesn't allow it. Instead, I fist my hand on my leg. My hips lift off the seat, and Noah moans around my dick.

Closing my eyes, I try to make this feeling last. The wet heat of his mouth brings me closer and closer to the edge, but then he's pulling off me. The cold air of the cabin hits my skin, and my cock tries to shrivel up.

My eyes fly to Noah's.

"I told you to keep your eyes on me. No closing them."

"Fuckin' hell," I mumble.

"And no complaining."

I've never had the desire to give the finger to the guy blowing me while simultaneously begging him not to stop.

When he takes me into his mouth again, I make sure not to look away. Watching as his head bobs up and down adds to the sensory overload.

"Noah," I warn.

His mouth is replaced by his hand. "Come on my chest."

My breathing is ragged, but I grind out, "Swallow. Less messy."

"You forgetting there's a shower in the plane bathroom? You were literally just in there."

That's all it takes. I come with a grunt all over his skin. My muscles tremble, and I haven't fully recovered when Noah stands, grips onto my hair, and brings his cock to my lips.

I welcome him eagerly, taking him to the root in my mouth, while my arms continue to shake and my breathing still falters.

"Damn," Noah whispers.

The plane hits unexpected turbulence, and Noah falls forward. His hands go to the headrest of my seat. His cock goes to the back of my throat, and it doesn't help the breathing situation, but I want it. Fuck, I want it.

"You ready for it?" he asks.

I hum and squeeze his ass cheeks, controlling his thrusts into my mouth. His muscles contract under my fingers, and warm spurts hit my tongue. My chest fills with something like pride or accomplishment. Making a guy come is the one thing that boosted my confidence whenever I doubted football. A shrink would probably say it's the intimacy I get from being with someone, but that's bullshit. It gives me a high.

After Noah's done, he shudders and pulls out of my mouth. Then he sort of falls on top of me, as if his limbs can no longer hold him up, and straddles my lap.

I haven't had the chance to even swallow before he takes my mouth with his in a searing kiss. This is usually the part where I'd run away from my hookup, so it takes me off guard that not only is this guy kissing me with the taste of himself on my tongue, but that I like it. Love it, even. Hottest sexual experience of my life.

Noah pulls away. "We need that shower. We'll be landing soon."

Reluctantly, I let him go, and he climbs off me. Noah's comfortable moving around the cabin naked, but paranoia kicks in. I stand and tuck myself away.

"Noah?"

He pauses at the door to the bathroom.

"There aren't like ... surveillance cameras in here, are there?"

He flinches back. "Wow. The high from coming really doesn't last long with you, huh?"

"I didn't mean—"

"No, you jackass. There aren't any cameras in here. I wouldn't film anyone while I got them off. At least, not without telling them. I'm not *that* much of an asshole." He heads for the bathroom again.

On shaky legs, I follow him. "I didn't mean it to sound accusatory."

Noah ignores me and closes the shower door behind him.

"I'm sorry," I say loud enough for him to hear over the spray.

He turns and pierces me with an exasperated gaze. "Hurry up and get in here."

I strip and join him, wrapping my arms around him from behind, because I'm not convinced he believes my apology. "I was honestly asking because I was trying to figure out if we had to find a way to destroy the footage. I wasn't going to be mad if there was a tape. It's just, Damon would kill me if a sex tape got out, and not thinking about this stuff has clearly bitten me in the ass before."

Noah leans back against me. His ass presses against my half-hard dick. My lips find the back of his neck and trail down to his shoulder.

Noah was right about one thing. I'm more relaxed around him now. Or maybe that's the aftereffects of a mind-blowing orgasm. It might be official: blowjobs fix everything.

"Do you realize you've had like three showers today?" I chuckle against his neck.

"What can I say, you make me feel dirty. And as much as I'd love round two, we don't have time," Noah says. "If we're not back in our seats for landing, they *will* come in here to get us." He turns in my arms, and I love the feel of him against me. I'm regretting not doing this the first time he asked. "But I promise there'll be more once we get home."

With a quick kiss and a rinse off later, I have to grab a new shirt from my duffel bag because mine is covered in my cum. "I told you it was messy. Even with the shower."

"I like messy. I like being marked."

And I'm hard again. Fuckin' hell.

"Don't give me that heated stare with your sweet brown eyes," Noah says. "We don't have time. Buckle up."

I slump in my seat and throw my head back, closing my eyes.

"Oh, and Matt?"

"Mmhmm?"

"Welcome to the mile-high club."

I grin and do my internal victory dance when I score a touchdown. I'm not one of the guys who dances in the end zone. I'm more of a fist pump, yell, and get tackled by teammates kinda guy. Or ... I was. I wonder if that'll change with a new team that knows I'm gay. If I even get a contract.

When Noah gives me a questioning look, I say, "You admitted blowjobs count. Guess I'm not a virgin, huh?"

Noah's face falls. "Damn it. Okay, you win this one."

CHAPTER EIGHT

NOAH

By the time our chauffeured car pulls up to my brownstone, it's late and I'm ready for bed but not necessarily to sleep.

The in-flight blowjob only took the edge off. Or perhaps it was the appetizer. I'm ready for the main course. I should probably take things slow with Matt, but it's not like we're doing this for real. We'll be pretend boyfriends who fuck. He won't ask more of me.

That's what Aron said in the beginning.

I don't have time to dwell on that thought because Matt grabs his duffel bag out of the trunk.

"That's what the driver is for," I say.

Matt scoffs, tips the driver, and then grabs my suitcase and wheels it behind him. "Scared you'll get calluses if you carry your own stuff?"

"It's his job."

"Come on, money bags, show me your mansion. I didn't get a good look last time I was here."

True. The night we met, I could tell he was there, but he wasn't really *there*. His mind was in survival mode.

"It's not a mansion. It's a small four-bedroom townhouse." That's worth about six million dollars. *Yeah, don't mention that.* "And one of the rooms is so small you can barely fit a queen bed in it."

"Oh, the hardship," Matt says.

I grit my teeth. It's not my fault I was born into a rich family. It's not my fault that when my grandfather died, he left me the brownstone in Manhattan or that my family dynamic is pretty messed up. My father was practically disowned by my racist grandfather when he got my mom pregnant, but for some reason, he never took out that anger on me, his biracial grandson. He spoiled me. I often wonder if he would've left me Dad's share of his estate had he known I was gay too. I inherited this place before I could even legally vote.

I get why Matt would look down on something like having your driver carry your bags, but it is literally part of their job, and it's the life I've led since I was born. It's reflex. I know not to say things like that to a guy who almost had to live in a trailer park growing up, though.

Seeing it through his eyes, I cringe when we reach the stoop to my place. I try not to be a dick to those on the family's payroll, but I guess I don't go out of my way to make them feel appreciated either.

"You've got to be kidding me," Matt mumbles as he stares at the house.

"Okay, okay, I'm a rich snob. Fine. You can say it."

Matt shakes his head. "Not what I was going to say at all. This place is amazing. An architect's dream." His hand reaches for the crown molding around the entryway.

"You do architecture as a hobby?" I quip.

"Nah. Always interested me though. My dad said I needed to go for something easier like a business degree and focus on football instead. I might've become an architect if I knew how to stand up to the guy."

That's pretty heavy. "But I thought you were born for football."

"No, I was born gay. Football was my escape growing up, which is pretty ironic if you think about it. Without football, I could've come out in college and fucked my way through the entire queer population at Olmstead. Instead, all I had were protein shakes, training, and the occasional hookup where I did all the work because I was too chicken shit to ask Maddox to return the favor."

"He didn't even offer?" I ask incredulously. "What a dick."

Matt laughs. "We were both pretending we were super straight. Hell, after I left, he still thought he was straight."

"Until he met Damon."

"Right."

"Okay, question," I say. "If you could do it all again, give up your football career and study architecture while fucking your way through college, would you?"

Matt purses his lips as he thinks it over. "No. I love football even if I was forced into it. It's been my life, and I ain't ready to let it go."

"Then you have your answer. You don't need to dwell on what could have been when you're living the dream."

"Am I, though? I'm currently unemployable, I was outed against my will, I'm hanging on by a thread—"

I grab his shoulder and squeeze. "We'll get that contract. You'll still play."

While I have no idea whether it's possible for that to happen, it does the job. Matt relaxes under my touch, and then he leans in and kisses me. I'm taken off guard because this isn't a hookup type of kiss. It's soft, and the hand cupping my face is gentle. It's appreciative, like he actually believes the shit coming out of my mouth. I hope I'm telling the truth, but I don't know a thing about football.

I step forward and press against him, and Matt moans when my tongue takes control of his.

"Inside," he demands.

Why's it so much harder to unlock a door when you're about to get laid? Oh, right, because Matt squeezes my ass, and my dick volunteers to open the door for me by trying to push its way through my pants.

We manage to stumble inside, drop our bags in the foyer, and toe off our shoes before I can't take it and pin Matt against the wall.

The grunt that escapes him when I line up our cocks and thrust my hips has me almost coming.

"Maybe you were right in the beginning." I breathe hard and speak in low murmurs. "Maybe this isn't a good idea."

Matt pulls away so fast his head bounces off the wall behind him. "Why?"

I cup his face. "Because once wasn't enough. I don't know my number with you."

"Your number?"

"How many times it'll take to get you out of my system." And that scares the shit out of me. Except for Aron and my douche of a high-school-slash-college boyfriend, there's always been a number, and I've always been able to predict how long.

A month, a week, a cab ride ...

There's something innocent and pure about Matt, which is hilarious when taking in his two-hundred-thirty-pound frame and muscular football physique. I want to show him new things. I want to show him how good it can be with the right person. Not a forever guy—I can't be *that* for him—but someone Matt can be himself around. I'm the last person who's going to judge him.

He kisses me hard and pulls me against him by gripping my ass. I want to fuck him. I want him to fuck me. God, I just want us to fuck each other—I don't care how, where, or who's on top.

The chance to do either dies along with my erection when someone clears their throat.

"When you're quite done," Dad says, standing at the archway between the foyer and the living room.

"Shit," I mumble and bury my head in Matt's neck. This is the big blowup I'd hoped for, and now that I'm about to get it, it's the last thing I want.

"Umm, Noah?" Matt asks. "You have company."

With a deep breath, I pull away and face Dad. "Hello, *Father*."

"Son." Dad turns the icy stare he's perfected onto Matt. "Mr. Jackson."

Matt holds out his hand. "Senator Huntington."

"What are you doing here?" I ask when Dad doesn't shake Matt's hand.

"Someone calls for the jet, I naturally assume it's you. And seeing as your phone's been off for days, this was the only way I could get through to you that this relationship needs to end."

"Yeah, that's not going to happen," I say.

"You're twenty-six years old, Noah. When are you going to stop playing around?"

"We're not playing around. We're serious." Lying to my dad has always come easy for me. *Of course, I wasn't one of the ones getting drunk on the beach. Of course, it's the professor's fault I failed poli-sci sophomore year. Of course, I'll come home for Thanksgiving.* I tell him what he expects to hear, because I know he won't be interested in the truth. Ever. If I told him I was helping out a friend by using our family's rep as leverage, I'd probably be disowned. Not that it would mean much. Thanks to Grandfather, I'm worth more than my father at this point.

"How am I supposed to spin this?" Dad asks.

"With all due respect, sir," Matt says and steps forward. "My agent and management team are working on salvaging my reputation and my career. Noah and I have not, and will not, do anything wrong or anything that will make you or your campaign look bad."

"My son being with a media nightmare is bad enough."

Unexpected protectiveness builds in my chest, and I swear a growl escapes. Apparently, I growl now. Great. I shake it off.

"Do you know what this looks like?" Dad says.

I shrug. "I don't know. Maybe it looks like your son believes love is love no matter who it's with. Even a down on his luck football star with a shady reputation."

"Find someone else. I've managed to stay scandal free my entire career."

I laugh, not only at him talking about Matt as if he's not standing two feet in front of him but because I've heard this speech before. "Who? Who should I find? You've never approved of any of my boyfriends, and we both know you never will. You want the trophy gay son for your campaigns, but you don't want me to *be* gay. People are cool with the queer thing if they don't have to see it, right? *No PDA—no one wants to watch that*. That's what you told me numerous times. I'm a token to you. With me you get the black vote and the LGBTQ vote, but you don't want me to actually be either of those things."

Beside me, Matt's hands fist at his sides.

Shit, I've said way too much in front of him. "It's time for you to go," I say to my father.

"You can't kick me out of my own home."

"This is my home, or did you forget that?"

He's always hated that I got more than him in Grandfather's will. Of his siblings, Dad got the least, and then his share was divided even more because of me. My cousins resent me because I'm the only grandchild who got anything, and I get the feeling that happened because my grandfather suspected my uppity family would try to cut me out in the future. Rich dude logic—they're never happy with what they have, even though they're wealthy enough to buy their own country.

Dad relents. "I expect you to be in the office tomorrow to discuss this further."

"No can do. Busy. Sorry." Okay, even I heard the sarcasm in that.

"You're needed on this campaign. I never make you come in, but there are strategies that need to be devised, and you are still one of my strategists, aren't you?"

"Only because you know if you fire me, the tabloids will catch wind of how shitty a father you are."

Dad's raging but trying to contain it in front of Matt. He's not a violent man. He barely shows emotion other than his usual stoic expression. The biggest thing he's ever done was threaten to cut me off. But right now, he stands there with his face turning red, and he's more than livid. It's the first time in my life where I've wondered what would happen if I pushed too far.

"When are you going to get over what I did for you in college?"

He talks to me as if I'm the one being a petulant child, and well, maybe he has a point, considering my relationship with Matt is a ruse to piss him off, but I'm not the one trying to control my father's life. No, that's the other way around. Always has been that way, and I'll be damned if I'll continue to lie down and take it.

"What you did *to* me, you mean. Not *for*."

"If that boy really was the love of your life, he wouldn't have accepted a measly fifty grand and tuition to leave you. Especially when he knew how much we're worth. Trust me when I say he"—he points to Matt—"will be no different."

Matt makes a strangled noise at the back of his throat, and I freeze. I can't move, and I can't think of a retort other than a big fuck you, but I don't know if it'll be worth it.

So we continue to stand here staring at each other with nothing left to say.

"I'll see you tomorrow," Dad finally says and walks out the front door.

My gaze is locked on where my father had just stood and said the one thing that he knew would get me to back down. Of course, he'd bring up Nathaniel and play on my insecurities like that. It's Dad. And it doesn't matter if he has a point, because Matt and I aren't real.

That doesn't change the fact the thought of Matt accepting a payout to disappear fills me with gut-wrenching dread. I should be encouraging him to take it. Free money. A bonus parting gift.

When I've swallowed my anger, I meet Matt's eyes. "Guess that was a total mood killer, huh?" I say, my mask of indifference back in place, even though my heart beats erratically in my chest.

"He bribed your boyfriend?"

Of course, he won't let it go.

"Don't want to talk about it." I go toward the kitchen to wet my dry mouth with a glass of water but turn at the last second. "And if you tell Damon or Maddox what happened, this deal is done."

"They don't know? Does anyone?"

"Why would I tell anyone my boyfriend—the guy I thought I was going to end up with forever—thought I was worth fifty K?"

"Uh, so they could track him down and kick his ass?"

Damn it, his answer makes me smile. "He's not worth it."

"Is he why you don't do real relationships?"

"Is your fear of being gay the reason you're still a virgin?" I snap.

Matt's mouth drops open, but he shouldn't be surprised. I'm aloof on the outside and an asshole on the inside. Ask anyone. I take his silence as the opportunity to leave the room and get that drink.

Footsteps follow after me. "Don't do that." God, he sounds like Damon.

"Don't do what?"

"Be an ass to change the topic away from your personal shit by trying to offend me. It won't work."

I chug the water. "I'm not discussing this with you. No, not even that—there's nothing to discuss. Should've known better than to fall for the scholarship kid, and I was the dumbass who then followed him to college thinking my dad couldn't do anything about it. Douche ex-boyfriend was a douche. Dad was a bigger douche. The end."

Strong arms wrap around me, and with the simple touch, my racing heart falters and begins to calm.

"Who would've thought the thing we had in common would be daddy issues," I try to joke.

"I'm sorry for thinking you had it easy because you have money."

I run my hand over his thick forearm. "Things aren't always greener."

"I'm also sorry for all the douches in your life," Matt says. "I promise I'll try not to be one of them."

Smiling, I lean back against him. "You're not so bad."

"When I'm not cranky, I know."

"You know, sex is known to make a cranky man happy."

Matt groans into the back of my neck, and his hips thrust forward, pushing his cock against my ass. "I'm up for it if you are."

He really is up for it. I can feel him hardening.

"Guess we're about to find out if you're a top or bottom," I say. He laughs against my skin, and I shiver. I close my eyes to enjoy the sensation.

"Pretty sure I'm going to be okay with either."

My eyes fly open, and I turn in his arms. "How do you know?"

One side of his mouth turns up. "I have so many toys at home I could probably open my own sex shop."

"Damn, that's hot."

Matt leans in and lays a kiss under my ear and then moves down my neck. His hands grip my hips and tug me closer. "And I've used them all. Every. Single. One."

My dick fills and throbs for release. The image Matt's painting ... *damn*. "Totally not being pervy, but I wanna see that sometime."

Matt laughs. "Not pervy at all."

"As much as I'd love to take your ass virginity right now, I want you to fuck me." I *need* it. I need to escape all the shit with my dad, and there's no better rebellion than being dicked out until I'm walking funny. And I've seen Matt's dick now. There's no way I'm going to be walking normally afterward.

"Not gonna say no to that," Matt whispers.

I lace my fingers with his and drag him up two flights of stairs to the third floor. Matt whistles as soon as we cross the threshold into my room.

"Are you going to do that every time you're reminded of how rich I am?"

"Yes."

"That's going to get old."

He whistles again, and when I glare, he throws his hands up in surrender. "Okay, I'm done. I think."

"Good. Now we can get to the fucking."

With a predatory gaze, Matt pushes me down on my king bed, and I love his sudden burst of dominance. He sheds his shirt before climbing up me and straddling my waist. His mouth dives in as he leans over me, and he grunts when my hips thrust upward. He pulls me up so I can take my own shirt off, and then he's unbuckling my belt and slipping his fingers in my pants and around my shaft.

I throw my head back, trying to hold back the shuddering and moaning. I could get addicted to Matt's strong grip.

My hands wander on their own, feeling the hard planes of Matt's insanely ripped biceps and chest. I find his nipple and squeeze gently, remembering he liked that on the plane. Quickly, he forces my hand away. Confused, I pull back.

"You're going to make me come."

"From nipple play? I want to do that now, just so I can tell people I'm that good."

Matt leans back on his heels and laughs when I try to tweak his nipple again.

"Damn, maybe you'll make an excellent bottom after all if you can come from that," I say.

"It's a talent and a curse."

"You should get them pierced."

"Can't. Work hazard."

"We'll come back to that later. Right now, I need you."

Matt stands from the bed. He loses his jeans and then his boxers, while he stares down at me with a hungry, feral look in his eye. It's hot as fuck, and I freeze.

My gaze doesn't leave his strong hand that makes its way to his cock and starts stroking slowly. Suddenly everything becomes too real. The air thickens, and I'm riddled with guilt.

Matt picks up on my hesitance, and he cocks his head. "What's wrong?"

"I dunno. Shouldn't it be ... more than this?"

"Huh?"

"Like, for you. It's your first time. It should be ... *more*." I don't know how else to say it. "It should be more than a quick fuck, and with someone better."

Matt sighs. "I've already told you I don't consider myself a virgin. This is purely trying something new. I don't need romance or love. I'm not a teenage girl on prom night."

"Don't sell yourself short. You'd look hot in a prom dress."

He flips me off, and the mood is light between us, but doubt has already seeped into my bones ... or boner to be exact. I'm not good enough to be someone's first. I hurt everyone who tries to get close to me before they can do it to me, and I don't want to do that to Matt. I've never considered anyone else's feelings when I did shit like this in the past. After hurting Aron, I don't want to put myself in a position to do it again. But I want Matt so fucking much.

Matt pushes me back down as he straddles me again. A naked football player on top of me means my dick automatically springs back to life. It's science—chemical reaction or what-the-fuck-ever.

"I know what this is, Noah. I ain't gonna get clingy if that's what you're worried about."

"It's not." I wouldn't mind clingy. I like this part of a relationship—the newness and the fun stuff. It's when an actual attachment is formed that it freaks me out. Matt has said he's not looking for an actual relationship. This will all end when he goes off to football camp for preseason training. We might have to keep up appearances after that, but it won't be for long.

"Stop thinking and start doing," Matt says.

"Technically, you'll be the one *doing*."

"Good. Agreed. Now hurry up and lose your fucking pants."

I lean up on my elbows as he eases off me. "You're already starting to sound like me. Damon's going to kill me if I turn you into another version of Noah Huntington."

"I'm sure there are worse things than being compared to you." Matt doesn't wait for me to get with the program. He climbs off me and yanks at my pants, sending them to the floor. My erection bobs on my stomach, and Matt smothers a moan by biting his lip.

"Suck me while you get me ready."

"Don't have to tell me twice." Matt lowers his head and takes me in his mouth all the way to the root of my dick.

"Shit! I might love your mouth a little bit."

He pulls off me and strokes my aching cock. "BJs are the one thing I have had *a lot* of practice with."

I grip his hair. "Don't really want to hear about that while you're getting me off."

"Nuh-uh. Not allowed to come until I'm inside you."

"Nuuurungggh."

Matt recycles my words to him from the plane. "Is that English?"

Bastard.

I can't wait any longer. Reaching for my bedside table, I pull out lube and condoms. "Just hurry up."

"It bodes well for me that you want this to be speedy. I'm not usually fast on the trigger, but ..."

I smile. "First time and everything."

Matt takes the lube and lathers it generously on his fingers. My nerve endings roar to life with the slightest touch. His mouth goes back to sucking me as his fingers stretch and work my ass, and damn, I'm in heaven. Or hell. Depends on how I want to look at it. Matt takes his time opening me, but it's not from hesitance. He somehow knows what he's doing, and he's enjoying me squirming beneath him, silently begging him for more with my body. My hips move on their own, trying to get Matt's fingers deeper inside me. Heat pools in my groin, and I suck in a sharp breath.

I grip Matt's hair and love the feel of my fingers running through his surprisingly soft, brown locks. I allow myself three more seconds before I just about explode. "I'm going to come if you keep going."

"You ready?"

With a nod, I go to lie on my stomach when he grips my waist in his strong hands.

"I want to see you," he rasps.

A mayday warning rings in my head. That's too much. Too close. Too … everything I don't need. Yet, I don't protest. I can't bring myself to.

Matt leans up on his knees and tears the condom open with his teeth. The sight of him rolling it down his thick cock has me whimpering. He adds more lube, and I raise my knees to wrap my legs around his back. When he slowly enters me, I'm glad he didn't let me roll over. The bliss on his face is going to be a hard image to get out of my head. His eyes shutter closed, and his biceps bulge as they hold him up, as if he's worried about putting his entire weight on me. I love it, but at the same time, it makes edginess seep into my chest. Restlessness.

Matt shudders and moves slowly in and out of me. "You feel so good."

I'm too stuck to reply. I'm frozen, staring at his face, his high cheekbones and rugged, bearded jaw, and the look of awe and amazement that shines in his eyes.

I can't handle it.

"It's about to get even better." I push him off me, and before he can stop it, I'm on my stomach and raising my ass in the air. "I want you to fuck me hard."

Seconds go by where nothing happens, and the coldness of the air on my bare ass makes my heart kick up a notch. I rest my head on my forearm and hope he's not about to call me out for being unable to face him.

Instead, his punishing hand grips my hip hard enough to cause a bruise. "You sure that's what you want?" His gruff, accented voice sends a shiver through me.

"Fuck yes."

Matt lines up his cock, but there's a brief moment of hesitance. Before I can speak, it's gone, and he inches inside. I have to bite down on my arm to keep from calling out.

I want pain, I want it rough, I want to remember why I hate relationships. Because with Matt and that one look that will be burned into my memory forever, I run a real risk of forgetting what it's like to have something more. The heartache, the mistrust, the fighting. I can't do it. I won't do it.

Matt doesn't give me a chance to adjust and gives me exactly what I ask for. He picks up his pace, and every hit of my prostate breaks me a little more.

The realization that Damon's right, and I actually do like Matt, freaks me out. I can't be the guy he needs.

Then he goes and covers me with his sweaty, beefy body, and I come unglued. The soft kisses on the back of my neck while he continues to fuck me are exactly what's wrong with this scenario.

Closing my eyes, I cherish every move, every thrust, because this is a mistake of epic proportions. It's a mistake I know I'm going to repeat time and time again, because when I screw up, I royally screw up.

"Noah." Matt's breathy voice sends me that much closer to the edge. "I'm gonna"—he grunts—"soon ..."

I love the unintelligible sentence and the fact he probably thought he said it right. I reach for my cock. A few strokes and I'm going to go off the edge. If I had the chance, I could probably come hands free with how he's pounding me.

He comes with a shout, and I suddenly regret being a stubborn asshole, because I want to see it. I want to see how he loses his composure.

Instead, I settle for his hand snaking around my waist and taking over stroking my cock. The second his fingers wrap around me, it's all over. My ass clenches around his still hard shaft inside me, and I come so hard I swear I can't remember the last time I'd felt physically exhausted from an orgasm.

When Matt pulls out and collapses beside me, I flatten onto my stomach and practically bathe in my own jizz. I should clean that up.

My eyelids are droopy when Matt climbs off the bed, but when I hear a "Holy shit!" I know he's found my bathroom which is bigger than my kitchen. I can't help laughing.

Drawers open and close, and before I can ask him what he's looking for, the water runs in the sink and then he's back with a warm cloth in his hand.

"Roll over," he says, his tone gentle.

For some reason I can't explain, I do as he says and don't protest when he wipes the cum from my stomach and off the bed. It happens so fast it takes until he's back in the bathroom for me to realize he's taking care of me. And I like it.

I roll back onto my stomach and bury my head in my pillow.

"What are you moaning about now?" Matt leans against the bathroom doorframe and folds his impressive arms across his wide chest. His naked body is nothing but phenomenal, and for a short while, I get to play with it. But I need boundaries before this gets out of control. Right now, I hold all the cards, and I'm not willing to share them.

Climbing out of bed, I grab a pair of sweats out of my drawer and throw them to Matt before finding myself a pair.

"I'll show you your room," I say and walk out before I can memorize the frown on his face. I'd much rather remember the way he stared down at me while he fucked me for the first time.

Matt stumbles after me down the hall. "Okay, what the fuck is up with that?"

I sigh. I'm not used to people calling me on my shit. "I prefer to sleep alone. We can screw around, do whatever in my bed, but to get a good night's sleep, I need my own space. And as we've already established, you're like a clingy bear when you're asleep, and you don't even mean to be."

"Did you just call me a bear? Aren't they fat?"

"You're more like a wolf with that beard." I lead him down the stairs to the biggest guest bedroom. "You can take this one."

"What a dump," he says dryly.

"I'll see you in the morning. Help yourself to anything you want. I'll have to do a grocery order, but there's beer in the fridge."

"Nutritional."

"Goodnight." I turn to leave, but he pulls me against him.

When his mouth meets mine, and his tongue forces its way into my mouth, I know without a doubt I've definitely made a mistake.

He pulls back and lets me go. "Goodnight."

CHAPTER NINE

MATT

Even though the streets of New York are filled with millions of people—literally—it's the first time I've been out in public in months where I'm not self-conscious. The thing easing my mind is the fact everyone still thinks we're in Bermuda.

I reach for Noah's hand and lace our fingers together.

"What are you doing?" he asks.

"I wanted to try something. This is *weird*. I'm holding a guy's hand in public and not freaking out over it. It's ... kinda awesome."

It didn't escape me last night when Noah shut down. Pretty much as soon as I'd entered him. When he rolled over, I realized I was making it too personal. He doesn't do serious. We're not having a real relationship. It's sex and then pretending to be in love for the cameras.

Right here, on the street, with no one following us, I want to know what it would be like to be with someone for real and how a relationship would fit into my life after the media shit storm dies down.

"Small things amuse small minds, right?" Noah says, gesturing to our hands.

"This isn't small. Not for me."

He winces. "Sorry. But I've been holding guys' hands for ... what, eight years in public? It's easy to take that for granted."

"If you're not cool with it, it's okay. I just wanted to know what it was like." I try to pull out of Noah's grasp, but he holds my hand tighter.

"I'm okay with it. It just felt ... boyfriendly, and I haven't had one of those in a long time for a reason."

After finding out the exact reason why, I can't blame Noah for being closed off. "All good," I say, but I still don't let go of his hand. The fact something so small is a massive accomplishment depresses the shit outta me. How is it I'm a twenty-three-year-old guy and something I should've experienced when I was a teenager brings a giant smile to my face?

"Where are we going?" Noah asks.

"I saw a coffee shop up here. I want to take advantage of going out while we can. In a few days, it'll go back to everything being crap."

"You storm into my room and wake me up so we can go get coffee? Had you let me sleep, it would negate the need for coffee. Also, the more we go out, the higher chance we have of being spotted."

"I'm taking whatever the world is willing to give me. I can't stay in your house all day every day. I will literally go crazy. I also need to find a gym close by that has day passes."

Noah stops walking. "I was going to keep it a secret, because I knew I'd lose you as soon as you found out, but my basement is full of gym equipment. You can work out there while you're staying with me."

"How long were you going to keep it a secret?"

"Until you asked me. And, look at that"—Noah checks his Rolex—"you lasted a suck, a fuck, and twelve more hours."

"You have such a way with words."

His carefree attitude toward everything is enviable. His life is far from perfect like I thought, but he doesn't let any of it get to him. At least, not on the outside.

I tug on his hand and bring him close to me. He grunts as he runs into my hard body.

"What are you doing?" he asks.

"Know what else I've never done in public?"

Noah's eyes dart around the street. "You can't give me a blowjob here ... oh wait, you *have* done that in public before."

I pinch his ass. "Not that. And the club doesn't count. The only reason that was public was because of those stupid photos."

"So, what haven't you done in public?"

"Kiss me," I demand.

"Is that a direct order?"

"Just do it already."

Noah leans in. "That's what you'll be screaming later."

My laughter is cut off by his lips on mine, and it's pathetic that I get an adrenaline spike from Noah kissing me on the side of the street. I don't know what it is about his mouth, whether it's the fact it likes to take charge and control my own or that this guy turns me on so much I'd be happy with any form of physical affection from him, but what I do know is I want more of him. I want anything he's willing to give me, even if it'll only be brief.

When Noah pulls back, I try to stop him—I want more—but he doesn't let me. "I'd love to keep kissing you right now, and though we're not in some small town in Tennessee, sometimes people aren't so cool about seeing two dudes make out. Even in New York. Sad but true."

"Right." Of course. I may have this new level of freedom, but that doesn't mean society won't try to shove me back in my cage.

Noah still holds my hand as we walk, and I love the feel of his smooth skin against my calluses. "Besides, if we kept going, it was going to turn into way more than kissing, and indecent exposure is a crime for some stupid reason."

I make a mental note to contact Damon and thank him for setting me up with Noah. He's becoming the exact thing I need in my life right now. His confidence and don't-give-a-shit outlook on life is enviable, and I want to be like him. Maybe not the relationship phobia, but I can't say I wouldn't be the same way if my dad did what his did. Had I been straight and had a girlfriend, I reckon my dad would've done everything in his power to make her disappear. Maybe if I was straight, I wouldn't have made it to the NFL at all, because I wouldn't have used football to hide behind. Maybe I'd be in the neighboring trailer next to my sister and her boyfriend with a baby momma and six kids.

I shudder at the notion.

Inside the coffee shop, Noah finds a table as I order. When I slide a coffee in front of him, he barely registers my presence. He stares at the table with his head in his hand.

"What's up with you?" I ask.

He startles and looks at his coffee and then at me. "Sorry. I didn't sleep well last night. This will help." He holds up his cup of coffee.

"I had the best sleep I've ever had." Sex probably helped.

After last night, I'm kicking myself for not risking being outed sooner. Does everyone know sex is that awesome?

Noah grins as if he can read my thoughts. "What're you thinking about?" Shit, maybe he can.

I lean in and speak low. "That we have three more days until our cruise comes back and that the only thing on my schedule is to work out and fuck."

"You know, if you retire from football, I'm pretty sure you could find someone and that could be your entire life."

"You think I should give up football?" I ask.

Noah shifts in his seat. "No, but if the whole contract thing doesn't work out, your future's not so scary."

"Didn't seem that way a month ago." My voice rasps, and I try to hide it. "I had nothing. If I don't get another contract, I'll have—"

"An opportunity to do whatever you want with your life. Go back to school and study architecture. Become a football coach. Live the life of luxury on the millions you've already earned."

Noah has a point. I have a finance guy who takes care of my investment portfolio, and my expenses are relatively small. I send money to my parents to help with my siblings, and I have my apartment in Philly which I stupidly bought instead of leased. If I sell the loft and invest the rest of my money the right way, I won't have to work another day in my life if I don't want to. But it's too soon for me to think about that. It's like I'm preparing to give up if I contemplate it.

"I ain't ready to say goodbye to football."

"And you say football isn't in your blood. Face it, Matt, you *are* football. Instead of blood, you're made up of pigskin."

"That's ... a pretty terrifying picture."

"You're welcome."

After Noah drinks at least half his coffee, I bring up a subject I should probably avoid if we're going to keep this fake relationship sailing smoothly. "Uh, so ... are you going to go see your dad today?"

"That'll be a big fuck no."

"Can I ask why you work for him if you don't want to?"

"Because he doesn't let me quit, and as I said last night, he won't risk firing me and have it get out to the press."

"So, no politicking in your future?" I ask.

"I'm not interested in the games you have to play to get ahead in that world. Politicians aren't there to help people. They're there to make themselves and their friends richer while screwing over those who actually need the money."

"No offense, but I don't see you donating your money to a good cause."

Noah's brow furrows. "I have financial advisors who limit my spending. I donate what I can, but the advisors are on the family's payroll. They're not going to let any of us blow our money. Think of me as a grown-ass man being treated like a kid getting an allowance. It's how things are done in my family."

"Why don't you—"

"Can we make this an off-limits topic?"

Knowing it's not my place, I drop it and lean back in my seat.

Noah finishes his coffee. "Ready to head back? I was thinking if you weren't so desperate for a workout and could hold off to hit the weights until later that we could go back to bed. And not to sleep."

I don't think I've drank a cup of coffee faster.

A daily trip to the coffee shop is the only time I see outside of Noah's townhouse for the next three days.

I get up at five a.m., work out in Noah's basement for a few hours, run to the coffee shop for my cool down, and then bring back coffee for Noah, and wake him with a blowjob. I learned the first time that coffee isn't enough of an incentive to wake him up.

"I could get used to this," he pants as I climb up next to him.

I reach for the bedside table for his cup and hand it to him while I take a sip of my own and lean against his headboard. "You could, but you can't. I'm going back to Philly today. We have to go pick up my car."

"Nah, it's all good. I gave Maddox and Damon the keys before we left the ship. They're bringing it here."

The hand holding my coffee pauses halfway to my mouth. "You ... you gave them permission to drive my car? And you swiped my keys?"

Noah winces. "I forgot about your rule and your precious Lamborghini, but come on, this way you don't have to deal with the media. I thought it'd be easier. If he crashes it, I'll give you my Beemer." Noah laughs when my eyes widen. "Babe, seriously. It'll be fine." We both pause at the slip of his tongue, but he recovers faster than I do. "Don't worry, I call all my hookups *babe*. It doesn't mean anything."

Oh. "Is that because you don't remember their names?"

"Not at all, Mike."

"Funny."

"And no, it's nothing like that. I guess babe is my go-to nickname when I'm with someone."

"Don't I feel special."

Noah puts his coffee back down before rolling over and

covering me with his hard body. "You are special. I don't let just anyone fuck me." His head dips, and he takes my nipple in his mouth. I don't know whether to be pissed off or turned on. He knows that's my Achilles heel.

"So, I'm the only guy you refuse to top?"

I've asked him. A few times now. He keeps saying he's fine with bottoming.

"I like what we've been doing." Noah works his way back up and kisses my cheek and then my jaw, and I have to agree, I more than like what we've been doing. Maybe I shouldn't complain. Noah's skirting the edge of welcoming intimacy and pushing me away. I'm wondering if it's his way of protecting himself.

When Noah takes my cup and sets it aside, I settle in for whatever he plans to do to me.

Noah moves down my body and tongues my abs. "Mmm, you're all sweaty."

"I can shower." I try to move but he pins me down.

"Don't. I like the way you taste."

I groan and lift my hips, trying to get him to go more south, but before we can get to the good part, the doorbell rings.

We both slink in disappointment.

"Did you lock the front door when you came in?" Noah asks.

"Umm, no. You told me I didn't have to, and I told you that you were crazy because you live in New York."

"So, you listened to me anyway?"

"Uh, yeah."

"If it's Maddox and Damon, they'll—"

"Yo, Noah!" Damon yells from inside the house.

"Do that."

"All good. I'm gonna jump in the shower," I say.

"Don't jerk off. I want a goodbye fuck."

"We'll see each other in two weeks for that benefit thing."

"And how do you think that'll go after coming countless times the last few days to nothing for two weeks?"

I purse my lips. "Good point."

"Hello?" Maddox calls out this time.

"I better go before they figure out we're up here messing around." With a quick kiss, Noah makes his way outta the room, and I collapse back on the bed. Guess I'll go for that shower. A really cold one.

The shower does its job in deflating my erection, but it doesn't dim the need I have for more of Noah.

By the time I drag myself from the bathroom, I have to sneak into my room and hope Maddox and Damon don't see me wrapped in a towel going between floors.

When I come downstairs, Maddox and Damon are making out on Noah's couch with Noah nowhere to be seen. What are they, fucking teenagers? Not that I could say Noah and I wouldn't be doing the same thing had they not turned up.

"Uh ... hi?" I say, and my voice goes unnaturally high-pitched. "What, a week away together and you still can't get enough of each other?"

Damon and Maddox jump apart. They're both a burnt brownish-red color.

"Did you guys wear sunscreen at all while you were away?" I ask.

Maddox frowns.

"Where's Noah?" I ask.

Maddox seems even more perplexed by that question, but I ignore him.

"Kitchen," Damon says.

"Got me a contract yet?"

Damon cocks his head. "Really, man? I've been on vacation. Give me a week to get back into things."

"Fine." I make my way into the kitchen where Noah's making the crappy coffee in his Keurig. He loves the stuff; I'd rather walk to the coffee shop up the street for the *real* coffee.

"I'm guessing you don't want one?" he asks.

"No thanks. Need any help?"

"You can go talk to Damon if you need to get business out of the way."

"Nah, they're making out on the couch. No one needs to see that, so I'll pretend I'm helping out in here." I pull myself up on the spare part of the kitchen counter.

"We eat off that thing, you know," Noah says.

I raise my eyebrow, because we both know we didn't eat food on here yesterday when he was bent over it and I was fucking him. Apparently, Noah unpacking Chinese food is sexy. That, and I wanted to shut him up about how boring my brown rice and steamed chicken looked.

"Don't look at me like that or there might be a repeat," Noah says. "I don't care who's in the living room."

"Pretty sure this won't stay a secret if we were to do that."

The heated stare he gives me has me not caring if Damon and Maddox were to walk in. That is, until Maddox actually walks in and our gazes break away from each other.

"Coffee ready?" Maddox asks.

"Yep," Noah says and slides over a cup. He takes the other two into the living room, and I'm about to hop off the counter to follow him when Maddox's hand hits the middle of my chest.

"Can I help you?" I ask.

He speaks low. "How long did you last before you fucked him?"

My face falls. "Huh?"

"Let's see, you were walking around in a towel; I had to maul Damon on the couch so he didn't see you. That could easily be dismissed if you were walking from the bathroom to your bedroom, but I'm pretty sure I saw you come from the third floor. Then, the first question you asked when you came down was about our trip, and the second was about Noah. That's when I knew for sure you were doing him."

"How?"

"I drove your car. I'm waiting for the questions about if I scratched it."

"Did you scratch it?" I ask and try to hide the panic in my tone.

"No, but I was still expecting the questions. So, tell me. How long did you last?"

I hesitate, wondering if I should tell him the truth. "Three days."

Maddox laughs. "I'm so disappointed in you. Three days? *Three*. It's Noah."

I slide off the counter. "There's nothing wrong with Noah. And don't say anything to your boyfriend about it because we were supposed to keep it professional."

"Oops. It slipped in? Is that how it happened?"

I ignore him, and his laughter continues to follow me as I head back to the living room and take the single armchair.

"I have to say I'm impressed," Damon says from the couch.

"Impressed?" I ask.

"Yeah, that you haven't killed Noah yet."

"It's been really hard," I say.

Maddox snorts behind me.

"Are you two coming tonight?" Damon asks.

"Tonight?" Noah and I say at the same time.

"Yeah, to that sports bar on Fifth. The usual people will be there. I figured Aron would've texted you." Damon's tone is half-fishing, half-accusatory, and I wonder how secret Aron and Noah's tryst really is. He said they were friends, but I didn't realize they still are or that they're in the same group of friends. That makes things more difficult.

"Oh, right. That," Noah says as if he were invited. My guess is he wasn't. "I might go. Matt's going home to Philly today."

"Maybe Matt can stay an extra night and come," Maddox says, and again, I suspect he knows about Noah and Aron too. And now he knows Noah and I are ... doing whatever it is we're doing, maybe Maddox thinks I should be there. For some reason. I'm not sure. Noah's contractually obligated to keep it in his pants, but if he wants to hook up with his ex, there's not much I can do about that.

"I'd be cool with that," Noah says. "If you want to come that is," he says to me.

"To a sports bar?" I ask.

"It wouldn't be a bad thing to have us photographed doing normal stuff."

"Hanging out with friends isn't exactly normal for me," I say.

"That's because you didn't have friends until now," Noah says.

Damon leans forward. "As long as you don't get drunk or argue with Noah where anyone can hear it, it'll be all right by your management team."

"You're my management team," I say.

"Exactly. And I can keep an eye on you."

"I guess I've got nothing better to do back in Philly."

"He's totally fallen in love with me," Noah says. "Can you tell?"

Maddox and Damon snigger. "Guess we'll see you both tonight," Damon says and stands.

And I guess I'm going out with Noah and his ex tonight. This should be fun.

CHAPTER TEN

NOAH

Inviting Matt tonight was a stupid thing to do, especially when I knew Aron would be here, but for some idiotic reason—I'm thinking my dick is responsible—I was focused on Matt staying another night and not the fact Aron is still pissed over how I ended things with him.

"On a scale of one to ten, how much is this Aron guy going to hate me?" Matt asks on our way into the bar. The paparazzi were surprisingly absent when we left the house, and they're not here either. I'd like to think it's because they've given up, but I think it's more to do with the fact they have no idea where we are since we weren't at the cruise terminal. That'll change quickly considering we're about to walk into a sports bar where Matt will no doubt be recognized.

"I haven't heard from him since he found out about us, but if that conversation was an indication, I'd stay out of glass-throwing range if I were you."

Matt grabs my hand—he's becoming really good at the PDA

thing—and pulls me close to him. "I think I'll be able to handle it." With his free hand, he raises his arm and flexes his biceps.

"Do those guns actually work for anything other than catching footballs?"

Matt leans in and whispers in my ear. "You know full well they have other talents."

After four days of countless rounds of handjobs, blowjobs, and fucking, I don't think I've ever had this much sex in my life. This is where I've been going wrong. I've never been with an athlete before. Matt's stamina is insane.

When my college boyfriend screwed me over, the only other guy I'd had regular sex with was Aron, and even then, our meet ups would be under my terms. Matt's different. He's always there and up for it. I thought it was a convenience thing for me, but the thought of him going back to Philly has me wanting to come up with ways to keep him in New York.

I tell myself it's because of the sex, but a part of me thinks that's a lie. I push that serious thought to the back of my mind and bury it as deep as possible in the part of my brain where I send rationality and maturity to die a slow and horrible death. Those bastards ruin everything for me, and right now I'm having fun with Matt. I don't have to think when I'm with him.

When we reach my table of friends, all conversations come to a halt.

"Don't worry," I say, "this is my friends' normal reaction to seeing me. My awesomeness renders them speechless."

There's a round of complaints from everyone and a chuckle from Matt.

"I think you've met everyone once before—the night you met Damon at my place," I say.

"Uh. Right. Yeah."

I get the feeling he has no recollection of that night, so I go around the table. "That's Rebecca and her fiancée, Skylar. The blond guy is Wyatt, next to him is Aron, and you already know the two assholes on the end."

"Hey," Maddox whines.

Matt's eyes linger on Aron for a second too long, and Aron's the first to glance away. Even from here, I can feel the tense energy coming off him.

Everyone says Aron's like the white version of me. We're exactly the same height, and he's toned and lanky like I am.

Matt takes the seat next to Damon, putting him three seats away from a pissed-off Aron. Brave man.

"I'll get us drinks," I say to Matt.

"Light beer," he reminds me.

"Yeah, yeah, calories, wah, wah, wah." Thank fuck I'm not a football player. No matter how many times I tell Matt to stop pushing himself while he's on break, he won't listen. He wasn't as bad on the cruise, but now he's determined to go back and prove himself if he gets a contract. He takes note of his calorie intake and exercises twice a day for hours at a time.

Screw that for a job.

At the bar, I'm half-expecting Aron to follow, but it's Wyatt who appears beside me, and I cut him off before he can start whatever lecture he came over here to give me.

"I didn't mean to hurt him," I say.

"I know. And I don't want to pick sides, but can you at least apologize to him for putting him through hell? You literally told him a month ago that you don't do relationships, and now you're parading Matt around. It's not exactly fair to Aron."

"I'm not parading Matt around. We're just seeing each other. It might turn into something serious, it might not. Give us a few months to work it out for ourselves." I realize now I definitely shouldn't have brought Matt here, but it was the excuse I needed to ask him to stay.

"Maybe you should come with a warning label," Wyatt says. His tone is light and joking, trying to make this less awkward, but I don't think that's a possibility now.

I huff. *"Caution: acts like a dick because he's an entitled asshole.* Has a ring to it."

Aron appears at our side. "I'm out."

His eyes find mine, and he waits as if I'm supposed to try to stop him, but we have nothing left to say to each other. I said I was sorry and I meant it, and I get that's not going to magically fix everything, but there's nothing I could say now to make it better either.

Aron eventually gives up, and unsurprisingly, Wyatt follows him out of the bar.

When I get back to the table, I slide Matt's drink in front of him and sip from mine.

"Thanks," Matt says. His hand goes to my forearm, and it's literally a two-second touch of gratitude that is nothing more than platonic, but the others don't see it that way.

I sip my beer and pretend they're not staring at me. I should know avoidance tactics won't work with my friends, because they don't stop. "So, yeah. Aron and I had a thing."

Everyone at the table is silent, but I know it won't last.

"You Noah'd him, didn't you?" Skylar says.

"Did you just use my name as a verb?"

"Yes," she says. "It means to act without considering the consequences. There's going to be sides taken and we have to be conscious of who we invite where and worry about offending someone, and—"

"No," I say. "If he can't get over it, cut me out. I'm the one who ended it, so it's my fault. Maybe coming tonight with Matt wasn't the best idea."

"Ya think?" Rebecca says and turns to Matt. "I hope you know what you're getting into."

Matt doesn't answer her.

I sip my beer again and do what I do best: pretend their words don't get to me. I know I fucked up. I act without thinking about how things will end, but it's not like I *plan* to do this shit. It comes naturally.

Skylar and Rebecca stare at Damon and Maddox as if having a silent conversation. Matt's gaze is fixated on me, but I refuse to acknowledge him.

A waiter takes our break in conversation as the perfect time to approach Matt and ask for an autograph.

Matt does it without hesitance, but Damon doesn't stand for it. He waves the waiter over once he has Matt's signature. "Tell your manager and the rest of the waitstaff that if you can prevent anyone from approaching Matt while we're here, he'll sign something for everyone on duty."

The kid's eyes widen. "Of course."

With a promise of a whole heap of signed merchandise, the waiter leaves us to our drinks and then circles us like a shark to prevent anyone else approaching.

"I don't think espionage is in that guy's future," I say.

"Yeah, he's about as subtle as you and Aron," Rebecca says.

"We're still on this?" I ask. "I'll back off. I hoped with the whole Matt thing he would've moved on by now. I won't come to anything else until he gets over it. How about that?"

"That's not what we want," Skylar says.

"Then what do you want? Because short of a time machine

to make me go back and tell past me not to go there with him, I'm all out of ideas."

"This is why hooking up with friends is a bad idea," Rebecca says.

"No shit," I mumble and look at Matt. "You've gone quiet."

He shrugs. "Don't think it's my place to say anything. It's between you and your ex."

Rebecca smiles. "Matt's way too mature for you."

"Probably true," I say. He's too everything for me. When he's not angry over being screwed by the Bulldogs, he's down to earth, fun, and damn, he's driven. Honestly, if it were me who got fired for being gay—he can say all he wants about it being about not being a team player, but the truth is he lost everything because of those photos that outed him—I would've ran away with my tail between my legs and hid out until everyone forgot who I was. Matt's optimistic and trying to find his way back into a world that doesn't want him, all because he's so passionate about football that he feels like his life is over if he can't play it.

I've never been that passionate about anything. Ever. And until now, I didn't realize I was missing out.

The others finally move off the topic of my shortcomings, but Matt still eyes me.

"You okay?" he asks.

"Of course. I'm always okay." I hate that I've known the guy a week and he already has a *I call bullshit* face he can pull at me. And that he's right. "Wanna go home? You're heading back to Philly early in the morning."

"If that's what you want."

I stand immediately. "We're out, guys. Maybe you can message Aron and Wyatt to come back."

"And so it starts," Rebecca says.

"Nah, here's where it ends," I say and turn to Matt. "You should go sign all that crap you promised before we head out."

I follow him to the bar and wait for him off to the side while he talks with the staff. The joys of being with a football player. I pity the women who have to do this permanently.

Damon appears next to me out of nowhere, and I flinch when he starts talking, as if preparing for a lecture. "Aron will get over it."

Not as bad as I thought. I relax a little. "I know he will. There's not much to get over."

He narrows his eyes. "Was that a dig at yourself or the relationship?"

"Both, I guess. Aron and I were never suited. We were bored. I shouldn't have crossed that line with him."

"Like you shouldn't with Matt. It's business."

"I know. In a few months, we won't ever see each other again."

"Might be sooner than that."

I pull back. "How soon?"

"Don't tell Matt, but I called my office today to check in. Apparently, there's a couple of teams taking calls about him. Nothing solid yet though, so don't get his hopes up. I should warn you, the closest one is in the Midwest. If you did start something, it'd be long distance, and as we've established, you can't even handle a relationship when you're in the same room."

"Got it. Warning received loud and clear. I won't fuck Matt."

Damon laughs. "How naïve of you to think I don't already know you're fucking."

"Are you and Maddox detectives now?" Matt told me about

their conversation in the kitchen, but he wasn't supposed to tell Damon about it.

"Your fake relationship doesn't seem so fake ... Are you serious about him, or are you repeating the same mistake?"

"It's just fucking and doesn't mean anything." Why does that feel like a lie? "I promise I won't break your precious golden ticket."

Damon rolls his eyes. "Come on, man, that's not why I came over here. I don't want to see either of you hurt."

"We'll be fine. We promised."

"Like Aron's fine?"

I wince. "Low blow."

"You want my advice?"

"Nope."

"Too bad. End it."

A big fuck you is on the tip of my tongue, but Matt finishes up talking with the staff, so Damon backs off.

We head out the front without so much as a goodbye to my friends. They mean well, I get that, and I did screw up, but it gets to me when they play the blame game.

"You oka—shit." Matt stalls in his tracks.

Paparazzi wait outside for us. Guess someone has a big mouth—or quick fingers on social media.

"And our break from the limelight is over," I say so only he can hear. "Come on. We got this."

Matt wades his way through the photographers like a pro, but in the car, his mood turns sullen. He doesn't say anything the whole way back to my place, but as soon as we're in the safety of my house, that's another story.

He grabs my arm. "You okay?"

"I already told you I'm fine," I say. "Shouldn't I be asking you that? The vultures are back."

"Did you notice there were less this time?" He says this as if that means something. I don't want to disappoint him by saying it might mean there was a bigger celebrity close by.

"I'm going to head to bed," I say. When I start up the stairs, he doesn't follow. "You coming?"

"Is that an invitation or are you asking out of some sort of obligation?"

My brow furrows. "Huh?"

"You can't tell me the shit your friends were saying hasn't gotten to you. You think you're going to do the same to me that you did to Aron, and they think so too. So, you're either inviting me up to cover the fact you're freaking out or you really don't care and you're repeating the same mistakes because you obviously never asked Aron what was going on during the entire time you were together."

"It's too late at night for psychoanalyzing." I turn on my heel and march up the steps.

"Goodnight then."

He's seriously not following me? Fine. He's leaving tomorrow anyway.

I continue up the stairs without looking back.

"Really?" Matt yells when I'm almost at the top.

I pause. "What?"

"I literally gave you an opening to talk about what went down tonight, and you're bailing."

"We're fucking, Matt. We don't talk."

That's a lie, and I know it. Matt's learned more about me in the week we've spent together than any of my friends have in years. For some reason, I've spoken to him about my issues with my father. Maybe I wouldn't have had he not overheard them, but the fact is, I've talked more with him than I have with any other person.

We get each other. We were brought up completely different but somehow have a lot in common.

"If that's how you want to play it, then fine, but if you ask me, I reckon your friends are full of shit."

I freeze on the steps and finally turn back. "You what?" I can't have heard right. No one takes my side. Ever.

Something a lot like gratitude tries to melt my cold, dead heart, but I don't let it. He's probably just saying it so I quit with the pity-party routine. I fucked up. It's my fault. There's no way around that.

"I get they're pissed because you and Aron have made it awkward between them." Matt slowly starts walking up the stairs to meet me. "But you're not the only one at fault here. Aron knew what he was getting into, just as I do. He broke the rules. He fell for you when you told him not to. He no doubt couldn't help that, and it's easy to say you shouldn't have started something with him in the first place, but you're not the asshole your friends are making you out to be."

"Yeah, I am." I have to be. I can't ... I don't like that Matt can see right through me.

"No. You're not." He steps into my space. "You don't let them know their words get to you. They don't know the guilt you feel." Warm lips drop to my neck. "This doesn't change anything between us."

I moan when Matt's hands find their way under my shirt. "Damon told me to stop."

"Do you usually do what Damon says?"

"I don't want to make the same mistakes."

Matt pulls back and grins. "I want to fuck you, not marry you."

"You say such sweet things to me." I drag him the rest of the way upstairs and into my room.

We tumble in a pile of limbs on my bed, and even though *I'm making a mistake* still alarms in my head, the feel of Matt against me wins out. It's addictive, and I'm definitely going to need a stint in rehab when he leaves.

The fact is, I wasn't lying when I said I don't know what my number is with Matt, and that thought alone scares the shit out of me.

I put my hand on his chest and push him just enough for him to back off with his hips still digging into mine.

"What's wrong?" he asks.

"Maybe we should stop."

He pulls back farther, misunderstanding what I mean. "Right now?"

I grip his ass and bring him closer to me again, and I almost lose my train of thought when his cock presses against me. "No, not now. But, I mean, you're going back to Philly tomorrow, and it could be a clean break."

"I'll be back in two weeks."

"For publicity."

He hesitates for a second and then shrugs as if it's no big deal. "If that's what you want."

It's not lost on me that I had this conversation with another guy not that long ago and he complained. I would've given anything for Aron to accept my terms as easy as Matt has, but lying here right now, something niggles in my chest, and it feels a hell of a lot like disappointment.

When footsteps sound across the carpet in the hallway toward my room, I smile and roll onto my back, preparing for Matt's usual wakeup call. It takes a few seconds for me to remember he's leaving today, and with how high the sun is and with it blinding me through the windows, I think I've missed my good-bye. For a minute, I get excited at the thought that he didn't leave, but that's dashed when my mother appears in my doorway.

Dad's very own Michelle Obama. At least, that's what he tries to sell her as to the public. To me, she's the woman who'll whoop my ass if I've done something wrong. And by the look on her face, I've done something wrong.

"Still in bed, I see." Her voice is scolding but her chocolate eyes are warm, so I can't tell if she's playing with me or is serious.

"Is there somewhere I should be?"

"Oh, I don't know, maybe a large office block in Midtown, holding pompons and saying 'Vote for my dad!'" Ah, so half-serious, half-teasing me about my life choices.

"You paint a fascinating picture there, but I don't see it ever happening." I sit up and make sure the sheet stays wrapped around me.

Mom rolls her eyes. "I'm your mother. There's nothing I haven't seen before."

"Yes, but I'm not two anymore."

"Even if your behavior lately says otherwise." Her gaze darts around the room as if assessing it. "Where's ..."

"His name is Matt, and he went back to Philly to take care of a few things. Why are you here? Did Dad send you?"

"Yes and no. He wants me to convince you to break up with your football player and come to work. I'm only going to do one of those things, so which do you pick?"

"I'm not breaking up with Matt."

"There." She smiles. "That was easy. Now get to work."

Damn her and her mother trickery.

"What's the point?" I ask. "Every single one of Dad's advisors rebuff my ideas, I'm practically invisible, and they aren't actually doing any good in the world. They aren't in this to fix anything. It's all personal gain."

"So, go in there and demand to make a change."

"I've tried. They practically pat my head like a dog, say 'good boy,' and then pretend I never said anything. It's why I stopped bothering going in at all, and guess what? The only person bitching at me to come in is Dad."

She sighs. "What do you want to do with your life, Noah? What do you care about?"

The one time I cared about something, he stomped on my heart and then shit all over it.

"You don't like politics—"

"It's not that I don't like it. I had every intention of following through with the plan you and Dad wanted for me. But when you sold me on the idea, I thought I could make an actual difference. Politics is a long game for short-term benefits. It's impossible to please everyone, so you please majorities just for the small chance to help out the people who truly need it. I want to try to improve the world, not make rich men richer."

"Give your father until the end of the campaign. Pay your dues, and then you can talk about making bigger changes."

"I've been paying dues for the past four years."

"No, you've been half-assing it. I need you to make an effort.

We're one year out from the primaries, and God knows if he doesn't make it this time 'round, there's another four years of hard campaigning in our future."

"If he doesn't make it this year, maybe it's time to give the White House up."

"Please. Your father's a stubborn mule. He's just going to keep coming back for more until the American public loves him."

I want to argue that strategy didn't work for another certain democratic nominee, but I keep my mouth shut.

"Okay," I relent. "I'll start making an effort again."

"You need to do something, baby. Messing around with the pretty football player can only last so long, and it's going to be crunch time before we know it."

I let out the loudest breath in history that somehow matches Mom's sullen mood. I get the feeling she wants to be the first lady as much as I wanted Matt to leave. But it's the life she signed on for, and she made her choice. She married into it. I never got the choice to be born into this, but it's my life anyway.

"Fine," I say.

Damn that woman. It's impossible to say no to her.

CHAPTER ELEVEN

MATT

Noah's name flashing on my screen makes me feel better than an ice bath after a grueling training session. I left New York eight days ago at the ass crack of dawn—well before Noah was awake. Since then, I've had not even a text, so I'm curious to know why he's calling but even more curious as to why that makes me happy. Especially considering our fling is over and it's back to the original plan—business arrangement only.

"You know if you were a real boyfriend, I'd be pissed," I say in way of an answer.

"Why?" his playful tone replies.

"Eight days, man. Don't leave your boyfriend hanging like that."

"Your phone has dials too, you know. You could've called if you needed something."

"Yeah, but I've been putting my apartment on the market, having meetings with finance guys, looking for storage places for all my furniture. I've been busy. What have you been doing?"

There's a small pause before he says, "Believe it or not, I've been going to work."

"You what?" I exclaim. "There must be a bad connection or something because I'm pretty sure you said you went to work. Which is campaigning for your dad."

"True story."

"You miss me so much you're voluntarily going to a place you hate every day just to forget me. Aww." I probably shouldn't provoke him when he spooks easily, but that's what makes it funny.

"Actually, Dad's biggest recruiter came by and forced me to start making an effort."

"Wait ... there's someone in this world who actually has the power to force Noah Huntington the fucking Third to do something?"

"Yeah. She goes by the name of Mom."

I can't help laughing at that.

Noah sighs. "I did have a reason for calling, you know."

"Which is?"

"Our suits for the benefit this weekend. Damon says they have to be matching but still look different, so what are you going to wear?"

I grin. "They're giving us what suits to wear."

"Oh."

"Which, if you had spoken to Damon, he would've told you. Which means you literally called for a made-up reason." Now there's definitely no way I can stop smiling.

"Damn it, fine. I tried to stay away, okay? Damon warned me, and the rest of my friends said I was doing the same thing to you that I did to Aron, and I didn't want to hurt you, so I figured you going back to PA was the perfect time to take a step back."

"And then?"

"And then I got horny."

I snort. "Eight days is a little insulting considering all I've been thinking about doing is dicking you out again."

A tortured groan fills my ears, and my cock stirs.

"It hasn't been eight days of nothing," Noah says. "It's taken me this long to reach my breaking point. Porn is doing shit all to help. My cock wants you, apparently. I tried to tell him no, but he never listens."

"That's sweet. I think. Although, I'm worried about the fact you're talking to your dick."

"It's only a problem if it talks back."

It's so tempting to cancel the rest of my appointments this week and run back to New York. "If I didn't have another meeting tomorrow with my finance guy, I'd be in my car already."

"What's with all the finance meetings?"

"I'm organizing for the worst. I didn't want to contemplate it, but if I don't get another contract, I need to make my money last until I figure out what I'm going to do with the rest of my life. I'm trying to sell my loft. There's nothing for me in Philly anymore—contract or not."

"You're getting a contract. I have faith."

"Damon's hopeful, but getting the finance side of things straightened out makes me feel better about it if it doesn't happen."

"When can you get to New York?" Noah asks.

"Not until the benefit. Can you come here?"

"I guess I can blow off work again."

"Don't do that," I say.

"If I don't, I won't be able to get out there until Friday night, and the benefit is Saturday so there'd be no point."

"You mean other than fucking for twenty-four hours straight before a dull, black-tie event where we can't be all over each other in fear of someone taking photos?"

"I like how you think."

An idea forms. "Hold on a sec. I'll call you back."

Shucking off my shirt and pants, I climb into my bed naked and then video call Noah. Nerves form in the pit of my stomach as I wait for him to answer. I've never done this with a guy. Well, there's still a lot I haven't done with a guy. I shouldn't worry about this though, because it's Noah. The nervous pain in my stomach turns to arousal when he answers the call with a wide grin.

"Why do I get the feeling my night just got a whole lot better?"

"Probably has something to do with my abs." I pan my phone down my body.

"I'm thinking I want what's under the sheet-covered portion." Noah licks his lips. "Hold up, I'm running to my room."

The image on my phone bounces with every step Noah takes until the point I almost suffer motion sickness by the time he gets to the third floor.

All I see is the ceiling of Noah's room when he throws his phone on the bed, but then it moves again, and I'm rewarded with Noah's naked body filling my screen. My eyes move over his hard torso and long limbs and rest on something else that's long and hard.

My mouth dries.

"Are we really doing this?" Noah asks.

"Looks like it." Pretty sure I've left the point of no return. Even if he was to cut the phone call off right now, there's no way I'm stopping. My hand reaches for my aching cock.

"I can't see what your hand is doing," Noah says. "I mean, your face is pretty and all, but it's not what I want right now."

I grab a pillow and set it up on the other side of the bed from me so my phone rests against it, giving Noah the full view. "What do you want me to do?"

Noah bites his lip. "Where's your famous toy collection?"

With a smirk, I lean over the side of my bed and feel around for the box I have stashed under there.

"Damn, that ass," Noah whispers.

"Could be all yours if you want it."

He moans. "You're going to break me one day."

"Was kinda hoping you'd be the one to break me."

Something unintelligible comes outta Noah's mouth, and by the time I find the biggest toy I own and roll back over, he's stroking himself hard and fast.

"Haven't even got to the good part yet," I say.

"The thought is enough to get me there."

Yet, he refused to top me when I stayed with him. I shake that thought away; otherwise, I'm going to be distracted, and distraction is the last thing I need while watching Noah get off.

His eyes land on the vibrator with the thick head. I purposefully chose the biggest one so he knows I'm not scared of having sex with him. He won't have to be gentle with me. I may've never been fucked before, but I've found plenty of ways to get myself off over the years.

"Dude, even my ass is clenching at the sight of that thing," Noah says.

I should come back with a funny retort, but my eyes are glued to his hand wrapped around his dick.

Noah breathes heavy. "Regretting not blowing off work and driving to Philly right now."

"Regretting trying to sell my apartment."

"I'll buy your apartment."

"Even then you'd have to wait two more hours to see me. Can you hold out that long?"

"God no. We're doing this now. Pinch your nipple for me."

One hand goes to my chest while the other makes its way back to my aching dick.

"Did I say you were allowed to touch your cock?" Noah asks.

"Oh, getting bossy now, are we? What are you gonna do if I touch it?"

"I could think of a few things. Maybe turn the camera away while I come so you don't get to see it." He slows jerking himself, and I don't reckon he's bluffing.

"You wouldn't."

"Wouldn't I?"

"Fuck." My hand stills on my stomach.

"Pinch. Your. Nipple."

I still don't know how it's possible for someone to piss me off and turn me on at the same time. It's a gift Noah has, and I can't tell if I like it or hate it. I follow his instructions and get that shooting sensation down into my groin that I'm addicted to. It elicits a gasp from me, and a moan from Noah.

"Damn it." He breathes hard.

My gaze finds his, and his hand has stopped. "What's wrong?" I ask.

"About to come."

"Can I touch myself yet?" I hope my voice isn't as tortured as I feel.

"Prep that ass. I want to watch."

I grip my cock and throw my head back.

"Nuh-uh. Just your ass."

"I hate you."

"No, you don't."

I reach for the lube on my bedside table. "No, I don't."

Noah's eyes intensify as they watch me lube up my fingers and raise my legs, but then his brow scrunches. "I can't see anything at this angle."

Shuffling around so I'm lying horizontally across my bed, I hang my head off the edge and give Noah direct line of sight. It's probably not the best camera angle, and vulnerability of being on display makes me pause, but all that goes away when Noah moans. Loudly.

A sharp intake of breath comes out of the small speaker on my phone when my fingers breach my hole and slowly work my ass. I palm my balls as my fingers move in and out of me, but I remember not to touch my cock. It leaks precum onto my stomach, and I have to resist the urge to give in to temptation to stroke myself. A few tugs and I'd be done.

"Pretend they're my fingers," Noah says. "I'm right there with you. On top of you. Inside you."

I close my eyes, picturing Noah next to me. I can't see him through the screen anymore, but in my head he's right here. He watches over me as he continues to stretch my ass.

"If I were there, I'd suck you into my mouth while my fingers fucked you."

The moan that escapes me is deep and guttural.

"I'd keep you on the edge of coming until you begged me to take that virgin ass."

"I want you to," I croak.

"Fit another finger in. You need to be ready."

While I do as he says, I use my free hand to find the vibrator and slick it up with lube.

"You're going to be feeling this for days," Noah says.

"I'm counting on it."

"Are you ready?" Noah's voice is strained now, so I know he's gotta be close. I lift my head and catch a glimpse of his frantic hand, and I wish he wasn't so far away. I want skin on skin. I want contact. I don't want to be doing this through a screen. "Do it now, Matt."

When I line up the giant head of the toy with my ass, Noah's breathing stops completely. I stroke myself with one hand, while pushing the vibrator in with my other. The coolness of the lube and sleek silicone makes my ass clench around it. The tight grip on my cock distracts from the stretching pain of the ridiculously large toy. I close my eyes again and pretend it's Noah inching his way in.

"So tight," Noah says, and it's as if he's here.

I can even smell his expensive cologne. Wait, that could be a sign of a stroke, right? My eyes fly open, but at the same time, I reach that glorious spot inside me my fingers can't quite get to, and my dick leaks so much I wonder if I've actually orgasmed.

But no, the pressure in my ass and the hardness of my dick only makes me want more. When I turn the vibrating function on, blood rushes to my head, and not the one hanging off the edge of the bed. The constant pushing against my prostate has me breaking a sweat and gritting my teeth as pleasure tries to overtake my entire body.

"You look so hot." Noah's whispered words encourage me to hold off.

I want to come more than I've wanted anything in my entire life, and I want to do it with Noah's name on my lips, but I want this to last.

"I'm going to come," Noah says.

There goes my plan of making it last. I lift my head in time to see Noah come all over his stomach and chest.

It takes less than three seconds for me to join him.

Breathing heavy and limbless, I can barely bring myself to right my balance. My head is heavy, and I have to move so it's not hanging off the end of the bed anymore.

When I finally do and catch sight of Noah, he's grinning from ear to ear.

"Think that'll hold you until Saturday?" I ask. I nervously chew on my lip, because we were supposed to end this already. We probably shouldn't have done that, but I don't exactly have control over my actions when it comes to Noah.

"We might need a real-life repeat."

"Count on it." I don't want to stop what we're doing. "I should, uh, go get cleaned up."

Noah laughs. "Later."

NOAH: *WHAT'S YOUR ADDRESS?*
        MATT: *WHY?*

NOAH: *SO I CAN SEND YOU A FUCKING GIFT BASKET. JUST GIVE ME THE ADDRESS.*

I shouldn't be in Philly. I definitely shouldn't have driven all this way without telling Matt first. Yup. Total mistake. But that doesn't stop me from heading straight to his apartment when he sends through the address.

I told myself I wasn't going to do this. I even went to the campaign offices this morning to work. Then I had flashes of that damn video call ...

A quick case of fake flu, and that's how I ended up here on his doorstep.

Of course, he has to go and torture me by answering the door in a towel. *Only* a towel. Then the fucker smirks. "You're the gift basket?"

"Best gift basket ever." I push my way into his apartment

and stop dead in my tracks. "And you go on about how rich I am. Look at this place." I spin in a circle and take in the sleek, modern furniture, hardwood floors, and the view of Philly out the large windows.

"Please. This place is worth a sixth of what yours is."

"And about three times the size."

"That's because it's not in New York." Matt folds his arms across his wide chest. His towel is only holding on by that tiny lip tucked in at the side.

My hands itch to rip it off him.

"Noah," Matt says and brings my focus to his face. "I thought you had to work."

I don't know what to say to that, so I go with a semi-truth. "What, friends can't fake being sick to get out of work, drive for two hours in crappy traffic, and then fight an old lady for street parking just to come say hi?" All those things happened, but I think we both know I haven't come here to say hello.

Matt runs a hand over his beard and tries to hold back a smile. "So, uh, are you here for the day, or ..."

"Something like that." I'm here for as long as he'll have me. My eyes go to his towel again. God, how I want it gone.

Matt grips onto it as he walks closer to me, and I can't tear my gaze away. "I think you're drooling."

I fist my hand at my side. "I am ..." I stare at his naked chest, his perfect nipples, his tight abs ... damn, those abs. This guy is breaking me, and all he's doing is standing there.

"Why are you here?" he whispers.

I suddenly don't know. I thought it was for sex—for an in-person repeat of last night—and I definitely still want that, but now that I'm here, I realize ... I just wanted to see him. After nine days apart, a video call isn't enough.

Shit. Don't admit that aloud. "I heard Philly has amazing cheesesteaks."

Matt laughs, deep and rumbly.

With Noah-like charm—meaning no tact—I step forward and cover the hand gripping his towel. I open my mouth to threaten to rip it away from him, but it's not necessary; his hand falls away without a fight.

"I came here to fuck you," I say. I'm scared it's written all over my face—the real reason I'm here: I couldn't stay away.

Matt lets out the loudest groan as if I zapped him with electrodes attached to his balls instead of offered him sex. "I wish that could happen, but I have a showing on the apartment in fifteen minutes. I thought you were the realtor when you knocked."

I stare down at his towel and back up to his face. "You answer the door to your realtor while only wearing a towel? If you had a real boyfriend, I don't think he'd be happy about that."

Definitely not happy.

Matt, however, loves my new jealous trait that I didn't know existed and can't stop smiling as he says, "I'll be sure to tell *her* to keep her hands to herself."

Abrupt subject change is needed. "Well, if we can't stay here, what are we going to do?" I take a step back so I'm not tempted to jump him anyway. "When's your financial meeting?"

"Had it this morning, so I'm free."

"Okay, so you can show me your city."

"You've never been to Philly before?"

"I have, but I want to see it how you do."

"Uh ..." Matt hesitates. "We could go see the Liberty Bell?"

"I'm sorry, are we on a grade school excursion? I want to see where you eat, where you drink ... okay, maybe we won't go to *that* club, but"—I shrug—"show me Matt's Philadelphia. It could technically be classed as Damon's homework." Sure, blame Damon for the reason I want to get to know Matt on this whole new level I'm unfamiliar with.

"Umm ... yeah. Okay." He nods. "Okay."

One would think I asked him to watch me fuck his sister with how uncomfortable he looks, but he shakes it off and heads for the hallway.

"I'll get dressed and we can get out of here when the realtor shows up."

As if on cue, the doorbell rings. "You put some clothes on, and I'll get the door," I say and watch as his ass disappears down a hallway.

The realtor does a double take when I let her in.

"Matt's in the bedroom," I explain awkwardly.

"Oh, right. You're ..."

I force my public-ready smile—the one I had to learn as a kid to stand by Dad's side at all his campaigning rallies. "Noah Huntington."

I shake her hand, but she continues to eye me warily. I want to ask her why she's staring at me like that.

She moves about the space, as if she's the one looking to buy it. "We shouldn't be long here. You probably won't have to leave if you don't want to. Although, it can be intimidating if the owner's in the home while we show people through."

"Don't need to worry. We have plans."

Her smile is tight, and I have no idea what her issue is, but when Matt comes out of the bedroom, it becomes clear.

Something's wrong.

Matt approaches, wrapping an arm around my waist and bringing his mouth down on mine for a soft kiss. I melt against him, not caring about the witness in the room, and push my tongue into his mouth.

When the realtor clears her throat, Matt pulls away. "Ready to go, babe?"

I purse my lips at the show he's putting on for her. "Uh, sure."

He grabs my hand, tells the realtor to lock up when she leaves as we'll be gone all day, and then drags me out of his apartment and to the elevator bank.

Once there, he lets go of my hand. "Sorry about that. While I was getting dressed, I got a phone call from Damon." Matt shoves his phone at me. "The more people who see us together, the better."

On Matt's phone, there's a link to an article about us.

Trouble in Paradise or Publicity Stunt?

"They're onto us? How?"

"Damon thinks there could be a leak in his office—like with the photographers at the cruise ship terminal—or it could be the fact we left the cruise early and I've been spotted here while you're in New York. It might be speculation for entertainment value, or it could be we're not doing a good enough job of convincing people this is real."

"So, what's the plan?" I ask.

"We have to go out in public more. We've been hiding, apparently." Matt pockets his phone. "Whose car are we taking?"

"I fought an old lady for a spot. I'm not moving my car. I also don't know Philly." My phone vibrates in my pocket, and when I dig it out, Damon's name flashes across the screen. "It's

Damon. Did you tell him I was here?"

Matt shakes his head and holds the elevator door for me while I answer.

"Hey, what's up?"

"You busy? I need you to get to Philly for some photo ops with Matt."

"Uh ... umm, yeah, I'm already on my way. Matt just called."

There's a pause. "That was fast. Okay, so I'll tip off some paparazzi in an hour or so ... unless you're going to be there sooner?"

He's so onto me. "I'll talk to you in an hour." I quickly end the call. "I think he knows I'm already here."

Matt tries to suppress a smile. "Scared about getting in trouble from the big bad Damon?"

"He did tell us to stop ..."

"It's cute you're scared of him. We're not doing anything wrong."

"Right," I mumble and get into the elevator and lean against the back wall. We aren't doing anything wrong. We're both grownups. "Hey, maybe I'm just psychic and knew you'd need me today."

"Sure, let's go with that and ignore it was actually your dick that brought you here."

"Fine then, maybe my dick is psychic."

"With crystal balls?"

"Wanna touch them? If you rub them, you get a wish."

Matt laughs. "I think that's a lamp, not a crystal ball."

"You should try anyway."

Okay, so maybe we aren't complete grownups, but that

doesn't mean this ... causal thing, or whatever we want to call it, is a bad idea. Even if my gut tells me otherwise.

"You should stop joking around before I take you up on the offer and I'm photographed in yet another compromising position. Damon's going to tip off some paparazzi, and they'll no doubt be following us."

"Yeah, he said that. We have an hour leeway to do what we want before they'll find us."

Matt releases a loud breath and plays with the hem of his shirt. "Do you still want to see my Philadelphia?"

"Is that a euphemism?"

My joke has its desired effect. He loses the tension in his shoulders and slumps next to me against the wall.

"We can go see the Liberty Bell if you're not up to—"

Matt reaches for my hand and interlaces our fingers. "I know one place we can go."

We're in the car for over half an hour before he pulls into the parking lot of the very last place I'd expect him to bring me.

"We don't have to—" I start.

He parks the car and turns the ignition off. "You wanted to see what my life was like living here? You're looking at it."

I glance through the windshield at the gray concrete building with a giant bulldog metal sculpture out front. It's intimidating, even to me.

"Matt—"

He ignores me and climbs out of the car. I almost don't want to interrupt him. He stares at the building as if having a moment with it. When he sits on the hood of his car, I tentatively open my door.

I slowly approach him, trying to figure out what type of mood he's in. If it were me, I'd be angry, but when I go to sit next to him, he shifts farther back and pulls me in front of him. My ass lands between his legs on the hood of the car, and his arms wrap around my middle. Even though we don't have to put on a show yet, I don't stop him.

His breath tickles my neck when he says, "It feels like my entire life has revolved around stadiums. Dad used to take us to college games because we couldn't afford NFL tickets. Most of the time it was just Char and me, because the others were too young, but when I think of my childhood, the happiest memories were the games Dad took me to. It was the only time it seemed like he cared."

That's depressing.

"Did you know you wanted to play football professionally back then?" I ask.

He shakes his head against my neck. "I was more worried about not appearing weak in front of Dad. I love football—it has saved me from a lot of shit—but the reason I got into it was to make sure Dad didn't know I liked boys. I mean, I was a kid so I wasn't one hundred percent sure myself, but the way Dad emphasized it with me made me think he knew all along. Or at least suspected."

I lay my hand on top of his on my chest. "What did it save you from?"

"For one, it got me out of that town. I had this ... friend in high school. I wouldn't say he was a boyfriend, because like when I was with Maddox, we both played the 'I'm straight but I want to suck your cock' game. If I wasn't good enough to play college ball, I'd probably still be in that town, married to some woman and fucking guys on the side. I wasn't great at school. I did the bare minimum to make sure I got C's so I wouldn't be cut from the team. I literally put everything into football.

There was no backup. When I lost my contract with the Bulldogs and my entire life was on those rag sites, I ... I honestly thought my life was over. And now, sitting outside the place I put four years of my life into, I see both my prison and my saving grace. It got me out of Tennessee, but I was still trapped ..."

"Hiding," I say quietly.

"Exactly."

I lean back and turn my head so our lips are mere inches apart. Trying to find the right words is impossible, so I settle for kissing him instead and telling him with my mouth that he's worthy of a life everyone deserves, and he should be able to do whatever he wants.

I'm not completely convinced that's football, even if he thinks it is. He says football is the only thing in his life, but he's never even tried for more. It saved him, and now it's his security blanket, and he doesn't want to leave it behind.

I continue to kiss him, partly to make him try to forget his issues but mainly because I don't know what else to do. I don't do the comforting thing; I'm not sure I'd even know how, but I want to. So, I do the one thing I know I'm good at—the physical stuff.

Matt's hand wanders up my shirt, skimming my abs, and my pants become uncomfortably tight.

I have to pull my mouth away. "You're determined to get me arrested for indecent exposure, aren't you?"

"We're fully clothed."

"Keep kissing me like that, and we won't be for long. How long was the realtor at the apartment for?"

"She should be gone, but Damon—"

My pocket starts to vibrate, and of course, it's him. "Do you reckon Damon has super hearing like dogs? Like if his name is being said in a two-hundred-mile radius, he can hear it?"

Matt sighs. "Guess that means it's time to get to work?"

"I'd rather go to bed."

"Of course, you would."

The paparazzi first find us as we're having lunch at a strategically chosen table outside a restaurant in a courtyard area. The view from across the street is perfect for them to set up their cameras, and we pretend to be annoyed but make sure to hold hands on top of the table and smile at each other as we call each of the vultures a name and give them each a backstory. They only get worse the longer it goes on.

"Baldy lives in his mother's basement for sure," Matt says.

"Where he has a closet full of skin suits."

"What are the chances of losing them if we leave?"

"Probably high, but that's not the point, is it?"

Eventually, we move on from lunch, the paparazzi follow us everywhere, and by the time we get back to Matt's apartment in the early evening, I'm exhausted.

We did the most mundane things all day. Shopping. Coffee. More shopping. Pretending to be interested in what we were looking at.

But that's not the most disturbing part. The thing that makes me unsettled is the fact that even though I hated shopping and the paparazzi were relentless, I had fun. Because I was with Matt.

I groan when I throw myself down on his couch. "I still have to drive back to New York."

"You can stay if you want." His gruff voice does things to my cock. "I'll even let you have your own room."

I hesitate because I want to stay but probably shouldn't. We were supposed to have a clean break. It was our perfect opportunity to step back, and then I went and drove a hundred miles just so I could see him.

End this.

"Thanks, but I should get back tonight."

Matt shrugs as if he's oblivious to my inner turmoil. I want to stay, I don't want to go home, but that's a bad idea.

"Want to at least stay for dinner?" he asks, and damn it, I think I'm going to cave.

"If it's pizza."

He scowls.

"With extra cheese and all the delicious stuff I bet you haven't been eating since coming home."

"Fine, you win."

"And beer."

"Are you going to stay the night so I can burn all those calories?" He waggles his eyebrows, and now I know without a doubt I'm going to cave.

"I'll have to head back first thing. My father's probably going to flip his lid when those photos hit the news. I told them at the office that I have the flu."

Matt grins. "Still can't believe you played hooky for me."

Shit.

"Umm, well, you know. My psychic dick did."

I haven't seen Matt smile as much as he has today, and I'm beginning to realize I'd do anything to keep it on his face.

Even stay the night when I know I shouldn't.

CHAPTER THIRTEEN

MATT

I'm late. Very, very late. Noah's already in his suit and ready for the benefit when I get to his place.

"Traffic was a bitch," I complain as I step into his house. "Someone wanted to come look at the apartment, and then they ran late, which put me behind and—" I throw my duffel bag on the ground in haste to kiss Noah hello.

"Whoa." Noah backs up before I can touch my lips to his. "Your beard. Or ... not beard."

I shrug. "Figured I should look respectable or whatever." My cheeks feel naked, but they warm at the sight of Noah in his tux. He looks absolutely fuckable.

I push him against the wall right by the stairs in the foyer and force my tongue into his mouth.

"We don't have time," he says but keeps kissing me anyway.

"Stupid people," I grumble. "Didn't even buy the apartment. I need something to take the edge off. Haven't seen you in forever." Three days is forever, right?

"I'm sure you can make it a few hours without needing to touch me."

"I'm not sure that's true." Hell, I'd settle for blowing him here in the foyer.

"Well, it has to be, because any minute now—"

There's a knock at the door behind us, and I step back in time for Damon and Maddox to come through the door wearing tuxes. It's not a surprise Damon's invited to this too. Although, I'm not sure if it's because he's representing me and has been getting almost as much publicity as I am or because he decided he needs to keep an eye on me and Noah. Probably the latter. If Noah and I screw this up, it's not just my career on the line but Damon's as well. If we really dissect it, it could put Noah's dad's campaign in jeopardy too.

No pressure.

"You guys aren't ready?" Damon asks.

"What gave it away, Captain Obvious?" Noah says.

"I can be ready in ten," I say and run up the stairs. "Where's my suit?" I yell out.

"In my room," Noah says.

I wonder if Damon will have anything to say about that.

Fifteen minutes later, we're out the door. On the car ride over to the Plaza, nerves and dread sit in the pit of my stomach. I have to be *on* tonight, and that always makes me antsy. I have to pretend like my career isn't in the toilet, that I'm completely happy, and I'm not looking at the daunting possibility that football is over for me.

I run a sweaty palm down my leg, but Noah reaches for it. Wordlessly, he runs his thumb over my hand, and he doesn't need to speak to tell me he's there for me. He doesn't need to reassure me, that's not part of his job, but that doesn't stop him.

As soon as we hit the red carpet, Noah works the media like being in the limelight is just another day for him. He's casual and his charming smile never falls. I'm convinced I look like a deer in the headlights. These aren't paparazzi. This is full-blown professional press outlets. My palms still sweat, but Noah doesn't acknowledge that. He holds my hand tighter, and it grounds me.

Once we're inside, Damon ushers me over to my PR rep, who proceeds to introduce me around to some people who I should know but don't. They look at me as if I'm the worst gay person ever. One, a guy named Neil, is the head of the National LGBTQ Network who's hosting the event, so in retrospect, I should know him.

"We're so glad you could make it tonight," he says. "Having you here, supporting us—"

"Thank you for inviting me."

I know it's an honor being recognized and appreciated at something like this, but more people start to converge, and I feel like I'm on the spot.

"What's it like being the first out player in the NFL?" a woman asks.

"Uh, I wouldn't know. I'm technically not part of the league right now."

Everyone seems to purse their lips in unison, and their thoughts are clear as day on their faces. They practically scream the unfairness of it all.

"Do you think being gay will affect your chances of playing football again?" Neil asks, but it's not as intrusive as if a journalist asked. He comes across as concerned more than anything else but also somehow threatening. Like if I were to say yes, he'd sic the gay mafia onto the league. The thought alone has me wanting to laugh, but instead, I'm frozen by the weight of the question.

"There are non-discriminatory laws in place, so it shouldn't," I say diplomatically.

"But that doesn't mean it won't," another man says.

I pull on my bowtie that suddenly feels too tight around my throat. "I, uh, didn't exactly come out in the most ... umm ... gracious way. I was let go on a morality clause."

There's a few awkward laughs, and I tell myself them being entertained at my expense is better than them thinking the same way as the Bulldogs—that I deserved to be let go because of what I did in that club.

"What does society expect when you're forced to hide who you are?" Neil says, and I decide I like him, even if I'm uncomfortable with this whole conversation.

"If you all just came out, it wouldn't be a big deal," the woman says, and I grit my teeth. By all, I assume she means athletes, but I don't want to ask for clarification.

Noah's in my line of sight but just out of reach. I try to send a telepathic message asking him to come rescue me, but apparently, I haven't developed superpowers in the last few hours.

Dang it.

As everyone continues to be determined to talk to me, and I'm introduced to more people I should know, it becomes torturous being so close to Noah but apart. We get no time together. We're both passed between groups of society's high elite. Everyone wants to talk to Noah about his father, and I'm bombarded with more questions about being an out football player, and by the end of it, I realize I've become the very person I feared I would when I was outed. I'm not seen here as Matt Jackson—football player. I'm Matt Jackson—*gay* football player.

None of my teammates are ever introduced as "that married football player" or "the hetero football player."

My eyes continue to track Noah through the room as he moves from important person to even more important person. Noah naked is one thing, but Noah in a tux? I almost like it more.

Almost.

By the tenth time I'm stopped by someone I don't know and forced to talk about my public outing, I'm tempted to drink my ass off. That won't look good in front of the press, so I stay stone cold sober and hate every minute of it.

The only reassuring factor is knowing that I'll be in Noah's bed tonight, hopefully doing unspeakable things to him. Or him to me. Really, whichever. I don't care. I thought after our Skype session he'd be eager to get inside me, but even during his visit to Philly, where he drove two hours just to fuck me, he chickened out. Not that I protested much. I was worried if I pushed the issue it'd end up with neither of us getting any.

When I finally pull myself away from people by faking needing to go to the bathroom, Maddox finds me hiding in the corner.

"How are you holding up?" he asks.

"I keep trying to find your boyfriend to ask if I can go home yet."

"I'd go with you in a heartbeat. Damon's schmoozing."

I eye the swirly dark drink in his hand, and without asking, I grab it and chug the rest. I screw up my face as I look at the empty. "Only Coke?"

"Didn't want to get ugly drunk while Damon's networking."

"Do you think if I threaten to get ugly drunk he'll let me go home?"

Maddox laughs. "You can try."

When I do finally catch Damon, it takes a couple of threats —all empty, which Damon knows—but when he finally says it's okay, I could kiss him. I don't though. I'll go home and kiss the fuck outta Noah instead.

The thought alone has my pants tightening.

But, this isn't my night. Traffic is a bitch again. So, by the time we get back to Noah's place—a hundred years later—I'm more exhausted than horny. I collapse onto his bed face first, not even bothering to remove my penguin suit. "Thank God, that's over."

"It wasn't that bad, was it?"

"It wasn't horrible, but I had to people. Peopling is hard."

Noah laughs. "Kind of the point of a benefit."

"You're used to schmoozing. I'm used to scowling at people to get them to leave me alone."

"You're great with fans."

"Because I have to be. If I had a dollar for every time tonight I heard how important gay men in sports are and how more of us should come out, I'd have more money than you." I bury my head into Noah's pillow.

A weight settles on top of me. "I know that side of your job sucks, and I'm sorry you've become this gay icon without asking for it, but those people tonight have a point. You can't tell me you're the only gay dude in the NFL. Damon wasn't the only ball player either. The more of you who come out, the easier it'll get for everyone."

"Why do I have to be the guy?"

I hate that my voice is small. It's not only being the first openly gay player that I'm worried about. What if it doesn't work out or if I get a new contract and then get cut, what message will that send to kids trying out for their football team? That we're not enough? We can't be the best?

There's a reason no one else has come forward. I lost my career because I was outed, and now I have to fight my way back. It's easy for people who don't live in my world to say everyone should come out, but they have no clue what it's like in a locker room.

"Doesn't have anything to do with getting caught with your pants down in a nightclub," Noah says. "In an ideal world, you would've done this on your own time, but we don't live like that."

"Don't remind me."

"One day, maybe." Kisses land on the back of my neck and then my shoulder. "Did I ever tell you about the time my dad outed me to the entire world?"

I tense. "What?"

"When I was caught with Nathaniel, instead of talking to me about it, Dad called his advisors. They said it could be beneficial to the campaign as long as they embraced it and didn't try to hide it. A few days later, he was giving a press conference telling the world how proud he was to have a gay son."

I roll over underneath him so we're face to face. "What the fuck? That's never okay."

Noah shrugs. "I was out to everyone except my parents. My friends all knew, it wasn't like I was hiding it, and if I'd protested, I'm sure my father wouldn't have done it ..." The suspicion in his eyes gives away the fact he's not entirely sure that's true. "But I've had a taste of what you went through, and I know it's hard. If I could make it better for you, I would." He lowers his voice as he lowers his forehead to mine. "I'd take your burden and make it mine to give you a break."

"*Why?*" I croak.

"Do you know how many times I stared at those photos of you in that club?"

The switch in direction makes me think he doesn't want to answer my question, so I don't push. "Did you wish it were you on your knees?"

"I've always thought you were gorgeous."

"Even now with my beard gone?" I rub my face along his jaw and neck. I already miss my beard.

"I did like the beard. Felt good on my balls while you sucked me off."

I laugh and talk without thinking. "Fuck, I've missed you."

He stills on top of me, and I know I've messed up. It's only been a couple days since I saw him in Philly.

"I mean in a *I want to fuck you* kinda way. Not anything more." I tell myself I'm not lying. He mentioned balls and made me laugh. Missing that doesn't mean anything. I just like having someone to joke around with after years of no humor in my life. Something in the back of my conscience doesn't believe me, but it's so quiet I can ignore the voice telling me to back away before I become the one thing Noah doesn't want—interested in more.

Noah relaxes, blanketing me with his body. "Guess you better start fucking me then."

"Suddenly, I'm not so exhausted anymore."

CHAPTER FOURTEEN

NOAH

Matt's sleeping face confuses me. Not because he looks more peaceful than I've ever seen him, but because I'm still staring at it long after he falls asleep. In my bed. Because I told him to stay.

Yup. That happened.

He said he only needed a minute to recover, and then I said it: *stay*.

I asked him to stay with me.

If I didn't know it already, I definitely do now. *I'm so screwed.*

"What am I doing?" I whisper to myself.

"Huh?" Matt murmurs. Damn. Light sleeper, I guess.

"Nothing, babe. Go back to sleep."

"Hmmlergh." His beefy arm pulls me against him, and I don't fight him.

I didn't lie to Matt when I said I can't sleep with anyone else in my bed. It's not an intimacy issue—though that probably has *something* to do with it—but the main problem is I can't get comfortable. When Matt and I were on the cruise, neither of us were conscious of getting close, so I always woke up with him glued to me. That's when the uncomfortableness creeped in. Not when he was actually holding me. I don't want to think about that too hard. It might open a can of *Why I Don't Let People Get Close to Me,* and I don't want to answer that question anytime soon. Pretty sure it sits right next to the cans of *Daddy Issues* and *Shockingly Depleted Self-worth.*

Gah, I need to go to sleep. I can freak out in the morning when Matt gets up at stupid o'clock to work out.

Only, when I wake up hours later with the sunlight streaming through the windows, Matt is still attached to me.

I nudge him off me. "Shouldn't you be downstairs getting all sweaty?"

Matt rolls his hips so his cock digs into my back. "I don't have to go downstairs to do that."

"You really did miss me, huh? I've created a monster. How are you going to go during the season?"

"You're too big to fit in my suitcase."

"Mmm, but your toys aren't." Images from our video call make my dick hard, and my body inches closer to Matt.

"Pretty sure my roommate won't appreciate that. That's if I get a contract. I tried to talk to Damon last night about this meeting coming up, but he said to wait."

I roll over to face him. "That doesn't mean anything."

"It does when he says it as if he's about to tell me I have terminal cancer. Then Maddox ran interference, keeping me away from Damon. Although that might have to do with the fact that every chance I had to speak to Damon ended with me asking if I was allowed to go home yet."

"Still, doesn't mean anything. He probably didn't want to talk about work where anyone could overhear."

"Maybe ..."

"You'll find out tomorrow, so there's no point worrying about it now."

"Easy for you to say." Matt's right though. It is easy for me to say not to worry because I have no idea what it's like to want something as bad as Matt wants football.

"You know what else is easy for me?" I push Matt onto his back and work my way down his body, laying open-mouthed kisses over his hard muscles. "Distraction."

"I like this type of distraction." His hands go to my head, gripping the nonexistent hair. "But do you have to shave your head? I want something to grip onto."

"Maybe if you're a good boy, I'll grow it out."

Matt moans, and I love it. I can lie to myself all I want and say I'm doing this for Matt, that he needs it to stop him from thinking, but the truth is, I need it just as much. Sex, I can do. It's everything else I struggle with. Matt understands that. He's the only one I've been with who gets it, and he doesn't push for more. When my mouth wraps around his cock, he arches his back.

Matt grabs me to pull me up so I can get in on the action, but I shake my head. I'm not going to be selfish. I hold him down to stop him from reaching for me.

Matt fists the comforter and lets me take control. I pull off him just long enough to wet my finger with saliva.

"Fuck yes," Matt hisses when I push against his hole.

I told myself I wouldn't do this with him. He deserves someone better than me for his first time, and I've been deter-mined not to fuck him, but it's pointless in trying to resist. I won't go there today, but I know it's going to happen eventually.

It's inevitable, because I'm not a strong man. Not when it comes to him.

The more time I spend with Matt, the more I worry this guy doesn't have a number. I might never get him out of my system.

"Noah ..."

I've never heard my name sound so good.

Matt looks at me like I'm more than my money. No one has ever done that. Even my friends. I don't help my case by playing the role of entitled asshole, but it's how I survive. The one time I showed my true self to someone, he ripped my heart out for a college degree and a fifty-thousand-dollar bonus.

The noises Matt makes as I suck him down go straight to my dick. I want him to come, and I want to swallow it all—something I don't normally do. Matt knows that, and the few times I've done this, he gave me warning. It's not the taste I hate but the amount. It triggers my gag reflex. Guys in the past have complained about it, but Matt doesn't care.

My finger massages his prostate while my mouth works him over, and my own cock begs to be touched, but I refrain.

"Coming," Matt says.

I don't move away.

"*Noah* ..."

I stay with him, loving every drop he gives me. The gag reflex kicks in a little, but not enough for me to pull away. I drink him up and wait for him to stop shuddering. And when he pulls me up this time, I don't stop him. He kisses me hard and long, no doubt tasting himself on my tongue, and he groans into my mouth.

"You didn't have to—"

"Wanted to."

"Noah—"

Uh-oh. Nope. I know that tone. We're not talking about it. "I need coffee." I try to climb out of bed, but Matt's too strong for me when he pulls me back and rolls on top of me.

"Not so fast. We have all day for coffee, and I need twenty-four hours of distractions. It's your turn."

As he slides down to return my favor, I welcome everything he's going to give me. Because it means I don't have to talk about the real shit going on in my head. I guess we're both great at distraction.

I don't kick Matt out of bed again Sunday night and wake up with him against me. My muscles ache, my skin is marked with bruises from his mouth and punishing hands, and I absolutely cannot care less.

"What's the time?" I mumble as a vibrating noise comes from the bedside table.

"Who the fuck knows."

"Are we late for your meeting?"

"It's not until two." Matt finally reaches for his phone and frowns. "It's OTS."

"Answer it."

He grips his phone tight. "What if it's the call telling me not to bother coming in?"

"Then not answering won't change that fact."

The phone stops ringing, and Matt lets out a loud breath. Then it starts ringing again. He stares at it as if it might explode when he hits the green button.

I hold my hand out. "Want me to answer? I can pretend to be your assistant."

Hesitantly, he hands it over.

"Matt Jackson's phone," I answer.

"Noah? Why are you answering Matt's phone?" Damon asks.

"Why are you calling him when you have a meeting in"—I hold out the phone and check the time—"four hours?"

"There's a ... situation going on here. Matt needs to come in immediately."

My heart plummets into my stomach and then lurches into my throat. Did we fuck up? Did someone find out we're not really together? I force myself to take a deep breath and not freak out yet. The way Matt's staring at me, with those brown puppy dog eyes, I don't want to scare him.

"If it's not good news, it can wait," I say.

"It's got nothing to do with the offer I have sitting on my desk for him. There's a guy here claiming to be his brother."

My eyebrows shoot up. "Brother? Which one?"

"Says his name is Jet."

I pull the phone away from my mouth. "Jet's in New York."

Matt's eyes widen. "What?"

"He didn't know how else to get a hold of him," Damon says in my ear. "He's not talking much. Just asking to see his brother. Got a bit of an attitude on him. Can you guys come in early?"

"We're on our way." I end the call and throw the phone on the bed.

Matt starts to dress, but I stop him. "We smell like sex. We need to shower."

"Fine," he relents.

We take a world-record-breaking short shower, and I offer to drive, because Matt's moving on autopilot. I can hear the silent questions running through his head, wanting to know why his brother's here, what happened, and how he can fix it.

"Which brother is Jet? The nineteen-year-old or twelve-year-old?"

"You remember how old my siblings are?"

"Shit, don't quiz me. It was a fluke."

Matt laughs. "Jethro's the nineteen-year-old."

"Where does he go to college?"

"He doesn't. I offered to pay for his tuition when he graduated high school, but he's determined to be a musician."

"So, he's come up from Tennessee and didn't tell you he was coming? Why didn't he call?"

"He won't have my number. My parents made it clear I wasn't allowed near my siblings anymore. They all disappeared from Facebook. My parents blocked me. I tried setting up a fake account and adding them, but they never accepted. Which is fair, I guess. I don't really want them adding random strangers, but I had to try. My parents probably monitor their accounts too."

"That's ... extreme."

"Nah, that's homophobic parents for you."

"Why do you think your brother's trying to find you?"

"I dunno. It's a lot of effort to go to when he didn't know if he could get a hold of me. I'm trying to not jump to conclusions, but I'm thinking something bad happened."

I don't say it aloud, but one good thing about Jet making an appearance is Matt's not freaking out about his meeting anymore.

As soon as we hit the reception area of OnTrack Sports, a slim but toned guy in a T-shirt, skinny jeans, and chucks stands to greet us. My eyes immediately trace his intricate tattoo sleeve on his right arm. His hair is long and shaggy but is the same shade as Matt's. A duffel bag and soft guitar case sits on the floor next to him, and if Matt hadn't said Jet was a musician, I would've walked right past him in the waiting room. He's cute but looks nothing like Matt.

"Jethro." Matt goes to hug him but pulls back at the last second as if thinking better of it. "What are you doing here?"

His brother doesn't have Matt's hesitance and brings his older brother in for a hug. "Hey, bro."

"What happened?" Matt asks.

"What do you think? Same thing that happened to you."

"Huh?"

If Matt can't tell his brother is gay, I seriously have to question his gaydar.

"I'm gay as all get out, dude."

Matt's mouth drops open, and I laugh at how adorable he is. "Since when?" Matt asks.

"Uh, don't know if you've seen the studies, but pretty sure I've been this way my whole life. But I'm guessin' you either mean when did I figure it out or when I came out. The answers being fourteen, when I saw you and that guy making out when you thought no one was home, and—"

"You were spyin' on me?" Matt's accent comes out thick, like Jet's. And yep, still love it.

"Not in a creepy way. I walked in, saw it, walked back out, and then realized kissing a guy was an option. I hadn't considered it before then, and I knew both of us would be in shit if I said anything. Also, that guy is married now. To a woman. But I'm pretty sure he's on Grindr. He has a tattoo on his ribs, right?"

Matt's eyes find mine, but he quickly looks away.

Jet continues his rambling. "As for coming out, it was at a family dinner two nights ago. They were goin' on and on as they do, but it's been a hundred times worse since you came out. Char wants to talk to those reporter guys sniffing around because she wants the money, but Mom and Dad lost their shit over it, and then that began their ranting about gays burnin' and we're to pretend you were never born or existed. *Don't talk to them dang reporters and embarrass the family. Wah, wah, wah.* I was over it, and I had to get out of there. When they asked where I was going, I said 'I'm gonna go set myself on fire.'"

Matt scoffs. "You didn't."

"Oh, I did. To be fair, I didn't think they were smart enough to get it. Probably should've tried to play it off like I was joking, but I didn't want to lie anymore. Dad gave me five minutes to pack everything and get out."

"Sorry," I say stepping forward, "but can we go back to the reporter part?"

Jet's eyes meet mine and then trail down my body. "Ah, the boyfriend, right? Senator's son. Apparently, you're a big deal." He holds out his hand, and I shake it. Then he turns to Matt. "When you rebel, you really rebel. Gay and with a black guy?" He laughs. "You should've seen Mom and Dad's face when they saw that in the news. It was awesome."

"The reporter?" I push again. It can't be good if they're going after Matt's family now.

"Y'all don't need to worry about them," Jet says. "Mom and Dad won't talk. The only one who might is Char. She's about ready to pop, and she's livin' in a trailer. She needs the money, and these guys are offering a lot. One of them approached me in the bar I play at and offered me ten grand to give 'em the scoop."

"Did you give them one?" I ask.

"Have you seen an article about my brother quoting me as a source? Do I look like a sellout?" There's the attitude Damon was talking about.

Matt's eyes dart around the small office area and speaks low. "Can you tone it down? These people are in charge of my career."

Jet throws his hands up in mock surrender.

"And why does Char need money?" Matt asks. "I send you guys money."

Jet looks confused. "Uh, no, you don't."

"What?" Matt growls. "I send our parents eight grand a month. Have done since I was drafted."

"We've never seen any of that money," his brother says.

I see the moment it all clicks in Matt's brain.

"What the hell do they spend that much money on?" Matt asks.

"They still go to the track a lot. Like every day. Dad retired as soon as you made it to the NFL, but—"

"He said he lost his job."

"Are you really that naïve?" Jet asks.

Matt grits his teeth, his jaw hardening, and I can't help reaching for him, but then a door opens leading to the offices, so I step back.

"Done with the family reunion yet?" Damon asks. "We have an offer for Matt."

I can understand what Matt means by Damon not being overly excited over the fact. There's no smile, no enthusiasm behind his words.

"Want me to come with you?" I ask.

Matt shakes his head. "Can you stay out here with Jethro?"

"Jet," Jet says. "How many times do I have to tell you to call me Jet."

"Sorry, JJ," Matt says.

"That's even worse," Jet mumbles.

I don't miss the shock on Damon's face when Matt kisses my cheek before heading into his office, but I'll deal with that later. I'll say Matt's keeping up appearances. For his brother's sake. For all I know, that's the truth.

Jet sits on the couch next to his guitar and eyes me again.

"JJ, huh?"

"Don't even start."

"Jethro Jackson. Sounds like a country singer."

"We live like an hour outside of Nashville. What do you expect?"

"And ... you need a place to stay?"

"Yeah. I was hoping to stay with Matt, but I guess if what the tabloids are saying is true, that means I'll be staying with you."

"Are you going to follow him wherever his contract takes him?" It's none of my business what this kid does, but the fact of the matter is, Damon said he has an offer for Matt, and I'm projecting my own question onto Jet. Unless it's a New York team or on the East Coast, I'll never see Matt. The thought of him moving across country makes me feel sick, and I realize I don't want him to leave.

"I don't know what my plans are yet," Jet says. "I'll get a job or try to get a booking agent while I'm out here. Maybe follow Matt if I have to, but I don't want to live off him like our fucked-up parents."

"Matt and I will help you with whatever you need."

Jet narrows his eyes, and it takes a second for my own words to sink in. My head's not with it today. It's spouting fantasies of shit that's not real. Matt and I aren't real.

And the outcome of this meeting may cement that. I need something to take my mind off it.

I turn to Jet. "Tell me your story."

"Chicago," Damon says, his tone serious and not at all comforting.

Easy decision. "Done. The Warriors may not have seen a Super Bowl in over ten years, but they always go far." Geographically, Chicago might suck, but it's what, a two-hour flight? Noah has access to a private plane ...

Don't take your fling into consideration. Football is the goal.

Damon glances at his partner and then back at me. "You haven't heard the details. The contract. It's ... not good."

"They're lowballing me because they know no one wants me?"

"They want you," Damon says. "They've been calling constantly, chasing after you. But they're bound by the salary cap. It's a one-year contract with the promise of renewing with a bigger salary and longer contract if you do well throughout the season ... if you even make it through training camp cuts."

I lean forward. "How low is it?"

He slides a piece of paper over to me.

"Are you fucking kidding me? That's like ... an undrafted entrant kinda deal."

"It's not ideal, but it's not *that* bad," Damon says. "They've offered you basically everything they've got. They have a few veterans on their last year, and that'll open up a whole heap more money if they choose to renew you next season. You can go home and think about it, but there's no doubt that they do want you. And they're not lying about the salary cap. We checked. We thought they might've been trying to get you on the cheap in case the team decides they don't want to play with a gay guy, but it checks out. The GM insists your sexuality won't be an issue. He'll make sure of it."

"Bullshit. There's always money somewhere. If they knew I hadn't secured a contract by the end of last season—"

"Your renewal with the Bulldogs was supposed to be a given, and the Warriors just scored a new QB."

Shit. I had read that. "Marcus Talon. Super Bowl champ two years ago. He's worth every penny they pay him."

"You don't have to take this," Damon says.

"But it might be your only shot." Of course, the old dude has an opinion on it—take whatever they'll give me because I'm lucky to get a contract at all.

He might have a point.

"I can't help thinking if this was offered to a straight guy with a scandal under his belt, it would be considered insulting, but I'm supposed to suck it up."

"Something else might come," Damon says. "The Warriors aren't expecting an answer until training camp. The GM knows it's a long shot, but he wants you. The coaches too. I've heard from nearly the entire management team."

"I'll think about it."

My feet propel me out of the office at a faster than normal pace. I tell myself to keep going before I do something I regret like tell my agents to fuck off or, worse, accept the shitty contract.

"Babe?" Noah says as I bypass him and my brother and head for the exit.

"We're going," I bark. I push the call button for the elevator harder than necessary, but it doesn't make me less frustrated.

"What happened?" Jethro asks and slings his guitar strap over his shoulder.

"I thought Damon said he had an offer," Noah says.

"He did. For about a fifth of what other guys with my stats get."

"*Ouch*," Noah says.

I turn to my brother. "You coming with us?"

Jethro averts his gaze as he admits, "Got nowhere else to go."

"I'll look into getting a hotel—"

Noah squeezes my hand. "He's cool to stay with us. I don't mind."

"Thank you," I mouth.

The elevator dings, and the three of us pile in.

"So, what're you gonna do?" Jethro asks.

"I don't know." My tone is defeated. *I'm* defeated. Maybe retirement is my only option. I'll become one of *those* guys, and people will continue to believe gay men don't belong in sports.

Or I could swallow my pride, ignore all the shit that'll be thrown my way, and accept the offer that's beneath my worth. Isn't that as bad as retiring though? Admitting that I'm worth less because of my orientation?

Fuck that.

But it's football, I remind myself. And the offer is still more than what most people make in a year. If I turn it down, my income will be zero until I work out what I want to do without football.

"Is it this or nothing?" Noah asks.

"Dunno yet, but probably."

We hit the parking garage and cram into Noah's BMW. With Jethro's duffel and guitar taking up most of the backseat, my brother has to somehow fold himself in half to fit.

"Lucky we didn't bring the Lambo," Noah says. "Where was the offer for, anyway? You never said."

"Chicago."

Noah stiffens but hides it with a fake smile.

Jethro leans forward between the two front seats. Somehow. I really don't want to contemplate my brother's flexibility right now, but what the fuck?

"The Warriors? Take it," my brother says. "Now they have Talon, they're gonna go to The Bowl next season, for sure. They've spent the last few years building their offensive line to kick ass."

"Football fan?" Noah asks.

"Our whole family is," I say. "We were raised on it. We were even quizzed at the breakfast table on highest stats in the league, teams tipped to win the Super Bowl before the start of each season. Dad is a freak when it comes to football."

Noah opens his mouth to say something but hesitates.

"What?" I ask.

"Are you sure you enjoy it? I mean, it sounds like it was forced on you. It's all you've known. Maybe you should try something else you could love just as much. Maybe even more."

"You don't know Matt well, do you?" Jethro asks.

"Umm—"

I stop Noah from answering that. "I don't expect you to understand. You hate the things your family has forced upon you. Public image. Politics. Money. I was lucky enough to love what my father forced on me. If I didn't love it, I wouldn't do it. I'd be a skinny ass like Jethro but doing something worthy like designing buildings instead of plucking a guitar."

"Hey," my brother complains.

I try to hide my smile. I've missed giving my brother hell. He's four years younger than I am, so he was the easiest target. Char gives as good as I do, and it seemed mean to pick on the younger ones. The thoughts of my siblings remind me of the ugly news Jet gave me before my meeting. None of my brothers and sisters have been given a cent of their money.

"So, when you say you haven't seen any of the money ..." I turn to my brother.

"I mean, I haven't seen any of that money. No other way to put it, is there? Yeah, Mom and Dad fed me and gave me a bed, and with four of us kids still living at home, that can't be cheap, but my guitar, my car—which I gave to Char when I got on a bus to New York—everythin' I own is because I paid for it from working at the movie theater."

"You still work at the movie theater?" I ask. "You got that job when I left for college."

"Yup. Well ... *worked* there. I should call them and tell them I'm not coming in this week. Or ever, if I can help it. I'm so done with that town. I understand why you never came back."

"You can stay with me as long as you want," I say. "And not going home wasn't by choice. Mom and Dad told me to not bother, and I was never offended by it because I didn't want to be there just as much as they didn't want me there. Thought I'd turn you. Guess they were right."

Jethro snorts. "Yeah. You totally turned me gay, bro. Better watch out for Wade. I bet we both gave him the gay cooties."

I shouldn't laugh. The morons that are my parents probably think that's actually true.

"If they should worry about anyone, it's Fern. She's super butch for a fourteen-year-old, and she's on the softball team."

"Way to stereotype, JJ."

He knees the back of my seat. "Don't call me that, asswipe."

"Sorry, Jethro."

Jethro smacks me over the head, and I laugh.

"Thank God, I'm an only child," Noah mumbles.

"How I wish you could've taken Noah home to Mom and Dad," Jethro says. "It would be like my birthdays and Christmases all in one seeing their racist, homophobic heads explode."

Noah reaches for my leg. "I might love your brother."

"Just wait. By the end of the week, you'll want to kill him," I say.

My brother hits me again. "I would protest, but Matt's probably right."

A month ago, I was alone in the world. Sitting here with my brother and a guy I'm beginning to care for, I realize I have people in my corner. My heart sinks at that thought because, with it, the weight of my decision becomes heavier. Now I have a brother to support and the potential to walk away from Noah with a broken heart. Or maybe break his.

I examine Noah's face as he drives, taking in his easy smile and relaxed posture and know I can't break his heart when he's not open to letting anyone inside it.

Which means the only one open to getting hurt is me.

I pace Noah's living room, listening to the same message I got when I tried to call Char after I was outed.

The number you're trying to call is unable to be reached.

"They move fast," I say. "They've already canceled her phone. Probably bought her a new one with *my money*." I thought they blocked my number, but after trying with Jethro's phone earlier, I decided to try from Noah's. That's not working either.

"Nah, they would've just bought a new sim card with a new phone number," Noah says.

"Not the point."

"Did Jet say he had Char's baby daddy's number?"

"And I'm just supposed to call some random guy and be all 'Hey, I heard you knocked up my sister. Can I talk to her?'"

Noah laughs. "Could work."

With a deep breath, I get *Bo's* number from the piece of paper Jethro gave me before going to bed. I have no idea what I'm going to say if he answers, so I'll just wing it.

"Can you stop pacing," Noah asks from the couch. "I'm getting dizzy just watching you."

"No."

"No what?" a guy's voice says through the phone.

I finally stop pacing and can't for the life of me say hello like a normal person. "Can I talk to Char?"

"Who the fuck's calling my girl?"

I clear my throat and try not to judge Char's choice in men. "Her brother."

There's a scuffling noise, and I let out a breath of relief when Char's voice comes on the line.

"Jet?"

"It's Matt, actually."

There's a long silence where I start pacing again.

"Ah. Mr. Bigshot finally pulled his head outta his ass."

"That's not fair. I had no way of contacting you. The only reason I do now is because of Jethro."

"Is Jet okay?"

"He's fine, he's stayin' with me, but he told me some things I had no idea about. First, you're pregnant?"

She swears under her breath. "I told him not to tell you if he found you."

"Why? I'm gonna be an uncle. That's pretty cool."

"No, you're not." Her voice is quiet, and my stomach sinks.

"Oh." Guess when it comes to taking sides, Char is firmly on team homophobe.

"Wait, no. Not because you're gay. I couldn't care less about that, but it's not like you're ever comin' home, are ya? Mom and Dad won't let you. Or Jet."

"About that ... Char, I ..." Shit, why is this so hard? "I'm sorry I haven't been there for you. Financially or otherwise."

"It's not your job."

"I know, but I wanted to help. I've *been* helping. Or, I thought I was."

"I don't understand."

"I've been sendin' money to Mom and Dad for four years, and they were supposed to split it between y'all. Jethro tells me they kept it."

"Asshats," she hisses. "I asked them to help out with the baby, and they said they're broke."

"I'm gonna fix this," I say. "I promise."

"Really?" The tears are evident in the way her voice cracks.

"I don't know how yet, but I'm gonna fix it."

Aww, now she's bawling.

"What's wrong, doll?" I ask.

She sniffs. "I ... I've been freaking out about having this baby. We live in a trailer, we got no money, and—"

"I'm gonna help. I, uh, don't have a contract right now, but I'm selling my apartment, and I have some money tied up in stocks and shit. I'll find a way."

"Thank you," she whispers.

"Can I contact you on this number again?"

"I'll program it back into my phone and text you. No joke, they canceled my phone without tellin' me, and wouldn't give me a new one until I deleted you and Jet from my contacts in fronta them."

"Maybe put it under a different name, in case they check up on you."

"Sure thing, new best friend, Miriam." She giggles.

"Works for me."

"I should go, but Matt?"

"Yeah?"

"I miss you. Give my love to Jet."

"I'd say give my love to the others, but they might let it slip that you're in contact with me."

"I'll make sure they know their older brothers love them."

"I'll make sure y'all are taken care of." Somehow. It's a big promise, and if one thing my meetings with my finance guys has taught me, it's that I can't afford to throw my money around. Not if football is no longer an option. The Warriors' contract won't help matters.

When I end the call, Noah beckons me over to him. "That sounded like it went well."

I nod. "Better than I expected."

"Well, I don't know too many people who'd be pissed at a handout."

He pulls me down on the couch so my head's in his lap. His fingers move through my hair, and I close my eyes, loving the feel of his hands on me. The events of today are pushed downfield. Hell, I don't even think they're in the same stadium right now.

"Okay, so now that's done, tell me what you're really thinking about the offer from Chicago," Noah asks.

My eyes fly open to find Noah's piercing blue-green orbs staring down at me.

"I don't want to think about it. I need to map it out when I'm thinking clearer. Right now, I'm still pissed."

"What are the pros and cons?"

"Ugh. You're not gonna make me do a list, are you? You don't seem like a list type of guy."

"I'll hide my legal pad from you, but saying it out loud might help." His hand freezes in my hair, and I rub my head over his lap like a cat to get him to keep going. "I'll keep giving you a head massage if you do the list."

So not going to pass up that offer. His hands are amazing. "The pros are easy. It's a promising team, I get to play football again, and it's Chicago. Being out there will be easier than somewhere God-loving like the Bible Belt."

"Cons," Noah says.

"Accepting that contract is like admitting I deserve less than everyone else because I'm gay. If I take it—"

"It doesn't mean you agree with it. It means you've been dealt a shitty hand, and you don't have much choice. Being forced to retire is just as bad as saying you deserve less. Retirement says you shouldn't be playing the sport at all."

"You think I should take it."

Noah doesn't answer right away, as if he's contemplating telling me the truth or a lie. "What are the other cons? The money?"

"If I don't take the contract, I get no income other than what my investments give me. And then I'd have to work out what I want to do with my life. So, the money isn't the issue. Fuck, I might have to be a college student with my brother. I don't like the sound of that."

Noah laughs. "I'm sorry, but no matter how hard you try, that kid is not going to college. He doesn't want it, even if you're offering to pay for it. You shouldn't push him."

Noah's been great with Jet, welcoming him into his home like it's no big deal. Those two clicked instantaneously, unlike Noah and me when we met.

"He should have a backup," I say.

Noah coughs in between saying "Contradictive."

"I know I don't have a backup, and that's my point. I never had the option to have one. Finishing college before being drafted was never going to happen. I had a family back home I had to support."

The hand stroking my hair stops again. "About that. While you were in your meeting, Jet told me what it was like growing up with your parents."

I try not to tense, but I know I fail when Noah starts massaging me again. "There's a lot of kids who have it worse," I say.

"They're verbally abusive, you had to share a closet-sized room with the two other boys, and from what I understand, the word faggot flies out of your dad's mouth every other sentence. And now you're paying them for treating you that way."

"I can't stop sending them money."

"Yes, you can. You were drafted when you were nineteen. You said you've been paying them eight thousand a month?"

I nod. "Supposed to be four thousand for them and four divided by the five kids."

"That's almost four hundred thousand dollars since you left home."

"Ooh, someone can do math."

Noah's fingers jab into my ribs.

I flinch. "Motherfucker."

"Two hundred thousand dollars divided by five siblings is forty thousand each. Nice college fund. A down payment on an apartment for Char ..."

Anger coils in my stomach. "I get it, okay? But we're not like your family. We don't make threats of cutting people off to get our way."

"It's not about getting your way," Noah says. "They're walking all over you after treating you like shit your whole life. You don't owe them anything."

"I owe my siblings. Jet's right when he said I left them behind to fend for themselves with our parents. But how can I fix it? If I stop sending my parents money, the kids get nothing."

"They're getting nothing now. Jet said your parents are spending every day at the track. Your parents cut you off, but you're unwilling to do the same to them when they're wasting their money. What if you set up trusts for the kids, and now you're in contact with Char, you can send her money directly? Then, if you really want to keep sending your parents money, tell them they have to deal with half of the income they usually get—which, by the way, is still a lot of money for people who live in the sticks and don't have jobs."

"How would you know what's a lot of money to people like us?"

"Median household income in Tennessee is forty-seven thousand a year. You're currently giving your family twice that."

"How do you—"

"I'm a strategist for my dad who's going to be running for president in two years. I know the stats of most states. Contrary to how I act, I am good at my job ... when I actually turn up for it."

"Impressive."

"It's your money, but I hate that your family is taking advantage of you."

I run my hand up Noah's arm. "I'll look into the trust thing." If I go with his idea, I won't have to worry about coming up with more money. I wish I could somehow give lump sums to the kids after finding out Mom and Dad gambled their share away, but with an uncertain future, I don't have the ability to do that.

Noah stares at me—those blue-green eyes assessing me—and I can practically hear what he's thinking. He's wondering if I'll really go through with it.

"I promise." I rub my head against his lap again because the man gives a mean massage.

"Can we please go to bed now?" Noah asks. "Your head's been rubbing all over my cock for the last ten minutes, and I want to explode."

"I'm allowed to stay in your bed again?" I ask.

"Only if you fuck me in it first."

The last two nights, I waited for Noah to kick me out and have been surprised when I've woken up next to him. I haven't slept this good since I can't remember when, and I've never hated training as much as I do right now. I've skipped the last two days which means I have no excuse tomorrow, but peeling myself away from Noah will be hard.

I climb off him and hold out my hand for him. "You know what else is good about the Chicago offer?"

He drags me to the stairs. "Moving bridges?"

"I was thinking that it's a two-hour flight from New York."

Noah stops in the middle of a step. I'm about to backpedal, because I've clearly crossed a line we aren't supposed to, and I get it. Even if it stings.

Instead of chewing me out for even remotely suggesting there was some sort of future for us, Noah smiles. "I'll keep that in mind. If I ever get desperate enough."

I chuckle. "Wow. Maybe I won't fuck you tonight, because clearly two days of sex is enough to make you forget how long and agonizing the last two weeks were without me. You didn't even make it the full two weeks."

"Oh, game on. I could so last longer than you without sex."

"You're forgetting that I went twenty-three years without it. Won't be hard to go back."

"Are you sure about that?" Noah looks at me expectantly, and I know I'll probably be the one to cave. I can't get enough of the guy in front of me.

I step onto the stair below his, which makes him a tiny bit taller than me. Slowly, I start moving in as if I'm going to kiss him. His eyelids become hooded, his lips part, and then at the very last second, I pull away and march past him. "Yeah, I'm pretty sure."

I can't stop the laugh as Noah mutters "Asshole" and trudges up the stairs behind me.

CHAPTER SIXTEEN

I follow my nose to the kitchen and stop short at Jet bouncing around. The kid reminds me of a hyperactive poodle. But in a good way.

"Where's Matt?" I ask.

"Where do you think?"

Ah, right. "Basement for his morning workout." I'm usually not awake for it, but the smell of food roused me from sleep.

"Yep. Breakfast will be ready in ten if you want to go get him."

"You can cook?"

"No. I'm just makin' a mess in here for funsies."

I shouldn't laugh, but I do.

"After Matt left, Charlene was the one who cooked for us. Then she left, but at least she was still close by and I could ask her for pointers."

The way he says that type of shit so casually—as if it's normal for the eldest at home to parent the younger kids—pisses me off. "Another dumb question here. Why don't your parents cook?"

Jet shrugs and goes back to preparing what smells like bacon and something sweet. "They're never home. And the kids are old enough now to fend for themselves. They're not missing my cooking."

"It smells good."

"Don't get too excited. It's plain ol' bacon and egg crêpes with maple syrup. Hope you're not a vegetarian."

"I can handle a lot of meat in my mouth."

Jet laughs.

"Totally didn't mean that to sound as dirty as it did. This sure beats the breakfast of champions we've been having." *Blowjob with a side of coffee.*

"From the takeout menus I've seen, breakfast isn't the only thing you've been lazy with."

"It's New York. You can pretty much get whatever you want delivered, but Matt's is always the same."

Jet smiles at me and together we say, "Steamed brown rice and chicken."

"God, I remember when he used to feed us that crap at home when he was in training." Jet shudders. The reminder that Matt has stayed in training mode this whole time reminds me he's nowhere near ready to give up on football.

The dreaded realization that Matt is going to leave me makes the walls around my heart begin to close up. They've crumbled these last few weeks, but I can't let them fall completely. I don't know if I could survive it.

"He's going to accept the Chicago offer, isn't he?" My voice comes out as a low murmur.

"Matt is football. Always has been. If it's his only chance to play, he'll do it." Jet eyes me over his shoulder. "You gonna move to Chicago with him if he goes?"

My heart thuds in my chest, and I don't know how much to tell Jet of the arrangement between Matt and me. "Nah. We both know we're temporary. He's ..." *Too good for me.* Despite my father's opinions of it being the other way around, it's true; Matt is too good for me. My father sees our money as a status. I see it as a curse—a reason to stay guarded so I don't end up blindsided again. I can't let myself get in too deep, because Matt's leaving. If it's not Chicago, it'll be another town.

"He's what?" Matt asks from behind me.

"He's a nosy fuck," I say and fake a smile as I turn to face him.

He doesn't smile back. He's covered in sweat, he's shirtless, and damn, sweats were a bad idea to dress in this morning. Can't hide anything in these pants.

"Tell me what you were going to say," Matt says.

I tell myself to spit out an ugly truth. "You've got football to focus on, and we said from the start this wasn't going anywhere." I glance back at Jet who's pretending he's not listening.

"Right. Okay." Matt still breathes heavy from his workout. "I'm gonna go shower."

When I drag my eyes off Matt's retreating ass, they meet Jet's scowl.

"Brutal, man," he says.

"Nah, Matt can handle it. He knew the deal going in."

Jet scoffs. "Never thought I'd see the day I was smarter than my big brother."

"Stay out of shit you don't understand, junior."

Now I'm entertaining to him. Great.

We have a deal. Neither of us are going to break it.

"I'm not going to piss off the guy who's giving me a free bed, so this is me *not* telling you that if you break Matt's heart—"

"What? You'll break my face? You're half my size, squirt."

"I was gonna say if you break his heart, you're an idiot because you ain't gonna find better than my brother. He practically raised me. So, if you hurt him, you're a fuckin' dick."

I can't help laughing. "I'm glad you held back."

"That's funny to you?"

"Yeah, it is." Because I think I'm losing my head. Matt's getting under my skin, and I'm not sure I like it. My usual reaction to being called a dick is along the lines of *duh*. But when it comes to Matt, the last thing I want to do is hurt him. He's been through enough.

Jet continues to glare at me, waiting for me to defend myself. Newsflash, kid. I'm not that type of guy.

"If you're going to be an ass, can you at least help me serve breakfast?" he asks.

"Sure."

When Matt comes back, he doesn't even acknowledge what was said ten minutes ago. Kissing my cheek, he grabs the plate in my hands. "This mine?"

"No, yours is here." Jet turns to Matt with a huge plate full of omelet. The colorless, egg-white kind. Eww.

Matt's face lights up over it. "Thanks for breakfast, JJ."

Jet scowls.

"Okay, you have to tell me why you refuse to call your brother Jet," I say.

"It's a stupid name," Matt mumbles.

"You're a stupid name," Jet says.

"So glad we can have a grownup conversation, guys," I say.

Matt takes his seat at the dining table. "You know what my full name is?"

"Matthew?" I say.

Jet laughs. "Nope. His full name is Matt."

"Jethro was given the privilege of a full name and he refuses to use it. Pisses me off."

"Aww, you want me to call you Matthew?" I ask. "Because I'll do it."

"And that doesn't explain JJ," Jet says.

"Oh, that's because I'm a dick," Matt says and turns to me. "When he was six, he told everyone he wants to go by JJ. It caught on at school, but then ..." He pauses and then his face drops. "I didn't think. I remember you loving the name and then hating it, but it just occurred to me what made you stop liking it."

"What was it?" I ask.

"Dad said it sounded like a drag name," Jet says quietly. "Ain't no son of his gonna be a f—"

"I get the picture," I say. "And, Matthew, you are a dick."

"I'll stop," Matt says.

"Hallelujah," Jet says. "Although, that totally gives me an idea to do drag for Halloween and send our parents an update. And, you know what? Fuck it. I'm taking the name back and owning it. Dad can't do anything about it from where he is."

"Sounds like an idea," Matt says. "Give the parentals a heart attack, and then you can look after the kids while I play for Chicago."

Jet and I share a glance.

"You're going to do it?" I ask Matt.

"Damon called today. The GM wants to fly me out there.

They're serious about wanting me, and I figure I should at least go meet with him."

"When do you leave?" I ask.

"Next week. It'll just be a day thing. Fly out in the morning and come back that night."

I force a smile and fake my way through a lie. "That's great news. Good luck."

Suddenly, my appetite is gone, even though Jet's food tastes amazing. The eggs are perfectly cooked, the bacon nice and crispy, but I have to force myself to eat it. It sits in my stomach like lead.

This is what was going to happen all along, so I don't know why it leaves a bitter taste in my mouth. Am I angry because I want him to stay or am I angry at myself for allowing me to get to this point?

I don't want him to leave.

CHAPTER SEVENTEEN

MATT

The last person I expect to pick me up from the airport is Marcus Talon himself—the new star quarterback for the Warriors.

He's a bit shorter than I am, with pretty-boy blond hair and a killer smile that's aimed at me in the arrivals section.

"Hey, man." He does the whole man-hug thing with our hands clasped between us and a shoulder bump.

"Uh, hi ... Marcus." It's not as if I'm expecting him to not know who I am, but I've met this guy maybe once. Our old teams had faced each other numerous times, but with both of us being on the offensive line, we've never gone head to head.

"Call me Talon. Everyone else does. Did you have a good flight?" he asks.

"Fine. Quick, which is good."

"My car's out front."

And yes, it is. With people crowding around it. Some being paparazzi.

I freeze in my steps. "How did they know I was here?"

Talon laughs. "Someone has a big head. Sorry to burst your bubble, but they're here for me. You're not in your town anymore. I own this place."

"Speaking of big heads, already taking over and the season hasn't started, huh?"

Talon claps my back, and sure enough, as we head into the fold, Talon's name is called out to the point the two syllables don't even make sense to me anymore. But it doesn't take them long to realize who I am and what that means. Questions of contracts are thrown at me, but I ignore them and push forward to Talon's bright red Ferrari.

Seeing as I'm only here for the day, I don't have a bag, and it's an easy escape into his car and out of the drop-off lane.

It's the first time I've been around anyone who belongs to my old world, so it's awkward to say the least. And then I go and make it worse by saying something stupid.

"You know, at least one of those guys back there will print that we're together now. So, uh, sorry in advance."

Talon doesn't seem fazed; he even smiles.

"Why'd the team send you? This a publicity stunt?"

"I asked to do it."

"*Why?*"

"Because I want you as much as Coach and the GM do." He gives me the side-eye, and my gaydar pings, but I reckon I'm reading into it.

"Okay. Again, *why?*" I ask. "You know shit's gonna go down that first day in any locker room I walk into. Why would you want to invite that into your team?"

"Because you're a good player, I want you on my line, and ... what they're doing to you in the media is wrong."

"I don't understand."

"Wow, are you a cynical bastard, or what? I don't have to be gay to know homophobia is still a problem. And we both know how this industry works. Lie to magazines all you want about why you were dumped by the Bulldogs, but we both know the truth. When you have the stats you do, no one should care what you do at home."

"I may be cynical, but you're way too optimistic if you think no one will care."

"So make them not care," Talon says. "This is about football. You're probably the most versatile tight end in the league."

Okay, so I was questioning his sexuality right up until he said *versatile tight end* with a straight face. No gay man could do that.

God, I wish I had his type of faith. Ideally, my talent would get me a pass, but that's not going to happen in the real world.

"I know the contract the Warriors offered you can't be much, but we're determined to make you sign with us. If we can take it to the Super Bowl this year, next year's contract will triple what they offered."

"It'd need to be more than triple," I mutter.

"That bad, huh?"

"Your fault. Apparently."

Talon smiles. "Someone has to fund the lifestyle I've become accustomed to." He pats the dash of his car.

"And just when I thought we could be friends."

"Yeah, yeah, Lambo man. I've seen your car in the tabloids. My baby could beat your baby in a fight."

I laugh. "We gonna race for pink slips and have a rumble?"

"Only if you don't sign the dotted line."

If the rest of the guys on the team are like Talon, signing the shitty contract might not be so bad.

My phone buzzes in my pocket, and when I take it out to look at the screen, I don't know whether to be pissed off or laugh. "Motherfucker."

"The photos from the airport hit the tabloids already?"

"Nah, Noah ... uh, my boyfriend, took my little brother for a campus tour of my alma mater. At least, he was supposed to. The bastard took him to *his* instead. He sent through a pic of them at the Newport entrance with goofy-ass grins on their faces." And even though it's Newport, I'm jealous as all get out that I'm not there with them.

"Ah, the old Olmstead versus Newport debate." Talon laughs.

"Olmstead wins on location alone. It's not in Jersey."

"Hey, I'm a Jersey boy born and raised."

"Shit. Sorry."

Talon laughs harder. "I'm messing with you, man. I'm originally from Denver."

Talon's easygoing nature makes me forget about locker room politics. I'm already comfortable around him, which is more than I can say for any of my teammates from the Bulldogs.

Talon pulls into the stadium and parks in the faculty parking lot.

"What are we doing here?" I ask.

"Training facility's here, and the GM is meeting us later, but I want to show you something first."

He leads me through the back tunnels and corridors, taking me out to the field, and when he opens his arms wide—as if saying *ta-da!*—I look at him as if he's lost his mind.

"I've seen the field. I've played here."

"But have you ever looked at it like home?"

I shake my head.

"Picture it, Jackson. I can't wait to make this place mine."

The smell of turf, the grass beneath my feet, the imaginary crowd going wild ... yeah, I could call any stadium home. It's not the money holding me back, but the thought the Warriors management thinks I'm a risk. The others might not like playing with a gay guy. This is something I'll have to face no matter which team I join, and if it's a choice between less money but a great team or the millions I deserve and a hostile work environment, I'd pick less money every time.

"Do you know many guys on the team?" I ask.

"There's Miller who I went to college with. Henderson did his captainly duties and invited me over for dinner with his wife and kids when I moved a few weeks back. Seems decent. There's a few others I've hung out with after games."

"Oh, God, you're one of those players who hangs out with the opposition after games?"

"What, you stick to your team?"

"No, I don't go out at all."

"Ah. Well, that'll change when you're a Warrior." He grins.

"Do you think ... I mean ... are the others ..."

"Do I think the team is full of homophobic wankstains?"

"Nice word." I laugh. "But yeah."

"I'm not gonna lie. The chances of *no one* on the team having an issue is small, but I guarantee you'll have backup from me and Miller."

"Good to know."

A voice calls from the tunnel. "What are ya doin' standing around gossiping?"

We turn to Jimmy Caldwell, the head coach for the Warriors, as he makes his way toward us with a football. He's as intimidating as he is impressively large. A two-time Super Bowl champion himself, he's someone who knows what he's talking about. He'd be a great coach to work with.

"Show us that arm is worth every penny." He throws the ball at Talon. "Wouldn't mind seeing Jackson in action either."

"Testing out the merchandise before buying, huh?" Talon asks.

"If we had it our way, we'd have already bought this one off the shelves." Jim gestures to me.

"I'm not a piece of stock," I say, my tone light.

"Yeah. You are," Talon says. "So am I. Should we show them how lowballing you could be a big mistake?" He takes off his sneakers and socks.

Barefoot football? As fast as I can, I strip off my suit jacket, roll my shirtsleeves up, and take off my shoes and socks.

The turf is soft beneath my feet, and while there's pressure to do well—as well as I can do wearing a suit instead of pads—I lose myself in the feeling of home. Running toward the end zone, all the bullshit fades away. Being outed, contract negotiations, a fake relationship that doesn't feel so fake anymore—it all disappears into a black hole of *I don't give a shit right now.* I'm where I'm supposed to be.

Talon gives a yell that he's about to hike the ball, and I turn, but he's underestimated my stride length, and I have to backtrack. The ball sails into my arms for a perfect pass, and Talon gives a loud *whoop.*

When I jog back to them, the coach has a wide smile. "You're fast for your size. We need that in a tight end. Our guys are all blockers."

"I can do both." I'm not boasting. It's the truth.

"You don't need to sell us on you, kid. We're supposed to be getting you to sign. You ready to meet the big man?"

I nod even though I don't need to meet him. They've already sold me.

"Hey, how did it go?" Noah's voice elicits both dread and happiness.

I can't tell him my decision yet. I want to live in our bubble for a little longer where we don't know our exact expiration date. Before it was just something we knew was going to happen eventually. Not anymore. I'm moving to Chicago, which is eight hundred miles of distance between us.

"I think it went okay. I'm just waiting to board the plane and thought I'd check in."

There's a pause, and I can feel the question he wants to ask but won't let himself. I don't want to answer it, either.

This was part of the deal. I'd get a contract and leave. Yet, I can't bring myself to say it aloud—as if that'll make it real.

"How'd JJ go at Newport?"

"He, uh, umm ..." His next words rush out of him like verbal diarrhea. "He liked Olmstead better."

I grin. "It was hard for you to admit that, wasn't it?"

"Yup."

"So, you took him to OU after all?"

"Yeah, but good luck convincing him to apply to either. He doesn't want to go to college."

I sigh. "Then what's he going to do with his life?"

"Isn't that his decision?"

To me, he'll always be the fourteen-year-old punk I left behind five years ago. "I guess."

"He has his head screwed on pretty tight."

Pride swells in my chest. "The flight's being called. I'll see you in a few hours."

"I'll try to stay awake, but I'm exhausted."

"I won't wake you if you crash."

"I want to hear how today went."

"We'll talk tomorrow. Night."

"Night, babe."

Halfway down the gangway, my phone vibrates with another call. It's a New York area code but a number I don't recognize. I've learned enough over the last few months not to answer. It's most likely a reporter.

I switch my phone to airplane mode and forget about it, but when we land at JFK, there's a voicemail waiting for me.

"Mr. Jackson." The authoritative voice on the recording is both terrifying and confusing. "This is Noah Huntington." Yeah, so not the Noah Huntington I know, but then I remember Noah is a number. He has numbers in his name when there should only be letters. "There's something Rick Douglas would like to talk to you about. I'm sure I don't need to tell you who that is. If you can call my assistant and organize a time to come into my offices here, I can make a meeting happen. Rick is an old friend of mine." He rattles off a number to call and then the message cuts out.

Noah's dad wants me to meet with the owner of the New York Cougars? Something tells me he's not doing it outta the goodness of his heart. With one phone call, the strings have already been attached. It's just a matter of how long they are.

But it's *New York*. Some strings might be worth it.

I listen to the message another time and take down the number. Then I make the call.

CHAPTER EIGHTEEN

Hanging out with Jet makes me realize something. All those times my friends have called me an entitled asshole and I've shrugged them off because I know deep down I'm nothing like my father, I never once realized they were telling the truth and I was too entitled to see it.

This nineteen-year-old kid knows more about the real world than I do.

I'm not an idiot. I know there are homeless people every-where—I've read the stats on them and seen them begging on the streets. But as Jet rambles like an ADD kid without his meds that if he hadn't found Matt he would've been well and truly screwed, it's crazy to me how close he became to being a statistic.

"Why couldn't you have stayed in your hometown?" I ask.

"The guy I was hooking up with is in the closet, so moving in with him would've been suspicious. Plus, I don't think we even liked each other very much. Don't got a lot of prospects in Shitsville, Tennessee. Char lives in a tiny trailer with her boyfriend and is about to pop a kidlet. Not to mention Mom and Dad would disown her too if she helped me out. I had a few friends, but none I was close enough to be all 'Hey, I got kicked out for liking dick. Can I crash on your couch indefinitely?'"

I can't help laughing. "You certainly have a colorful way of coming out to people. What would've happened if you couldn't find Matt?"

"There's this forum online, and I got in contact with a few guys in the city. Thought I could crash with them until I figured out what to do. I spent what money I had on trying to get here."

"You were going to stay with guys you met online? Did your parents never teach you about stranger danger?" What am I saying? From what they've both told me, Matt's parents did nothing to teach anything. Except how to hold a football so Matt's gay stops showing.

"It's not like that." Jet takes out his phone, opens the forum, clicks on a thread titled *Rainbow Beds,* and holds it up to my face. "People who have a spare bed or couch post availability in here, and anyone who needs a place to stay after getting kicked out can find somewhere to crash. Kinda like Airbnb but gayer."

Either I'm a pessimistic bastard or Jet's more naïve than I thought. "Still sounds like a great way to get locked in a basement and have someone wear your skin as a body suit."

"Nice image. The hosts probably aren't heavily vetted, but there's a lot of people who have no other option."

"Can I look?"

Jet hands me his phone, and as I scroll through the threads, I feel like the biggest dick in the world. I live in a four-bedroom townhouse alone … well, I will when Matt and Jet leave. If they leave. I sigh. I really don't want them to leave.

But here are people who live in studio apartments offering up a couch, a pull-out futon, or even a floor for people in need.

It's dangerous, sure, but the idea behind it is inspiring. With the right backing, the proper channels ...

"Why can I see an imaginary lightbulb above your head?" Jet asks.

"This is brilliant. It should be something bigger than a thread on a tiny forum. With some money behind the idea—"

"Key word being money. You're forgetting that shit doesn't grow on trees."

"You and Matt are so cute. I swear to God." They're really oblivious to how much money I have.

"Cute?" Jet asks. "You better not be hitting on me. Not only are you with my brother, you're, like, super old."

"Fuck you very much. Twenty-six is not old, and I'm not trying to fuck you. I'm in love with your brother, jackass." My eyes widen. "Don't tell him I said that." Why did I say that?

That wasn't supposed to come out of my mouth. It's not even supposed to be a thought in my head.

I try to convince myself it's part of the act. Yup. That's all it is.

Part. Of. The. Act.

"You haven't told him?" Jet asks. "Didn't you say it in that interview for that magazine?"

My heart races. "There's something you need to know about Matt's and my relationship."

I don't know what's the truth and what's a lie anymore. This started as a business arrangement, but it's changed into so much more. I care for him. I want the best for him. But that's not me. That's all I have to think to have the reality check that this is all fake.

Matt promised he wouldn't fall for me, and as far as I can tell, he hasn't broken that promise. So I need to keep up my end of the bargain and not break the confidentiality agreement.

"I said that stuff in the interview because from a publicity perspective, saying we're in love is better than saying he's the guy I'm doing until he gets an NFL contract."

"You don't want him to go to Chicago though. It's obvious in the way you tense whenever the contract is mentioned."

I look at my feet. "Like you said, Matt is football. No way he'd choose to stay with me over his dream."

"He might. You don't know if you don't ask."

"Okay, this convo went wayward, and you need to shut your mouth about what I said. Matt and I have always been temporary. Now, back to this idea. I have the funds to make something like this massive and nationwide. I mean, we'd have to start off small first and make sure it's viable. The people taking others in would have to be heavily vetted, and it'd be a lot of work, but I want to do this."

"You're serious." Jet states it as if someone just told him the zombie apocalypse has started. It's a mix of disbelief and misunderstanding.

"I want to at least talk to my father about it."

Jet slumps. "Well, there goes that idea."

"Why do you say that?"

"I've seen your dad on TV. I don't know how to say this without offending you, so I'm just going to say he looks like the type of politician who spouts family values and then gets caught in a seedy motel with a prostitute."

I laugh. "So glad you tried not to offend me, Jet." God, I love this kid ... like a brother, that is. And I can't be offended if it's the truth. I mean, I don't know for sure if Dad has affairs, but I doubt it. He's too worried about his image. Having grown up in our cold house, though, I know there's no shared love between Mom and Dad. Their happy marriage is a political arrangement. A lot like Matt's and mine.

"You're welcome," Jet says, either not picking up on my sarcasm or not caring.

"How about this, then; I'll take my idea to my father, and if he says no, I'll see my financial guys and work out if I can do it on my own."

"Financial guys," he scoffs. "Who talks like that?"

"Uh, your brother, for one. He's been talking to his guys about the future of his portfolio."

"Ah, the fancy lives of the rich and famous."

"And what are your plans for the future, musician boy?"

"Worst superhero name *ever*."

"Do you hope to be rich and famous one day? Singing to your millions of fans? Screwing every fuckboy in sight?"

"Wouldn't be much of a difference to my life now ... well, minus the millions of fans." Jet waggles his eyebrows.

"If you say so, stud."

"Okay, fine. You can count every fuckboy in my hometown on one hand. It's not much of an accomplishment."

"Did the college tours change your mind about enrolling?"

"Nope. Cemented college isn't for me."

"Do me a favor?" I ask.

"Sure."

"Break that news to Matt while I'm at work tomorrow."

Jet laughs. "Deal."

"I want to start an LBGTQ charity," I blurt out.

Dad's advisors look at me as if I've grown two heads, so I repeat myself but slower this time.

"We have the Huntington Foundation that gives to many charities, including numerous LGBTQ causes," John—Dad's campaign manager—says.

"I'm thinking more along the lines of a homeless shelter for teens. It's more complicated than that, but that's the best way to describe it. Or, rather, it's more like a couch surfing app for homeless teens." I knew that one would go over the old guys' heads, but I say it anyway, and yup, confusion all over their faces. Should've kept with the shelter explanation.

Rob, an advisor, leans forward in his seat and looks at Dad. "I don't think it's the best move for the campaign right now. You'll already have the LGBTQ votes because of Noah." He tips his head in my direction. "Pushing it too far could lose the conservative democrats."

"Okay, let me put it this way," I say. "I'm going to start this charity, and this campaign can be as little or as much involved as you want. This is more of a heads-up."

"How do you propose you fund this project if I'm not involved?" Dad asks.

It's hard not to laugh at that. He knows I have my own funds, but he likes to keep up the pretense that I'm his heir and not worth as much as him. "I'll talk to my financial guys and make it happen."

Dad rubs his chin like some caricature of an evil villain. "I'm all for it."

I fully expect him to fight me on this, so the prepared argument is ready to let loose, but then I realize what he said. "Huh?"

"Can I have a minute with my son?" Dad asks.

His minions obey immediately.

"You're agreeing with me on this?" I ask.

Dad stands. "I'm done, Noah. You win."

"Win what?"

"We both know you don't want to be here, and as much as I want you to do this with me, you're a pain in my ass more than a help. I can't fire you, and you quitting will bring more questions than answers."

Still taking his image into account first. "But by leaving the campaign to fulfill my life-long wish of charity work, we all win," I say.

Dad approaches me and squeezes my shoulder. "It's a great idea for a charity, son. The stats show it's one that's needed. I'm not doing this to get you out of my hair. You're the one who doesn't want to be here. I'm trying to give you what you want because I'm done fighting you. You have to know by now that everything I do for you is in your best interests, and I'm tired of trying to prove that."

Still not taking responsibility for what he did to me back in college. He's never once apologized and doesn't see what's wrong with his actions. Maybe I would've worked out on my own that the shithead back then was a shithead. Maybe if Nathaniel hadn't been threatened and bribed, he wouldn't have run for the hills and we'd still be together. Dad may think he's doing what's best for me, but it always comes down to him and his campaign. Nathaniel's image wasn't good enough because he didn't come from money, so he made him disappear. If the politician thing doesn't work out, he has a promising career as a magician.

I can count on my fingers and toes how many times I've

been told I delayed his political career simply by existing. Dad got Mom pregnant out of wedlock, and instead of getting rid of me or paying Mom off, he chose to have no scandal under his belt. But an interracial couple in the White House is scandal in itself—especially back then. It's taken twenty-six years for the opportunity to even arise. My coming out delayed it again, but I guess I should be thankful that he didn't ask me to hide it forever like other politicians have done with their own sexualities.

Dad treats Mom and me as if we should be thankful he embraced us instead of turned on us. He will do anything to save his campaign, so while I want to believe he's agreed to this charity for me, I'm reluctant to accept it.

"I'm proud of you," Dad says. "For not thinking about yourself for once. This charity will do great things for people who weren't as lucky as you growing up."

Ah, there's the guilt trip I'm expecting. We have money; we're not supposed to have hardships.

"We'll work it so the charity is linked with the campaign, but you won't have to come to the offices anymore."

I honestly don't know why he's suddenly willing to let me go, other than he's been trying to find a way to do it for a while now and I've given him the out that's agreeable with *his* terms, but I also know not to challenge it or ask questions. "Thanks, Dad."

"Go," Dad says. "Take the rest of the day and prepare a list of what you think you'll need, and if you need someone to help you get the ball rolling, you can take one of the staffers."

Part of me can't believe it was that easy, but again, I'm not going to question it. As I drive home, though, and relive the conversation over and over again, suspicions begin to arise.

Perhaps it's the cynical side of me or perhaps I just know my father. His actions don't make sense, but I can't see an upside for him to give me this.

I went in preparing to fight my case, so I'm still confused when I drag my ass in the door.

I find Matt and Jet watching a hockey game, and I do a double take.

"Was I at work for four months?"

"Watching last season's playoffs," Matt says. "Maddox told me Damon's signed Ollie Strömberg. Wanted to check him out."

"Aww, there's plenty of Damon to share around," I mock.

Jet laughs. "I wonder if agents have their favorite clients, and it's like sibling rivalry trying to get Daddy's attention."

"I could kick Strömberg's ass if it came to it," Matt says.

Jet turns to me. "How did it go?"

I smile. "I got it. My father was my biggest supporter. Surprisingly."

"Got what?" Matt asks.

"I'm heading up an LGBTQ charity for kids like Jet who got kicked out of home."

Matt's eyebrows soar high. "Really?"

"Yes. The asshole has a heart. Moving on," I say.

"No, not that," Matt says. "Your dad agreed to this?"

"I checked all the news outlets to make sure Armageddon wasn't upon us. Apparently, we're safe." My lips quirk. "He said he was proud of me and it was a good idea."

"Might want to check those news sites again," Matt says quietly, but there's something in his tone. Hope?

I recognize it because I'm pretty sure it's how my voice sounds. I'm desperate to believe my dad has changed or something snapped in him that made him realize what a shitty father he's been, but I can't shake the feeling he has ulterior motives. I'll push that to the back of my mind, because I'm getting exactly what I want.

Matt stands from the couch. "After my workout, we should go celebrate."

"Actually, I'd really like to get started on this." I turn to Jet. "And I want your input. You know the forum."

"I'm in," Jet says.

Matt moves closer to me. Leaning in, he brings his mouth to my ear. "You being selfless and excited about helping people is kinda hot."

"Maybe I'll show you how selfless I can be later when I let you fuck me."

"Uh, guys," Jet says, "still in the room which is really small. I don't need to know the details. Thanks."

Matt squeezes my hand. "Later." With a kiss, he heads for the basement, and I throw myself down on the couch across from Jet.

"Let's get to work."

CHAPTER NINETEEN

MATT

After my workout, Noah and Jet have their heads close together, looking at something on Noah's laptop that sits on the coffee table. Noah's got his long legs stretched out, and Jet lies on the couch behind him, looking over his shoulder.

Hmm, cozy.

I find them after my shower in the same spot. And after doing a load of washing. I half-want to ask if they'd suddenly become conjoined twins, but their low murmurs let me know they're still busy.

I haven't told Noah about my meeting with his dad yet, but it's set for tomorrow. I want to hear what he has to say before I tell Noah. If it's that he wants me to stay away from his son, Noah doesn't need to hear it. The fact he's given Noah responsibility and a huge project to run, I want to believe he can see Noah's not going to relent on the political career he so desperately wants him to have. Maybe he's given up and wants some form of relationship with his son. Getting his boyfriend a meeting with the Cougars' owner might be his way of greasing the wheels.

One could hope that's what he's doing, but like Noah, I'm suspicious. This is the man who had absolutely no reservations about saying how I'm not good enough for his son while I was standing right there in front of him.

"What's for dinner?" I ask.

"Sounds good," Noah says.

Guess dinner is up to me then. "Steamed chicken and rice all round?"

"Totally," Jet says.

Okay, now I know they have no idea what I'm saying. I call and order Chinese food but am not a total dick. I order them real food instead of the shit I force myself to chew down on a daily basis.

They don't even stop for food, choosing to eat while they work.

Seeing as I've been getting up at ass o'clock every day, I doze off on the couch while waiting for Noah and Jet to finish for the night.

"Yo, chainsaw." Jet's voice startles me. "Care to take it upstairs? I have no idea how Noah sleeps with you and all that snoring."

My vision's blurry, and it takes a second to work out I'm still in the living room.

Noah gives me a weak smile. "I'll be up soon. I swear."

I stagger to my feet, dragging my ass up to the third floor. Undressing and climbing into bed still half-asleep, I crash out immediately. But when a warm body slides in behind me however long later, I can't help rolling over and plastering myself to him. My leg goes over his hip, and he lets out a little laugh.

"Are you climbing me in your sleep?"

"Mmm." I can't open my eyes.

"Go back to sleep," he whispers. "And for the record, I like your snoring."

I smile in the dark.

"I've never slept better than when you're in bed with me." He sighs. "But I guess that's one of those things we shouldn't talk about."

Pulling back, I force my eyes open. "Huh?"

"Nothing, babe. Goodnight." He rolls away from me and faces the other way, but if he thinks he's getting outta cuddling, he's sorely mistaken. Turns out, I'm a cuddle whore in bed. I only hope I remember this conversation in the morning because I have no idea what he means. I didn't realize there were things we weren't supposed to talk about.

My hands sweat as I sit in the waiting area of Noah Huntington II's office. Wiping them on my suit pants does nothing to dry them. It's a hundred degrees in here, and I have to refrain from reaching for my tie to loosen it.

I was vague about my plans to Noah and Jet, and I reckon they're under the impression I'm meeting with Damon about Chicago.

When Rick Douglas steps through the doors, he stalls for a split second as he sees me. The subtle shake of his head, as if he's disappointed, has me confused, but he pushes whatever it is away and approaches me with a warm—but I'm guessing fake—smile.

"Jackson."

"Mr. Douglas." I shake his outstretched hand and try not to wince when he grasps my sweaty palm.

And then? Nothing but silence. Brilliant.

"Umm, sorry, I don't even know what this meeting is about."

He narrows his eyes. "You ... you have no idea why we're here?"

"I can venture a guess, but I don't understand why we'd be doing ... that here. Without my agent."

Now he cocks his head as if I've confused him somehow. "You really don't know, do you? I thought ... Uh, never mind what I thought. But—"

"Mr. Huntington will see you both now," the receptionist says.

I gesture for Rick to go first, and we're welcomed by Noah's father holding the door open for us. Even though Noah Huntington II is only in his late fifties, he looks mid-sixties at least. I wonder if politics has aged him, or perhaps that's part of Noah's doing with his refusal to conform.

"We'll get straight to the point," Mr. Huntington says as we take our seats at his desk. "Rick has an offer for you."

"So why hasn't *Rick* gone through my agent?" I ask.

"We're all friends here," Noah's dad says.

Rick passes me a sheet of paper with a sum on it. An amazing sum. Like Tom Brady type of money.

"And the catch?" I grip the armrest of my chair with my free hand and prepare for what I already know is coming but am hoping I'm wrong. I'm not dumb. I'm not worth that much.

"You move out of my house," Noah's dad says.

My brow scrunches. "What, you worried I'm going to try to make a claim for it if something was to happen to Noah? That townhouse has been in your family for generations. I wouldn't—"

"He's not worried about the house," Rick says, and my suspicions are confirmed.

"You know there's no future with my son. Move out, buy your own place, and play for the Cougars. It's no secret in the football world that no one wants you."

Rick glances between Mr. Huntington and me. "Right."

"You get what you want, and Noah stays out of the spotlight," Noah's dad says.

I want to tell him to fuck off, but Rick-freaking-Douglas is sitting next to me, and while I'm not going to accept his tainted offer in a million years, he's a big deal in the NFL. I have to be professional.

But Noah's dad's trying to get rid of me the same way he did Noah's college boyfriend, and that pisses me off.

Even if this money would set me and my siblings up for our entire lives, it's not worth losing Noah over. Not to mention every time I'd put on a Cougar's jersey, I'd be wearing my guilt. My shame. My sellout.

Fuck that.

"Thanks, but I'm gonna have to politely decline. If Noah doesn't want me around anymore, it's up to him to tell me."

"You don't have to answer right away. Sleep on it," his dad says.

"I don't need to. I'm not accepting a bribe." I turn to Rick. "You're lucky if I don't go to the league about this." I stand from my seat and place both my hands on the oversized desk that's probably overcompensating for something lacking in his life and lean in to get in Mr. Huntington's face. "I can't be bought. You forget I grew up poor. Money means nothing to me, because I know I'll survive without it."

"Will you be able to survive without football?"

I falter, because I don't know the answer to that question. Football has been my everything for as long as I can remember.

"I know you care about Noah," Mr. Huntington says. "So do I. Which is why it's best for everyone if you step back. I'd hate to think how he'd feel if you gave up football for him when you two don't have a future. You wouldn't want to come between him and his new charity, would you?"

I'm not sure if that's a threat or actual concern for Noah's new venture that he's extremely invested in. Noah once told me he doesn't care about anything. He doesn't have a passion. But ever since he came home and told us about the charity, I've never seen him more focused.

I want to ask him to clarify what he means, but before I can, he says, "Think on the deal. You want back in the NFL, and this is your in."

I turn to Mr. Douglas. "No offense, but you look as happy about this situation as I do." I look back to Noah's dad. "There's no point being in this city if I can't be with Noah."

Truer words have never been spoken, and that's when I realize I'm falling for the guy.

Idiot. Idiot. Idiot.

"Yes, well, if I had friends on the West Coast, they'd be sitting here instead of Rick," Mr. Huntington says.

I have to get out of this office before I do something I regret —like confess my true feelings for Noah to the man who wants me to leave and the other who could break my career in half. I storm out, trying to keep hold of any type of composure, but I only make it to the lobby when black spots cloud my vision and I have to stop.

My hands go to my knees, and my head slumps.

"Mr. Jackson, are you okay?" the receptionist asks.

I wave her off but don't stand back upright yet. If only I could just ... breathe.

"You did the right thing." Rick's voice is the thing that brings me out of it.

I stand tall—totally faking any resemblance to confidence. "How could you have put your team on the line like that? It's clear you don't want to sign me." My chest rises and falls, and this guy can't even give me the respect to look me in the eye.

"You know in movies where the bad guy does the good guy a favor and says 'Just repay it when the time comes'?"

"Yeah?"

"The time has come for me to pay my debt, but I'm glad you have the morals of a saint. Not many would've turned down a multi-million-dollar contract like that."

"Well, relax. I'm not interested in a deal where I'm sure to keep my bank account stuffed but the bench warmed."

The Cougars' tight end bench is deep, but the lack of playing time would've been worth staying with Noah if the offer was real, but it's not. Rick would sign me in name only, and I'd have to give up Noah for it. Then Rick would either cut me or not find any field time for me.

Rick extends his hand for me to shake. "I thought ... when he tried to set this up, I thought it was you using your connections to get a contract. I ... I'm sorry I misjudged you." He looks away again, breaking eye contact, and I already know I won't like what he has to say next. "I've already sent the offer to your agent. Noah was adamant you would've taken it, so it was sent before we even had the meeting."

I scoff. "He wasn't adamant. My agent will encourage me to take New York because it's more money. Mr. Huntington is trying to push me into a corner."

"Move to Chicago."

"How did you know about Chicago?"

"Football's a small world."

Yet, he didn't tell Noah's dad about it, and I have to wonder why.

"And if you want my advice, don't take your boyfriend into account. The Warriors are in need of someone like you."

So is Noah, I can't help thinking. From the beginning, I've been awed by him and his disregard for the shitty things in life. He owns it and his attitude. But that doesn't mean he's not hurting on the inside.

All I want to do is make Noah happy, even though he doesn't want me to do that. And it'll never happen with his dad breathing down our necks. Little does he know, I'm leaving Noah anyway. That was our deal. It doesn't matter if I want more. I won't become another Aron to him. I won't go back on my word.

Maybe it's time this thing ended earlier than we planned.

Damn it.

I storm out of Noah's dad's offices and hit the call button on my phone.

"Damon King."

"Emergency meeting. Now."

"Can you come to OTS?"

"Nope. But you can meet me at a bar."

"It's the middle of the day. Does this have anything to do with the offer from the Cougars?"

My long strides stop in the middle of the street. "You've already seen it."

"It's a great offer. We're going to urge you to take it."

"No fucking way am I touching that contract."

"Matt, what aren't you telling me? How did you know about the contract?"

"Come meet me."

"Do *not* walk into a bar in the middle of the day. The tabloids will go crazy. Where are you?"

I glance around at my surroundings, still unfamiliar with this city. "Midtown."

"There's an Italian restaurant two blocks away from OTS. Walk there, get a table, and order a drink. And some lunch. I'm on my way."

Damon finds me with two scotches under my belt and an untouched chicken salad in front of me.

"Okay, what's going on?"

"I'm taking the Warriors' deal."

He pauses. "New York is more money. Like a shit ton more money."

"It's also more competition for field time. The Warriors need me. The Cougars don't."

"That's a valid argument, but the money more than makes up for it, so that's not why you're saying no to this offer. Did something happen with Noah? Are you fighting or—"

"You know ... about us?"

"Yeah. I know. Confronted Noah about it and told him to

stop. He said he would, but I've also known the guy for eight years, so I knew he was lying. What happened? He break your heart and now you want to move? New York's a big city. You won't have to see him."

"No one's breaking anyone's heart." Not yet at least.

"Then I'm going to need a bigger explanation as to why you'd turn down a contract that's more than you're worth. No offense."

I take a large gulp of my scotch and finish it off. "You guys didn't wonder why a last-minute bid came in for the PR nightmare? If something's too good to be true, it is." I get the waitress's attention and point to my empty glass.

Damon shoves my salad closer to me. "Eat something so you don't get hammered on an empty stomach. Look, you need to tell me what's going on. As you're my client, I promise not to say anything to Noah or Maddox or anyone you don't want me to."

I sigh into my empty glass. "Rick Douglas is good friends with Noah's dad. Although, considering he was blackmailed into giving me a contract, I think *friend* is a pretty loose term."

Damon blinks at me as the words tick over in his head.

"The terms of the agreement are I get the NFL back, and his son stops dating Matt Jackson and steps out of the spotlight."

Damon loosens his tie, and as the waitress approaches with my drink, he takes it out of her hand and chugs it. "Gonna need another one." He winces at the burn. "No, make it two."

"Either contract, I'm screwed," I say once the waitress is out of earshot once again.

"Noah said you guys were temporary anyway, so what would it matter?"

"I don't care how temporary Noah and I are. I'm not doing that to him. Even without the bribe in play—if this were a real contract—I'll be scrambling for field time. That's even if I make it past training camp. The payoff isn't the only deal breaker here."

"You could go to the league about the bribe."

"Fuck that. I'm already in the media enough. I don't want to add blackmailing scandal to the list."

He purses his lips. "You should tell Noah about his father."

I shake my head. "Not gonna hurt him like that. There's no point. I'm not taking the deal."

Damon's fingers drum on the tablecloth as he eyes me. "You know, don't you?"

"Know what?" I ask in exasperation.

"Did you ever wonder why Noah went to Newport instead of an Ivy League? He could've bought his way into anywhere—not to mention his entire family are Harvard alums—so why go to Newport? We couldn't work it out. I remembered seeing Noah freshman year. I mean, he's Noah. You can't not walk past him and ignore the fact he's insanely hot and moves like he owns everything. He was always with this other guy. We suspected they were together, but they were never blatantly obvious."

"Where're you going with this?" I know exactly where he's going with this, but Noah claims his friends don't know.

"Sophomore year, Noah comes back to school alone. Joins all the LGBTQ unions and starts sleeping around. When we became actual friends, I asked him what happened to the guy he always hung around with freshman year, and he shut down on me. He'd only tell us that he moved schools. We all figured that guy's the reason Noah is ... well, Noah-ish. We came up with theories. We've all met Noah's dad, and we've all heard Noah complain about him. Doesn't take a genius to work out a payoff was involved."

"I have no idea what you're talking about." I try to keep my voice even.

Damon smiles. "You're a horrible liar, and I take back what I said to Noah a few weeks back. The fact you want to protect him means you have my blessing. Not as your agent, but as his friend. If you want to be with him for real, you should tell him. As your agent, I have to tell you to take the New York deal, because that's what my bosses will want you to do, but as *your* friend, I'm telling you I'll do whatever you want me to."

"Telling Noah will only make him feel guilty when he has to break up with me like he did with Aron. He didn't mean to hurt Aron, but y'all made him feel terrible about it. I won't put that on him. It's my own fault. I broke our deal."

"Maybe he's broken your deal."

I scoff. "Not likely. Like you say, he's *Noah*."

"He never told any of us the real story of what happened with his boyfriend in college. Not even Aron."

"He wouldn't have told me either had I not overheard it between him and his dad."

Damon stands to leave. "I'll get started on your Chicago paperwork. Unless you can think of a reason to stay in New York and retire from football after all?"

I don't know what to say to that. If it comes to picking between football and Noah, I don't know if I'm ready to make that decision. But if he asked me to be with him—give up the NFL and stay for him—I don't think I'd be able to say no.

I'm so gone for this guy.

"Think about it and tell Noah how you feel. Let me know what you decide."

Sure, because putting your heart on the line is that fucking easy.

CHAPTER TWENTY

NOAH

After meeting with one of the hosts of *Rainbow Beds* and getting a better idea of what I'd need to do to make the forum into a charity and turn it successful, I walk in the door to my townhouse and am almost bowled over by Jet coming the other way.

"Whoa, where's the fire?" I ask.

"Matt told me to go away for a few hours. You're either in trouble or about to get laid, and I don't want to be here for either, so I'm out."

"Uh, okay. Umm ... see ya." I remain at the entrance, wondering what I could've done to piss Matt off but come up blank. That doesn't necessarily mean anything though. Oblivious should be my middle name. Plus, I tend to do douchey things without realizing.

Inside is quiet when I grow the balls to make myself walk in farther. "Matt?"

"Bedroom," he calls out.

I amble up the stairs, still confused, and I find Matt pacing the carpet of our—my bedroom. "Okay, what's going on?" I ask.

Matt stalls and stares at me. His mouth opens but nothing comes out.

"You're doing the stroking out thing you did when we first met."

"Where were you?" he asks.

"Meeting with some people about the project. Why?"

He shakes his head. "Nothin'. Don't matter."

Don't matter. Why's his accent coming out? "What's wrong?" I ask.

Matt fakes a smile and steps toward me. "Just want you." He wastes no time as he ditches his shirt and then hooks his fingers into my belt loops and brings me against him. "Missed you."

Missed me? He saw me this morning.

I'm still confused when our lips come together and his domineering tongue forces its way into my mouth. The Matt I know is passionate, but the aggression behind the kiss is desperate. Too desperate. A hand grips my hip tight, and the other snakes around my back to pull me closer.

My cock gets excited and wants to dive in, but my brain tells me there's something wrong.

"Matt." I try to back up, but he comes with me and kisses me again. I break away. "*Matt.*"

"I want this. *Us.*"

I stumble back. "Oh." Is he saying what I think he's saying, or am I reading into it because they're the words I crave to hear?

"Wait, before you freak out, I mean I want this afternoon to be just us."

My heart deflates. "I'm confused."

"I ... I saw Damon today."

Realization cuts through my gut, and I want to vomit. "You're moving to Chicago."

His nod is subtle, but the slight movement is still enough to rip a hole in my fucking chest.

I force a small smile. "I think I'm supposed to say congratulations or whatever."

"Unless ..." He looks away. "Unless there's a reason for me to stay here." His voice goes up at the end, almost as if it's a question, but at the same time it sounds like a statement.

Now's the time to lay it out there. I want him to pick me. Love me. Make me his life instead of football. Then I recoil at the notion. I have no right asking anyone to choose me, even if I desperately want them to.

I didn't mean to fall for Matt, and I never in a million years expected to, but I care for him more than I care about myself and that's never happened to me before. Except maybe with Nathaniel and look at how well that turned out.

"There isn't a single reason to give up football." I hate that I can't tell the guy how much I want him to stay, but if I forced him to do that, he'd eventually resent me. He can't give up his career for someone he has no future with. And I'm not under any illusion that we'd make it in the long run.

Dad's been vocal about not wanting us together. It's only a matter of time before he makes a move and Matt does what Nathaniel did to me.

This is the right call.

"So, this is it then," Matt says.

"No. Nowhere near it." I pull him forward by his belt and bring him against me again. "We have until you go. And then public appearances. We won't be together, but I want to keep seeing you."

"Like a fuck buddy situation?"

God, I want to hold onto anything he's willing to give me, but I don't think my heart could take it. "Like a *we're always going to be friends* type situation."

"Friends." He practically gags on the word, and I don't blame him.

"We knew this had an expiration date. Now we know when it is."

"Training camp's in a few weeks. I need to be in Chicago before that to find a place to live, and—"

"Maybe I can help you find a place." I hold my breath, preparing for him to cut ties right here and now.

"You'd ... you'd come to Chicago?"

The second you asked me to.

That's not what I say, though. "This started out as doing each other a favor, but I can honestly say you know me better than anyone else in my life. I'll help you get settled in Chicago any way I can, and I'll always be here for you."

"Right. Settled." Matt tries to step back, but I don't let him.

"Babe," I murmur. "I still have the right to call you that a while longer, and I don't want this to end on a bad note."

He stiffens as my arms snake around him and I bury my head in his neck.

There's so many unspoken words between us, but we're both too chickenshit to bring them up.

"I want you to know you're important to me."

Matt's hands wander down my back. "Be with me," he whispers.

I wonder if he realizes how that sounds, but before I can ask him to, he clarifies.

"I don't want to wait anymore. I wanted you to fuck me the day I met you, and—"

"Liar," I say with a chuckle.

"Okay, fine. Like a week after I met you and you let me past all your bullshit. But that doesn't change the fact I want you inside me."

I groan. "Matt—"

"If you can't give me anything else, give me this."

I want to give him everything, but he's right. I can't give him more than physical connection.

It's not lost on me that I had nearly this exact conversation with Aron not too long ago. Only, with Matt respecting my wishes and honoring our deal, I want nothing more than to scream at him to fight for more.

My resolve is on a thin ledge, begging to jump. I want to fall, and I want a life with Matt, but our situation is impossible.

My lips trail soft kisses from the bottom of his ear and down his neck, as my hands move over his back and down to his ass.

"Noah." His voice is like a tortured moan, and it throws me off my game.

This needs to be about sex, but the whole goodbye thing is getting in the way. There's a difference between knowing it's going to end and staring at the finish line.

Each day, that line will get closer and closer, and I know I won't be ready for it.

Words like "stay" threaten to fall outta my mouth, but I won't do that to him. I *can't* do it to him. I can't ask him to give up his dream for me.

I never thought I'd let anyone crush me the way Nathaniel did ever again. Yet, here I am with another broken heart. I don't know how it got this far. One minute we're fucking, and the next I'm caring. I don't do this. This isn't me. I can't have relationships, so I don't get attached.

What's so good about Matt—not Matthew—Jackson anyway?

His tongue teases my lips, and then I remember. Oh, right. His mouth, for one answer.

But he's so much more than that. I should've known to run away as soon as I started to care.

So, about twenty-four hours after meeting him?

Shit. If I really think about it, everything I did for him on that cruise, it wasn't because I felt empathy toward him. It wasn't because I felt sorry for him. It's because the moment we met, I knew he was mine to protect.

This has been screwed since the very beginning. And now I'm here, saying goodbye to another man who has no issues breaking me.

"Noah," Matt whispers again.

"I'm here, baby."

CHAPTER TWENTY-ONE

MATT

"Let me take care of you," Noah whispers against my skin. *Ask me to stay. Want me to stay. Don't turn this into goodbye.*

When Noah's mouth is on me, football seems like a waste. I'm ready to throw it all away for the man standing in front of me, but he refuses to even contemplate it.

One reason. That's all I need. One reason to stay. He can't even give me that.

So, instead of calling him on his shit because I promised I never would, I let him devour me, touch me, love on me instead of love all of me.

His fingers slowly unbutton my pants, and I can't catch my breath.

"Hurry," I say.

"Gotta go slow. Make it good."

"Don't. Don't be nice." I can't handle it right now.

Noah falters in his movements and pulls back. He eyes me warily before a mask of indifference takes over. "If that's how you want to play it." Something growly comes out when he talks, and it makes my dick jump.

Without any finesse, Noah shoves my pants and boxer briefs down to my ankles, and I step out of them.

"On the bed. Hands and knees." But now his tone is distant and reminds me of hookups I've had in clubs. The lack of interest in their eyes ... it was always about getting off. Noah's never used that voice with me, and it guts me that he's turned it on now, but at the same time, I need it.

I need him to be the cold, oblivious rich guy who only cares about himself, because no matter how much I don't want it to be, this is our goodbye. We may have weeks before I leave, but we've both mentally checked out to protect ourselves.

I do as he says and shiver with nerves when I hear the soft thump of his clothes hitting the floor. The bed dips behind me, and strong hands grip my wrists and pin them above my head. It makes my ass stick up in the air even farther as my forehead lands on the mattress.

There's no physical way possible for me to be harder than I am right now. The anticipation, the heartache, and the need swirl around me, ending with me on the verge of begging.

I'm so ready, but Noah doesn't give me what I want.

His mouth is tender as he kisses my shoulder, down my spine, across my back to my hip, and then my ass cheek.

I'm stuck in a torturous world where I want more but can't bring myself to ask.

When his tongue finds the top of my crack, I freeze.

"Umm, what are you doing?" My heart thuds in my chest.

"Shh. No talking. I'm taking care of you." His tongue lands on me, and my cock leaks. Electricity shoots up my spine and my gut tightens.

"Fuck." I've never been rimmed before. Never thought it was anything I was missing, but holy hell, as his mouth teases and prods me, my body turns into shaking, limbless jelly.

When a finger replaces his tongue, I let out a whine.

"Only about to get better, baby," Noah whispers. "I promise." His finger slips past my ring of muscle, and there's nothing I want more than to reach for my cock right now, but the second my hand moves from above my head, he swats it away. "Don't even think about touching yourself. I'm going to make you mine, you understand?"

I nod.

"I'm going to mark you and love you so hard that whenever any other man does this to you, you'll only think of me."

I should be pissed that he wants to ruin me, but I know he's already done that. I opened myself up to let Noah in, fully prepared to let him go when we were done, but he wormed himself in so far, there's no way he can get back out. He's in my heart, under my skin, and will always own a piece of me.

Instead of saying these things aloud, I let him do what he promises.

His mouth and fingers work in sync, teasing my hole, my balls, my cock—every inch of me.

When I finally hear the crinkling of a condom wrapper, I let out a breath of relief. I don't know how much longer I can endure his torture without giving into the molten lava inside me ready to explode.

I'm gripping the pillow so hard my knuckles are white. "I'm ready."

"Not yet." Noah's lubed fingers stretch and tease, while he fumbles with the condom.

I grumble but then when he hits my prostate, I let out a round of expletives.

Noah chuckles. "Okay, now I think you're ready." With one last kiss in between my shoulder blades, Noah straightens up, and his cock pushes against my hole.

Then nothing happens. The silence thickens the air, and his pause pisses me off.

"Fucking hell, Noah, if you don't fuck me this fucking second—"

In a swift move, he thrusts inside.

"Fuck, oh fuck—*fuck*."

Noah stiffens on top of me. "Shit, did I hurt you?" He tries to pull out, but I stop him.

"Don't even think about it," I grit out. "Feels good. Amazing. Need more."

His hips make the smallest of thrusts, testing it out.

"Doesn't hurt," I assure him.

This push and pull we have going on tears me in two. This is supposed to be about sex, and Noah being tender and caring ruins that.

Yet, when he pulls out and flips me over onto my back, I get lost in those aqua eyes that are stupid. I can't tear my gaze away. And when he leans in and kisses me softly—lovingly—I lose the ability to protest. When he moves in and out of me with the same type of worship, I can no longer hold it together.

He cups my face, and it's too much. This isn't fucking. This ... I don't know what this is. I want it—crave it—but it feels like our end.

I hope he's wrong, because if I ever meet anyone who could compare to the man inside me, I don't want to be thinking about Noah while I'm with him. Hell, I can't even contemplate anyone else right now when it's like my whole world is in this room.

I adjust to his languid movements, but if he doesn't start pounding me soon, there's a real possibility I'm going to start crying, and no way am I doing that.

"Noah," I croak.

"Yeah, baby? What do you need?"

"I need you to stop being a pussy and fuck me."

Noah bursts out laughing, and I join him, although it sounds forced—even to my own ears which are pounding with my erratic heartbeat.

He either senses I need this torture to end or I'm a better liar than I think I am, because he pushes himself up onto his knees and lifts my ass to meet his harder yet still slow thrusts.

Without him on top of me, my dick stands at attention, begging to be touched, but with Noah hitting my prostate over and over again, I know if I reach for it, it'll be all over.

I block out Noah's mumbled words of *tight* and *hot* and *amazing*, and every other term of need and affection because I know I won't hear the one thing I want. I want words of *forever* and *stay* and a need that doesn't include anything primal.

He promised to bruise me and mark me, but I didn't realize he meant the type of bruises that don't heal. The pain in my ass will fade, the hickeys on my skin will disappear, but he'll still leave his mark inside me.

I thought it impossible to have a heart full of warmth yet have that same heart shatter at the same time.

"I'm close," Noah warns, and I snap out of my self-pity.

"Touch me," I whisper. "Take me with you."

Take me always. I swallow that shit down and come on a hoarse cry as soon as his fingers wrap around my cock.

When I think I'm done, Noah pulls out, rips off the condom, and comes all over my stomach. I convulse again until Noah collapses on top of me.

Sweaty and panting, we stay like this until the cum on our skin is cold and the air between us is suffocating.

"Matt ... I—"

"We need to shower." We need to not be tangled together. I try to push him off me, but he holds firm.

"I need you to tell me we're cool."

I nod.

"Tell me this hasn't changed anything. We're still friends."

I swallow hard. "The best of."

He didn't say I had to tell him the truth.

When JJ—who's suddenly fine with me calling him that and insists I do it—walks through the front door, he calls out, "Is it safe to come back yet?" He takes tentative steps, and when he turns the corner from the entrance that leads to the living room, he has one hand over his eyes and the other outstretched in front of him to prevent him from running into anything.

"Fuck me harder, Matt," Noah says and then starts making sex noises.

JJ lets out a girl-like squeal and turns to run, but our laughs stop him. Slowly, he spins to face us with a tiny gap in between his fingers covering his eyes. When he takes in our fully clothed forms and the laptop open on my lap, he slumps. "Not cool."

"But funny," Noah says.

"What are you doing?" he asks me.

"We're looking for a place in Chicago for you and Matt to

live." Noah squeezes my leg, and the affection hurts. Ever since this afternoon, he's been more attentive and touchy-feely. It's as if he needs reassurance, but what I need is to start distancing myself. Walking away is already too hard, and he's making it worse.

Is he trying to kill me?

"Oh," JJ says. "*Oh.*" The disappointment is clear as day on his face.

"What's wrong?" I ask.

He runs a hand through his shaggy hair. "I, umm ... well, I totally just got a gig here, but no way will I be able to afford rent in New York on the salary."

"What's the job?" Noah asks.

"Playing in a band. They don't get many gigs but they're pretty good. Even played at Club Soho."

"Club Soho?" Noah jumps off the couch. "Are you serious? They've discovered a shit ton of famous bands there."

"I know. It's the reason this band was looking for a lead singer. Their last one apparently ditched them for a record deal."

"That's awesome." Noah rounds the couch and hugs my brother, and it pisses me off. When I told him about Chicago, I got a grumbly "Congratulations, or whatever." Hell, not even that.

I shake all jealousy away and focus on JJ, because I already have a Noah headache from overanalyzing everything that went down today. "If this is what you want to do with your life, you need to give it a proper go. I know you said you don't want a handout, but let me help—"

"I'm not taking your money," JJ says.

"Even if you get a job to supplement your income from gigging, you won't make rent. Let me—"

"You can stay here," Noah says. "Rent free. As long as you need to."

My gaze flies to his. "You'd ... do that?"

JJ's entire face lights up at the possibility. "I'll cook for you or clean or—"

"I'm not gonna say no to your cooking," Noah says. "But it's not a big deal. New York is stupid expensive, and I've got the room."

JJ turns to me. "Are you okay with me staying?"

If I'm honest, no, but the reasons I want him to move with me are more selfish than anything else. I'm sick of living alone and having no one. That doesn't mean I can ask JJ to give up his dreams so I don't come home to an empty apartment—especially when I'm going to be gone a lot when the season starts. "It's your life."

"What if I don't accept handouts, but if you ever want me in Chicago, I'll let you pay for my first-class plane ticket?" JJ grins.

"It's a two-hour flight," Noah says with a laugh. "You can handle being in coach."

"Says the guy with his very own Gulfstream," I mutter.

Noah playfully slaps the back of my head.

"When do you have to report for training camp?" my brother asks.

"Have to be at Milwaukee University in three weeks."

"Milwaukee?" Noah asks. "Training camp isn't in Chicago?"

"Only a handful of teams hold training camp at their own stadium," JJ says.

"It saves the turf and staying together in the one hotel

supposedly creates bonds between teammates, and all that crap," I add.

"I guess when you're in Milwaukee, you'll have nothing to do but bond. Why *Milwaukee*?"

"At least it's not Hoboken." I try to hide my smile.

"If it was Hoboken, you'd be close to home," Noah says.

That wipes the smile off my face. *Home.* If he wants me to see this place as my home, then why the fuck isn't he asking me to stay?

He stares at me like he knows he fucked up, and the silence drags on for a beat too long.

"So ..." JJ says. "Uh ... this is awkward."

Guess we aren't doing a good job of hiding the fact Noah and I are in some weird limbo state. We're over, but we're not.

"I have to go make some calls about *Rainbow Beds.*" Noah bounds up the stairs faster than John Ross's forty-yard dash.

"What was that about?" JJ asks.

"We, uh, broke up."

"What? When?"

"Today." I massage my temple as I think about what the hell it all means, because I don't actually know myself. "It's weird. Basically, we're together until I leave for training camp. So ... we gave each other notice of intent to break up? Is that a thing?"

"It's a weird thing." He throws himself on the couch next to me. "Are you sure you're okay with me staying then? Won't me living with your ex-boyfriend be weird?"

"Nah. Noah and I are still friends. He's also agreed to keep up appearances if he's needed. 'I have a boyfriend' is apparently more believable to homophobes as to why I won't hit on them in a locker room than 'You're not my type.'"

JJ snorts. "So, three more weeks, huh?"

"I was thinking I might head out to Chicago sooner than that. Get set up and move all my stuff."

"You can afford to pay someone to do that for you." His tone and his gaze hold nothing but suspicion.

"I don't know how much longer I can stay when I know it's over. The more I'm here ... the more I don't want to leave."

"So don't leave." JJ says this as if it's that easy.

"He doesn't want a relationship—he's not a forever guy. I need to accept that. We were both upfront from the beginning."

"But ..." JJ chews on his lip.

"But what?"

"Nothing. I just thought you'd both fight for each other more. You're like disgustingly in love, so it sucks that something insignificant like distance is going to break you up."

"Jet ..."

"Oooh, shit, he's bringing out the big guns. Calling me Jet? Are you dying? Is that what's going on here?"

I can't look at him as I say, "There's something you don't know about Noah and me. We were never really together. It was a favor. My agent said I needed to look like I was in a stable relationship and had to clean up my 'party' image. The media painted me to be some gay playboy with an alcohol problem and all that other crap. Noah's been pretending to be my boyfriend this whole time. He's a PR stunt."

"Bullshit."

"It's true. He's nothing more than my ticket back into the NFL."

"I'm not calling bullshit on how you met. I'm calling bullshit that he was never your real boyfriend. You're practically living together, and you're always all over each other, and don't think I haven't heard you fucking, because I didn't go out and buy noise-canceling headphones for nothing. I'm *jealous* of what you guys have, and if neither of you can see it, you're both fuckin' blind." He stands in a sudden rush, startling me. "Oh my God, song idea."

I don't have time to blink at him let alone stop him before he's running upstairs to his bedroom. The door slams and then not even five seconds later, his guitar starts strumming a tune.

My gaze goes back to the laptop in front of me, and my heart rips through my gut at the sight of Chicago apartment listings. What the hell am I doing?

CHAPTER TWENTY-TWO

NOAH

H*e's nothing more than my ticket back into the NFL.*
I pretend I didn't overhear their conversation and tell myself to ignore what Matt said. He's putting up a front for his brother.

Still doesn't take away the sucker punch to the gut every time I hear those same words in my head over and over, because let's face it, I've never been good at following anyone else's instructions so I sure as fuck won't listen to myself.

I hear the words when I sit on the couch next to him and he claims to be thirsty and disappears into the kitchen. I hear them when I join him in the shower after his workout and he claims to be finished and leaves me in there by myself. I hear them when he says he's too tired and stressed about the move for sex.

In the three days since I overheard that conversation, Matt's done nothing but pull away from me.

We still share a bed at night, but he's checked out. He's not really here.

He finds any excuse to leave a room when I walk into it.

He's hungry and he needs to take a leak are his favorites. To need to pee so much, he must be drinking six gallons of water.

He's also pulling longer training sessions in the basement. Jet notices it too and shakes his head every time it happens.

Deep down, I get it. I understand. But damn, if it doesn't hurt.

He's doing the exact thing I asked him to do when we started this. To keep it simple.

Yet, when I wake up to a cold bed, I miss his warmth and his stupid thick arms that like to cling to me when we sleep.

I roll over and look at the time on my screen. The bright light blinds me in the dark hour of four a.m.

For a crushing moment, I think he's gone—that he's snuck out in the middle of the night and isn't coming back, but once my eyes adjust, I know that's not true. His clothes are still strewn around my room, and his phone is plugged into the charger on his bedside table.

I amble out of bed and find a pair of sweats. There's only one place he could be, and it's too damn early to be working out.

As suspected, I find him in the basement. He sits on the bench in the middle of the room, all sweaty and panting while he chugs a bottle of water. He hasn't noticed me yet, and I lean against the doorway with my arms folded. When he's done with his drink, he hangs his head in his hands.

"Isn't it too middle of the night for a work out?" I ask.

Matt startles at my voice and raises his head. "Couldn't sleep."

"I know the feeling."

We stare each other down, neither one of us willing to talk or tell each other what we're thinking. I don't know if I want to know what he's thinking. I sure as fuck don't want to ask him the real reason he's down here at stupid o'clock.

With an outstretched hand, Matt beckons me over to him. "Come here."

His serious tone makes me do it without hesitation, but as I get close, he reaches for me and brings me down on top of him so I'm straddling him on the narrow bench.

My hand tangles in his sweaty hair, and his perspiration covers my bare chest. Some would find that gross, but a hot, sweaty Matt is what I've come to live for since meeting him.

Despite our wobbly balance, Matt takes my mouth with punishing force. He teases me with his tongue and nips at my bottom lip.

All this guy has to do is kiss me and I'm as hard as granite. I try to grind against him, but on this ridiculously small space, it's impossible without toppling over.

"Fuck this," Matt says and pushes me to the floor.

I land on my back with a thud, and then he's right there, blanketing my body with his.

"I need you." His lips trail my cheek, my jaw, down my neck.

"Have me," I rasp.

He backs off for a split second to stare up at me. "There's no time to fuck. I need fast, and I need it right now."

Maybe I'm telepathic, because I swear I hear the "before I change my mind" on the end of that sentence.

There's no finesse in the way we lose our clothes or in the way he flips 'round so we're on our sides and he can wrap his lips around my cock, while his is right there for me to take.

Unlike him, I'm not in the mood for fast and dirty, even though my hips have other ideas. They buck and squirm as Matt takes me to the back of his mouth, and his hand squeezes my ass cheek to keep me from being able to retreat. Not that I could right now anyway.

I use my hand to jack him, while my tongue teases his balls. There's a reason I usually don't like this position. I like to focus on giving everything to my partner, but I can't when he's determined to get me off as fast as possible. I can't concentrate with the familiar tightening of my balls and warmth rushing through me, continuously building and building to the point I can't even think, let alone remember how to suck a dick.

Matt moans around my cock, and it sounds like he's trying to say *Noah*. It brings me back from the ledge and snaps me out of my selfish focus. Before I get to work, I cover my finger in saliva and reach around to Matt's ass.

He practically whimpers when I take him into my mouth and breach his hole at the same time.

The whole thing becomes sloppy on both sides. We're unable to focus but can't stop. We mindlessly fuck each other's mouths and lose ourselves until I don't even know which one of us comes first.

The orgasm hits hard but lasts so long I lose the ability to swallow. The rest of Matt's release lands on my neck and chest, but Matt takes all of me until I forcibly have to remove my cock from his mouth.

Catching my breath takes longer than usual, and by the time I snap back to reality, I'm cold and covered in Matt's cum, sweat, and saliva. Definitely something worth waking up at four a.m. for. But something's wrong. Matt's no longer touching me, and when I sit up, he has his arm over his eyes, refusing to look at me.

"Matt ..." I reach for his towel beside me and wipe myself down before I climb on top of him.

He doesn't remove his arm from his eyes. "I can't."

"Can't what?"

"I ... I can't do this anymore," he whispers. He grabs me around my waist and moves me off him and then sits up so we're side by side. "I'm sorry. You told me not to fall for you, and I promised I wouldn't, but if we keep going like this, there's no way I'm going to be able to walk away from you."

My throat constricts.

"I don't want to put you in the same position you were in with Aron, so I'm bowing out now. I'm already too far gone, and I'm sorry I broke my promise. Football is my life, but when I'm with you, it's insignificant. It's a silly game I get a lot of money to play. If you'd let me, I'd give it all up, but I know it's not what you want." He pauses and waits for a reaction I can't bring myself to give. "Please let me off the hook. Let me go now before it gets worse."

Let him go before you can hurt him more.

"I'm sorry" is all I manage to say.

"You don't need to be sorry. You did nothing wrong here. I did."

We both did. This is so much more than I've ever had—than I've ever wanted.

"I'm gonna head back to PA today, clean up some loose ends, and then go to Chicago early before I need to report to Milwaukee. I found a place yesterday, and it's available now."

"Yesterday," I murmur. "You decided yesterday you were leaving." I grit my teeth, my jaw hardening. "So that's what this was? A goodbye?"

"I didn't ... I shouldn't have ... I'm sorry. We shouldn't have done that."

When he gets off the floor and stands, he holds out his hand to help me up. I move in a stupor and can't seem to be able to do anything for myself. Matt throws me my sweats, while he slips on his gym shorts, but I remain frozen, staring at a room I barely use as it is. Now it'll always remind me of the time the guy I loved begged me not to hurt him. Again, I find myself on the edge of asking him to stay—to choose me. All I have to do is say the words, and he'll do it.

But I can't do it to him. He'll end up resenting me or leaving me. Probably both.

I *won't* do that to him.

The thought of moving to Chicago's been niggling at me, but the last time I gave up everything for a guy, he left me anyway. It'd only be a matter of time before Matt did the same thing.

I won't do that to *me* again.

Matt is football. Asking him to give it up would be like asking him to breathe without oxygen. I thought he didn't know what he truly wanted because he was forced into football, but part of me now knows that was the beginning of me falling for him. It was wishful thinking that he'd give it up willingly and choose me instead. Now that it's a possibility, I don't have it in me to ask him to do it, just like I don't expect him to ask me to give up my life here.

And I hate that I can't let myself do it—that I'm letting a past relationship from when I was a fucking kid get to me so much that I can't see myself having a future with anyone, let alone the only guy I've ever truly wanted in years.

I want to go back to before I ever met Matt, because back

then I had nothing, and I loved it. I did whatever I wanted when I wanted, and I didn't give a shit about anything. I want to go back to before I knew what love is because I was blissfully unaware of how unhappy I was.

Now, losing the guy who made me feel again, that familiar numbness and entitled asshole mask I've always worn before him slips back into place.

This is the end, so I do what Noah does best. I let Matt go and pretend I'm not dying on the inside.

CHAPTER TWENTY-THREE

MATT

TALON: *FIRST NIGHT IN TOWN. DRINKS?*

I groan. That's the last thing I want. My new apartment may have a decent view of Chicago outside the floor-to-ceiling glass windows, but it's full of boxes. I've literally just arrived, so I have to psych myself up to face a brand-new team, the upcoming press conferences, and then training camp. Not to mention I'm completely heartbroken. Not to be melodramatic or anything, but the last few days have been hell. Jet came back to PA with me to finish packing all my shit in the now empty loft that's in escrow. It gutted me that when I left to drive across the country, my brother went back to New York—where my heart still is.

MATT: *NOT TONIGHT.*

The knock at the door comes immediately and confuses me. I stare down at my phone and then at the door. It better not be—

"I know you're in there," Talon calls out. "And we're not leaving until you let us in."

Us?

I swing the door open, and Talon pushes his way in with a huge smile on his face. Shane Miller, offensive tackle for the Warriors, follows him. The giant takes up the entire foyer. People think I'm intimidating, but Miller is mythical creature-like huge. Six foot five, at least. Muscles the size of Tennessee.

He claps me on the shoulder, and even that hurts. "Welcome to the fold, Jackson."

"How did you guys know where I live?"

"Called your agent," Talon says.

"And he gave it to you? That doesn't sound like something Damon would do."

"Nope. Refused to. Client confidentiality plus needing to prove I'm me and all that. Then his boyfriend grabbed the phone and gave it to me. Had me answer some bullshit question to prove I was me. Any football fan would know my stats, but hey, not gonna complain."

Fucking Maddox.

"Well, you two are welcome to help me unpack, but I'm not going out."

Miller laughs. "Ooh, new kid doesn't know the game yet, does he?"

"Game?" I ask.

"It's not so much of a game but more of a lifestyle," Miller says. "Always do what Talon says."

"That doesn't sound like a fun game. Or lifestyle," I say.

"I'm thinking of turning it into a franchise opportunity," Talon says. "Come on. One drink with your new teammates. I read that article. The one that said your last team thought you weren't a team player. So, time to right wrongs or whatever."

"W-who ... who else will be there?" I hate my voice cracks.

Talon's brow furrows. "A few guys from the team. It's not like the whole ninety-man roster will be there."

A knowing smile crosses Miller's face. "Ah. I think someone's worried how the team's going to react to bringing the gay guy along. Am I right?" There's no malice in his words, only fact, and he's hit the nail on the head.

"Want to know what happened when I was outed with my old team? One of the captains turned up on my doorstep, and I thought he was there to support me for some reason I can't even comprehend now. Instead, he verbally abused me and tried to take a swing."

"What the fuck?" Talon asks.

I nod because that was pretty much my reaction when it happened.

"What did he say?" Miller asks.

"The same old homophobic shit. That I was no doubt perving on the entire team, blah, blah, blah. It's his job to protect the others from guys like me, blah blah blah."

"Did you report it?" Miller asks. "Because that's not okay."

"Report what? My contract was done, and he never touched me. I saw it in his face—the moment he realized what he was doing. The end of his career flashed before his eyes, so he backed off before any punches were thrown, but I knew he wanted to. And I'm not stupid enough to think I won't get more of that."

Miller and Talon share an undecipherable glance. "You know the team better than either of us," Talon says to him. "Who do we have to watch out for?"

Miller shrugs. "It's not like we run into a parade of gay guys whenever we're out, and I haven't seen any of the team since Jackson's news leaked. I doubt any of them will make noise. At least, not at training. No one wants to get cut for running their mouth."

"So, I just have to wait until the season starts. Great," I say.

"Maybe going out tonight is an even better idea than I originally thought," Talon says. "We can scope out if there's going to be any issues before preseason starts and the media breathes down our necks."

He has a point. This could be used as a warm-up for what I'm going to face in a few weeks, and it'll be without anyone watching over us—the media or team management. "Okay. I'm in."

"Okay, I'm out," I say as we arrive at Intelligence near Grant Park. Talon and Miller ignore me.

The name of this place matches the uppity vibe coming from the bar. This isn't the type of nightclub I'm used to, but that's a good thing. This place has a dress code, for one. Always have to be wearing a shirt. Never seen that rule before.

There's no flashing lights or deafening EDM either. The mood lighting is dim, and the one bar has a bright blue LED light illuminating it from underneath. It's upscale and less tacky than my old hangouts.

It doesn't take long to find the rest of the team. Football players are rowdy at the best of times. Give them alcohol and all you have to do is follow the manly grunts and shouting.

The closer we get to the VIP area that's filled with muscular bodies surrounded by scantily-clad women trying to get close to the players, the harder my heart pounds.

Security guards send the girls away, but we all know it's a

futile act. They'll be back. And while I step aside to watch them pass, a voice cuts through the club.

"Holy. Shit."

I don't know which one of my new teammates it belongs to, but my stomach drops. All eyes turn to the three of us as we approach the long table.

"It's true?" Scott Bell, a linebacker I've come head to head with on the field many times, asks me. "You signed with us?"

I manage a nod but avoid eye contact at the same time.

The silence drags on a beat too long for being in a loud nightclub, but an echoing whoop fills the space. My eyes travel over the group and land on DeShawn Jenkins, a running back, smiling at me.

"We're going all the way this year, boys. Jackson, drinks on the new guy."

"Guess drinks are on Talon then," I say.

A round of laughs and oohs breaks out.

"Besides, he earns more than all of us. He can afford it," I add.

The ice breaks, and the guys make room for Miller and me while Talon heads to the bar but not before he flips me off on the way.

Drinks flow, and even though the conversation is easy—it's mostly about the upcoming season and then ribbing one of the guys about getting married next week—I sit back and laugh at the right moments and pretend I'm invested. The truth is, the unease doesn't leave me. I'm waiting for the other shoe to drop. Maybe that's what my first season as an openly gay player will be. Constant waiting for the remarks. Passive-aggressiveness. Slurs. I hope to God it's not, because sitting here right now, it's impossible to fully relax. I can't be this uptight on the field or I'll fumble more than Brett Favre.

At one point, Miller leans in. "How you holding up?"

I fake a smile. "So far, so good." Could be worse, but it only takes a few more minutes for my fears to become a reality.

"Okay," Bell says and throws himself in the spare seat opposite us. "I'm just gonna ask it. Because everyone here knows we're all thinking it."

Miller stiffens beside me and goes to get out of his seat—presumably to go for Bell—but I hold him back. I want to know what kinda shit this guy is going to say first, and I won't let Miller get into trouble for me.

"You're dating that Huntington guy, right?" Bell asks.

Fuck, it's even worse than I thought. I was prepared to answer questions about being gay. But Noah? It hurts to even think about him, yet we still have to pretend to be together for the public's sake.

I take a large gulp of my beer to wet my dry mouth. "Yeah."

Now I wait for the real questions. How does it work? Who does who? Who's the girl in the relationship?

Ugh. Ugh. Ugh.

"Is his father a real douche? Like, isn't he supposedly the next president or whatever?"

I'm too young to have a heart attack, but Bell's determined to keep me on my toes.

I glance around the table wondering if this is actually happening and realize all eyes are on me. They're all waiting for me to answer.

I clear my throat. "Noah Huntington the Second is a very compassionate man who I respect and admire. He's going to make a great president."

No one reacts, and I guess they can all see through my bullshit.

"Day-um," Bell says. "They got you trained good."

I crack a smile. "Oh, and he's also the biggest douche I've ever met."

"I knew it," Bell says and slaps the table, while everyone laughs.

I hope that comment doesn't come back to bite me in the ass, but more than that, I wish it didn't remind me of Noah's and my goodbye.

Apparently since I left, Jet hasn't seen much of him. He's either in his room or *out*. Whatever that means. It's not like I get a say in where he goes or what ... or who he does.

God, he better not be sleeping with anyone. I'd like to say it's because publicity-wise, he's still supposed to be with me, but I know that's bullshit. I couldn't care less what the press says about us anymore. I don't want him to fuck anyone else because he's mine.

Gah! He's not mine. Not anymore. He never was.

Miller leans in close to me. "You okay? You spaced out for a second."

I lift my beer. "I'm going to need something stronger."

"In that case, I'll be right back."

The club starts to get busy, the dim lights turn completely off, and then harsh neon lights come on, basking the club in a seedy ambiance that I'm more used to.

Miller waits in a long line at the bar, so I take the opportunity to hit the head while I wait for my next drink. It's probably paranoia, but when I stand, I swear half the guys at the table watch me as I leave.

Tonight is going better than expected, but something still doesn't sit right with me. Sometimes paranoia is warranted.

Especially when I finish at the urinal and turn to find Jenkins standing by the door.

I try to remain stoic as I wash my hands and not give away that my heart pounds in my chest. "You know, following the gay guy into the bathroom isn't going to do wonders for your rep."

Deep breaths. If it comes down to it, let him swing first. Defend yourself but don't fight.

I let out a grunt of frustration. I haven't had to think like this since I started going to gay bars scoping for a hookup. I had to be prepared in case someone recognized me or if I came across those horror stories where closet cases fuck you and then fuck you up because of their own issues. Luckily, I was never in any of those situations, but I was prepared all the same.

Jenkins shifts from one foot to the other. "I just wanted to say ... I mean ... I'm giving you a friendly warning."

Friendly warning. Pfft. Right.

"Aw shit, that came out way less than friendly." His hands rise in surrender. "I'm cool. My cousin is gay, and we went to high school together. I'm not the one with an issue, but I've seen a lot of ugly shit happen, and I don't want that for you. I wouldn't wish it on my worst enemy."

"If you're trying to reassure me any, you're doing a piss-poor job of it."

"Sorry."

"So, there are guys on the team with an issue. Got it. It's expected." It sucks, but I'm not surprised. "And let me guess— they're all the ones who eyed me as I left the table to come in here."

"They're not going to do anything. We all got a phone call

about you when they were trying to recruit you. We were told if you signed, and we did anything, it'd be our asses on the line, not yours. But I thought you'd like a heads-up on who to avoid."

"Fuck, that's probably the worst thing management could do. Now it looks like I get special treatment because of my orientation. That's going to piss the phobes off more."

"I dunno. It rang out pretty clear that there'll be a zero-tolerance policy when it comes to you. I think that's better than sitting back and hoping for the best."

"Maybe I should've retired," I mumble and head for the exit.

Jenkins follows me. "No way, man. You, Talon, Miller, and Carter are taking us to the Super Bowl."

"Carter ..." He was one of the ones at the table.

"One of the guys to look out for, yes. We'll make sure to put him on the other side of the field to you."

Being a wide receiver, Carter's going to be fighting it out with me for ball time. Football players are competitive by nature. We all want to cross that end zone, and some people are bigger fame whores than others. Add Carter's issues with me being gay, and I might have my first problem.

"We're going to be unstoppable," Jenkins says.

"At least one of us has faith."

The team's getting stronger and stronger every year. If stupid shit like my sexual orientation doesn't get in the way, we have the talent to go the whole way, but right now I'm skeptical we'll even make it through training together.

Back in the main bar area of the club, we run into Talon and Miller who've separated from the rest of the group. Miller's juggling two drinks and a handsy woman at the same time. Now that's talented. Talon has his hands occupied by the round ass of a tall redheaded woman.

"Either they move fast or we were in the bathroom a hell of a lot longer than I thought," I say to Jenkins.

"Come on, you know what it's like with these women." He laughs when I raise a brow at him. "Then again, I guess not, but you can't tell me you've never been cornered by a jersey chaser."

True. Right before I generally made an exit from wherever the hell we were.

"Yo, Jackson," Miller yells. "Drinks." He hands them both to me.

"Both?"

"You said you needed something stronger." Now Miller's hands are free to roam over the blonde glued to his side.

Meanwhile, Talon's trying to find the ginger's tonsils. I throw back the drinks. The usual burn is multiplied, and I wonder if they're doubles. At least the numbness should kick in soon.

Talon rips his mouth away long enough to say, "We're out. Miller, you and ... uh ... your gorgeous date coming? After-party at my place."

"I'm out too," I say. After Jenkins cornered me in the bathroom, I don't have any desire to go back to the table and try to decipher which of my teammates have put me on their shit list already.

Jenkins does the man-hug back slap thing. "See you guys at camp."

Where I'm sure it'll be just like high school all over again.

Football is my dream, I remind myself, because it's easy to forget with all the bullshit.

The five of us stumble our way out of the club, right into a group of paparazzi.

Damn it.

Talon practically tosses me his date, and she falls into my arms as the lights from the cameras go off in Talon's face.

Miller, the girls, and I are able to avoid the frenzy and escape up the street.

"I know I should feel bad, but thank fuck, Talon's bigger than I am here," I say.

"Yeah, I do not want to go through what you guys do," Miller says.

The redhead's arms wrap around my waist. "Are you going to come back with us to Marcus Talon's house too?"

I can't help laughing, and by the look of it, Miller's trying to hold in his own laugh.

"Barking up the wrong tree, sweetheart," he says.

"I thought ... well, you know," she says in an obvious tone— like her innuendo should be obvious. "The more, the merrier. That's what Marcus Talon said, right?"

My eyebrows soar high, and shit gets awkward super fast. Not only because she keeps saying Talon's name in full but because Miller can't look at me.

I laugh my surprise off, but I don't know if I sell it. "Your math is out, honey. Two guys, I get. Three guys, I get. Four guys ... you get the picture. If I were to join you, that'd break dude law, and neither Talon or Miller would go for that."

Not to mention even if they did, it'd be a dumb idea to hook up with a teammate.

Plus Noah.

Damn it. Can't I go five minutes without thinking about him?

"Dude law?" the blonde asks while simultaneously being draped over Miller.

"Thou shalt not touch during a devil's three-way," Miller says with a smirk.

"I'm gay and even knew that was a thing," I say.

The blonde appears confused as she pouts her lip. "But there's four of us. Is it still a devil's four-way?"

"On that note," I say, "I'm going to catch a cab home." I turn to Miller and hand over the redhead so he has one girl on each side. "Have fun with that."

I almost get to the end of the block, but Miller calls out.

"Wait, Jackson." He's ditched the girls and is already halfway to me. When he reaches me, he casts his eyes down. "Look, this ... thing. With Talon and me. It's just something we used to do in college. It's not like we touch or anything. We're—"

"Don't worry, I won't think you're queer because you have a four-way. It's none of my business. It doesn't involve anyone but you guys ... well, and those jersey chasers over there. Just don't let the press catch wind of what you're doing. You think the past few months have been fun for me? Wait until an orgy gets leaked."

He runs his hands through his hair. "Shit, you're right. We're not in college anymore. We shouldn't—"

"Ready to go?" Talon yells from where he's caught up to the girls.

Something happens to Miller's face when he sees Talon. All reservation is gone as he says goodbye to me and follows them. I tell myself to pretend I didn't see or hear anything, because it's not my business and I'd rather stay oblivious.

I make my escape while I can and grab a taxi at the end of the block, glad to be outta the stupid wind. Fuck this city.

The night wears on me, the alcohol finally kicks into my system, and I'm no longer in the company of distractions. Friends don't let friends drink and text. That should go for taxi drivers too. They should make it part of their service. Because now that I'm alone, I do the one thing I promised myself I wouldn't. I click on Noah's name and type out three words he doesn't want to read.

I MISS YOU.

CHAPTER TWENTY-FOUR

NOAH

"Get up," a voice says and tries to shake me awake. I'm on my stomach, there's drool on my pillow, and I have absolutely no idea what time it is.

I crack an eye open. "What the fuck, Jet?"

"It's seven p.m. Get. The. Fuck. Up."

"I don't think you're allowed to talk to your landlord like that."

"You're not my landlord if I don't pay you. You're more like an adoptive older brother. Which means I get to annoy you."

I roll onto my back. "Why do I need to get up? I was awake for like thirty-something hours getting stuff done on the *Rainbow Beds* project. I want to sleeeeeeep."

"I have a gig tonight, and you're coming."

"*Why?*"

"Because all you've done since Matt left is work and sulk."

"Noah Huntington doesn't sulk. Over anyone."

Jet steals my comforter off me. "Does Noah Huntington shower? Because he needs to. Go."

"I don't want to." It doesn't escape me that the nineteen-year-old is being more mature than me right now, but I don't care.

The real reason I was up all night was because I was staring at my stupid phone.

I miss you. What kind of shit is that? What am I supposed to do with it? Message him the words I've been desperate to say to him since he left?

Come back.

Don't leave me again.

I love you.

Fucking Matt. He's messing with my head even though there's eight hundred miles between us.

"It's your choice whether you shower or not, but you're going out either way. So, you have the choice of looking like a hobo or you can shower and get all old man sexy and forget about my stupid brother."

"Seriously, quit with the old shit. Twenty-six is not old."

"Whatever, old man."

Jet hovers in my room while I shower, like I need a babysitter, and still refuses to get out when I return in only my towel.

"You gonna just stand there and watch while I dress?"

"I need to make sure you don't get back into bed."

"You're a brat."

"At least I'm good at something."

I cock my head, because now that I'm really looking at him, I realize he's not in here for me at all. He fidgets with the hem of his shirt, and he keeps shuffling from one foot to the other as if he's impatient, but I don't think that has anything to do with it. "You're nervous. About your gig."

He folds his arms across his chest and tries to look defiant. "Fuck off. I've done heaps of gigs before."

"Not in New York. Not at somewhere as important as Club Soho."

Jet scowls and drops his arms. "Fine. Okay. I need you to freaking hold my hand like I'm a kid on my first day of school. The band booked this gig, and I still don't know half their songs. Seeing as Matt's not here, you're now my surrogate big brother. Suck it up."

I can't help laughing, even though I shouldn't. He's scared about going on stage and needs my support, not mocking. "You know, if you'd have told me that from the beginning, I would've moved a lot faster. I thought ..." I run a hand over my shaved head. "I thought you were being all pushy about Matt."

"Well, you do need a kick up the ass about that too, but that's not the real reason I'm in here."

"Okay, here's the deal," I say. "I'll go with you to your gig if you promise not to mention your brother again for an entire month."

He narrows his eyes. "A week."

"Two weeks."

"Deal."

We shake on it and then I dress so we can get our asses out the door for Jet to make it to the club in time for setup.

Club Soho is the type of club that has gone through a million transformations since its early days in the nineties. There's been a wide scale from grunge to hipster and everything in between. It's unfortunately still in its hipster infancy, but I assume that will change again in a few years.

With black walls, wooden tables, and bartenders with beards long enough to braid, the whole place makes me antsy, but I don't know why. Maybe this is the new me. Ever since Matt left, I've found any type of socializing daunting.

Jet drags me to the bar. "Hey, Scott, this is my brother Noah. Give him whatever he wants."

Scott's eyes flitter between us. "Brother?"

"Yeah. My brother. What's your point?" Jet tries to hold in his smirk.

I lift my chin to the bartender. "He's being a dick. I'm *with* his brother. As in ... all domesticated and shit."

I die a little at the lie, which is weird for me. Lying comes as second nature to a politician's son. I learned from the best. But pretending to be happy with someone who moved away and I haven't spoken to since he left ... it stings.

I order a scotch and find a table along the back wall, tucked behind a load-bearing pole. I think I'll sit here all night and hibernate.

After a soundcheck, the club starts to fill, and Jet disappears backstage. My phone burns a hole in my pocket, but I know all I'll do is read that damn message again, so I refrain from taking it out.

Four drinks later, the band comes out to a deafening roar of applause, but Jet doesn't take to the stage. I bet he's sweating bullets waiting to be introduced as the new guy. My leg bounces nervously for him.

The bassist takes to the mic. He's got more tatts than Jet—a full two sleeves. Ear gauges, mohawk ... he's the stereotypical rocker, unlike Jet who looks arty and soulful.

"Hey, Club Soho!"

The crowd cheers once again, and they get a chant going. "Benji, Benji, Benji."

"I know, I know," the guy says. His Australian accent is

thicker than Jet's Southern one. Interesting mix. "It's been a while since we've been back, but anyone following us on Twitter will know we've been *abandoned* by he who shall be furthermore known as Voldemort, and we've been searching for someone to replace him since. So, here he is, the bloke who has saved our asses. Fallout welcomes Jet Jackson!"

Pride swells in my chest as Jet makes his way front and center of the stage and gives the audience an arrogant smile. "Promise to go easy on me," he says into the mic.

Before anyone has a chance to heckle the new guy, the band breaks out into a cover of Train's "Drive By" and the crowd goes nuts.

Jet is ... amazing. I mean, I've heard him singing from his room and fiddling with his guitar when he's writing music, but with the atmospheric crowd and his incredible presence, he comes alive as he bounces across the stage with Jet-like energy.

It sucks Matt's missing this.

Without much thought to my self-imposed talking ban, I take out my phone and FaceTime the guy I wish I could get out of my head.

He answers with a sleepy yawn, his brown hair sticking up at all angles and looks sexy as fuck. An *I hate you* is on the tip of my tongue, but with the loud background, he wouldn't hear it anyway.

I hold up my finger, because I have no idea what he's saying when his mouth moves and then flip the phone the other way so he can see the stage instead.

Jet kills the song, but maybe I'm biased. Then again, if the group of girls standing near my table are anything to go by, I'd say he's won them over too.

Good luck, ladies.

During the second song—one of the band's originals—my phone vibrates in my hand. I don't know when Matt ended the call, but there's a text message.

MATT: *GO OUTSIDE AND CALL ME. PLEASE.*

I want to tell him no, but even eight hundred miles away, he has a hold over me that I can't shake. My eyes go back to the stage. Jet's in his element, and I'm sure he won't even notice if I duck out for a second, but I still use it as an excuse.

NOAH: *JET DIDN'T WANT ME TO LEAVE HIM ON HIS BIG NIGHT.*

It buzzes impossibly fast.

MATT: *HE'S KILLING IT, AND YOU KNOW IT. I NEED TWO MINUTES. IT'S ABOUT A PUBLIC APPEARANCE COMING UP.*

I don't fully believe him, but it does the trick. I'm out of my seat and heading for the exit before the song is finished.

When I find a quiet spot on the street, halfway in the alley beside the bar but still on the sidewalk enough to be mugger-safe, my finger hesitates on the call button.

With a deep breath and a reminder to keep this business and not personal, I hit dial.

"Thought you were going to blow me off." His voice is sexy and sleepy, and of course, my brain gets stuck on the words *blow me.*

"What's this public appearance?"

"Straight to it then, I guess."

"You promised."

Matt sighs. "How's Jet doing? Apart from kicking ass on stage."

"He's picked up a job as a waiter, but he hates it. I like it because he brings me dinner when he's done."

"Nice."

The conversation dies an awkward death, and I'm transported to the first few days on the cruise where we didn't know each other yet and everything was difficult and strained. I half-wish I could go back to then when I was still oblivious to what it's like to truly be with someone.

Our relationship may've been fake, but I've never felt anything more real.

And it's all Matt's fault.

Fucker.

"I cut my parents off," he says quietly.

"You what?"

"I took your advice. I've set up trusts for the kids, have organized to send money directly to Char, and told my parents they can take whatever I give them or get nothing at all."

I let out a humorous laugh. Even when Matt's trying to be mean, he still cares. "How much are you still giving them?"

"Enough to survive. Half of what I was. The rest goes to the kids like I originally wanted."

"Well, for what it's worth, I'm proud of you."

The stupid thick silence grows between us again.

"I spoke to Damon today," Matt eventually says. "He thinks it'll be a good idea if you're there for my press conference announcing my contract with the Warriors."

"No problem. I said I'd do whatever you need. That was the original deal."

"Noah—"

"Matt, I can't do this. I can't talk on the phone and pretend everything is okay and pretend I don't miss you like crazy. I'll do the public appearance, and I won't have to fake having feelings for you, but I can't ... I can't torture myself and pretend we're friends because we're not. You know it and I know it."

There's a pause before he quietly says, "All you had to do was ask me to stay."

"All you had to do was not leave."

And there's the truth. If he'd decided to give up football because he didn't want that future, that's one thing, but asking me to *make* him give it up? There's a huge difference between the two, but he can't see that.

As someone who has changed their entire life plan for a guy, there's no way I'd let him do it for me, and I don't want to go through that heartache again.

Yet, here you are, an annoying voice reminds me.

"I should get back inside. Jet was super nervous, and he'll probably freak if he knows I left."

We both know it's a lie, but he doesn't call me on it.

"The press conference is in two weeks. Right before training camp kicks off."

"Text me where and when, and I'll be there."

"Thank you. And thanks for looking out for JJ."

My mouth is dry, and I can't bring myself to say I'd do anything for him. And his brother.

I have two weeks to come to terms with the fact I'll be seeing Matt again. Two weeks to learn something I've never had: self-restraint.

CHAPTER TWENTY-FIVE

MATT

My throat constricts from the tie trying to choke me. I can't stand still, I fidget like crazy, and then my palms start sweating.

Talon nudges me. "Dude, what is wrong with you? It's a press conference. You could do these in your sleep."

"*Dude.* First openly gay player. You try being in my shoes."

We're the only two players being interviewed today. Talon, because he's a megastar, and me ... well, because I'm me. And we're both the new guys.

Even though this will be my first press conference as the gay guy, that's not the reason I'm nervous. I'm dying to see Noah, and at the same time I'm dreading it.

I'll gladly sit through an entire day of media asking inappropriate questions, but facing Noah? I won't know whether to maul him or keep my distance.

The locker room of Milwaukee University smells like feet and ass but I'd rather be in here than out there. The first time I'm going to see Noah in weeks will be in a room full of cameras.

Talon grabs my arm this time. "Is something else wrong? Is it just the gay thing or—"

I shake my head. "Noah and I are having issues. I ..." I contemplate how much I should tell him, but I think I might be having one of those episodes. Like when the paparazzi cornered Noah and I at the cruise ship terminal. Noah called it a panic attack, but I reckon that's extreme. It's majorly freaking out. That's not an attack. "We haven't spoken since I moved to Chicago," I admit.

"But that was weeks ago."

"No shit, Sherlock."

"Did you break up?"

"No." The response flies out my mouth on reflex. "Yes? But he's coming here today to support me, so ..."

"No wonder you're a mess."

"All I have to do is get through this press conference and then I can beg him to move here or do long distance or ... I don't know."

"Yeah, the whole football thing kinda sucks for relationships. I had a girlfriend who couldn't even handle the college level."

"Not making this any better, Talon."

"Sorry," he says.

Coach Caldwell and the GM appear in the doorway. "Ready, boys?" Coach asks.

Hell to the no. "Let's do this."

"Want me to hold your hand?" Talon mocks.

"Fuck no," I say quiet enough so only he can hear.

"Right. Don't want the boyfriend thinking you've been messin' around on him."

"Don't want the media to get ideas."

"That too," Talon says.

The coach and the GM lead us through the halls of MU and arrive at the auditorium where a makeshift press room's been set up. We take our seats at a long table with a microphone and glass of water in front of each spot. The auditorium's first few rows are filled with reporters, and cameras and lights are directed at the stage.

Vomit threatens to rise in the back of my throat with how many people there are for this, but then I see *him*. Very back row away from all the press. His lips turn up into a cocky smile, but his eyes are lifeless compared to the shining blue-green eyes I'm used to.

The media circus disappears, their words drowned out by the fact I can't take my gaze off Noah. Damn, I've missed him. It's only been a few weeks, but they've been the longest of my life. I want nothing more than to run up there and tackle him to the ground.

Then I remember our goodbye, and my heart breaks all over again. Yet, I still can't bring myself to look away.

I'm only able to drag my eyes front and center when they ask Coach the chances of me making it onto the roster this season.

"There's no doubt in my mind he'll dominate in training and come out on top. Unless he's injured"—he taps the desk twice to touch wood—"you can guarantee Matt Jackson will be on the Warriors' lineup come game one."

Yeah, he says that, but he can't know for sure. I can't go in there thinking I have this in the bag. It'll be all the more devastating when I get cut.

My eyes find Noah again, and I realize being cut wouldn't be the end of the world. It might be the start of mine.

A reporter to the right stands. "Matt, sources say you were offered a contract with the New York Cougars that was worth almost nine times the amount for Chicago. What made you choose the Warriors?"

My heart sinks into my gut, and I freeze up. My brain goes blank because all I can think about is what Noah's face must look like right now. And as much as I wish I could restrain myself, I spare a glance in his direction. Yup, shock, anger, and hurt are present on his cleanly shaved face. *How do I get out of this one?*

"It, uh, wasn't quite that much," I say into the mic, and my voice croaks as if I'm lying. Which I am. It was more than that but totally not worth the cost of losing Noah.

Then I realize I lost him anyway. Noah's dad won. And I bet my left nut he was the one who leaked that tidbit to the press. Insurance—I guess. A way to put a wedge in between us.

I stare down the reporter and try not to grit my teeth as I speak. "The Warriors have a great team this year, and I have no doubt that with Jimmy Caldwell coaching, we're going to make it to The Bowl. I want that championship ring more than I want money."

I'm either going crazy and can hear Noah's voice or he actually says out loud *You want that ring more than you want me.* But when I look in his direction, I know it was my imagination, because he's gone, and I can't even chase after him.

Coach takes over for me, talking offensive strategy and how a guy like me is important to the team, but I don't stop watching the back of the auditorium where Noah slipped out.

A throat clears off to the side, and my eyes go to Damon who also flew in to be here for this. He discreetly points to the exit, silently asking if I want him to go after Noah, and I nod.

I'm going to be stuck here awhile if their next line of questioning is anything to go by. When they ask the GM how he feels about being the first team with a gay player, I want to stab my ears with a butter knife. I knew it was coming, but if I hear that question, or any variation of it, one more time, I might come close to asking all the reporters who they go home to at night and how it affects their jobs.

Damon sneaks back in during the middle of the GM's speech about team inclusivity and the zero-tolerance policy that means nothing in a locker room. The subtle shake of Damon's head lets me know everything I need to. Noah's probably back on his Gulfstream right now, waiting to head back to New York.

Talon sees and reaches over to clasp my shoulder in support. The press will think it's a move for team solidarity, but it's because he knows my heart just walked out the door and isn't coming back.

After being let out of the longest press conference in history and the media files out, I go straight to Damon with Talon on my heels.

"No idea where he went?" I ask.

Damon shakes his head. "He was gone by the time I went out to find him. You didn't tell him, did you?"

"Of course, I didn't tell him," I snap. Damon's eyes dart around the small space to make sure everyone has left. "Sorry," I say a little calmer, "but what good would it have done?"

"Well, you'd still be together, for one," Damon says.

"What's he talking about?" Talon asks.

I stare between him and Damon and then look at the

ground. "Noah's dad bribed me with the New York contract. If I took it, I had to break up with Noah."

"But you broke up anyway," Talon points out.

"Because he didn't ask me to stay."

Talon's mouth turns into an O. "Oh."

"I have to find him and explain why I didn't take New York." I go to leave, when Talon pulls me back.

"We have a team meeting."

"Fuck!"

"You go to your meeting," Damon says. "I'll find Noah."

"And if he's already on his way back to New York?"

"Then he's an idiot," Damon mutters. "Leave it with me."

I take out a keycard to Talon's and my hotel room. "Room twenty-five oh seven. If you find him, give him this, and get him to wait for me to explain before he runs off on me." I turn to Talon. "Let's get this shit show over with."

It's our first team meeting with the entire ninety-man roster and coaching staff to kick off training camp. I doubt they'll take roll call, and I guarantee some of the veteran players won't turn up, but they'll definitely notice if I'm not there. After all, I half-think this could be a test. Let's see how the team handles the gay guy on day one.

The bar meetup a few weeks ago has nothing on what I'm about to walk into.

We head across campus to the college stadium. With the Damon holdup after the press conference, Talon and I are the last ones to arrive, and all eyes land on us—the two morons in suits. The rest of the team wears their workout gear while they sweat under the afternoon sun. Guess training started without us.

By some coincidence, or perhaps my phobe radar alerts me,

I catch Carter's scowl first up and have an involuntary stare off. It's broken by Miller and Jenkins calling us over to them.

"Nice tie," Jenkins says and shoves Talon playfully.

"Hey, careful with the merchandise. Jackson and I are precious."

"Precious is one word for it," Miller mumbles.

Talon gets Miller in a headlock. "What was that? Didn't hear you."

Coach Caldwell stands in front of us all. "Cut the shit, Talon. Everyone, take a seat."

It never escapes me that being a football player is a lot like being a kindergartener. We all sit on the turf, while the coaches stand before us like they own us. Nothing reinforces this more than when Coach starts going over the rules.

My face heats, and I know I'm going red, because it feels like it's all about me. Conceited, maybe, but when management tells us to come to them if they have any issues with other players, it's not hard to guess they're preparing for the worst.

As hard as I try to listen to Coach, my mind keeps drifting to where Noah could've gone and if it's too late to fix this. If he's gone back to New York, there's nothing I can do. I'm stuck here for the next month.

When the team meeting lets out, I'm hopeful Damon's found him, but there's a text on my phone from Damon saying he's handling it and to go to the hotel and rest up. I don't know if it's my agent or my friend telling me to do that, but I read it in a serious tone, because there isn't any question about it. It's an order.

CHAPTER TWENTY-SIX

DAMON: *WHERE ARE YOU? AND IF YOU SAY NEW YORK, I'M GOING TO KICK YOUR ASS.*

Guess it's time to face the music. The music being Damon chewing me out for leaving Matt in the middle of a press conference, but can he blame me?

With a few drinks under my belt, I decide to return the calls and messages Damon's sent in the last few hours. As soon as I got out of that auditorium, I was lost. Both physically and mentally. I walked aimlessly around campus and around Milwaukee. No surprises here: there is nothing to do in Milwaukee. So that's how I landed my ass on a barstool at six p.m. That was two hours ago. I haven't moved since.

NOAH: *DON'T GET YOUR BALLS IN A TWIST. I'M AT A BAR. GOOGLE GAY BARS IN MILWAUKEE, AND I'M AT THE FIRST RESULT. CAN'T REMEMBER THE NAME NOW. SOMETHING ABOUT ASSES.*

It takes a few minutes for his message to come through.

DAMON: *ARE YOU SERIOUSLY AT A BAR CALLED NUTS AND BUTTS?*

I snort.

NOAH: *YEAH, THAT SOUNDS ABOUT RIGHT. THOUGHT IT WAS FUNNY.*

DAMON: *DON'T MOVE. I'M ON MY WAY.*

NOAH: *YAY!*

DAMON: *EVEN IN TEXT, I KNOW YOU'RE BEING SARCASTIC.*

NOAH: *ME? NEVER.*

I'm in that glorious level of drunkenness where I still have all my motor functions but I don't give a shit about anything, which means I'm ready to face Damon. He needs to give me some fucking answers. He knew about the New York contract, and I want to know what the hell is going on.

Matt had the chance to stay in New York, yet he still chose Chicago. It doesn't make sense. I don't care if Chicago is a better team than New York. The fact of the matter is, he had a chance to stay with me and have football, and instead, he chose his career—and a pay cut—over the possibility of us. It also means his bullshit plea to ask him to stay was an empty gesture. He knew I wouldn't do it, and he was going to leave no matter what.

It's all *bullshit.*

Nathaniel chose money.

Matt chose football.

When is someone going to choose *me?*

My eyes catch on a tall blond guy making his way toward me. His burning blue gaze travels over my arms and chest and then back up to my face as he cracks a smile.

Oh yeah, he'd choose me. At least for a night.

He leans on the bar next to me. "I'm Lennon."

Wow. He isn't even trying with the fake name.

I give him a quick nod. "McCartney."

His smile becomes tight. "Yeah, never heard that one before."

"Huh?"

He pulls out his wallet and shows me his ID. "My name really is Lennon."

I stare at the ID and wonder if it's fake. That's taking anonymous hookups to an extreme though. "Did your parents hate you?"

He laughs, and it's deep and rumbly. "I still give them hell for it. When they complain I haven't visited in a while, all I have to say is 'You called me Lennon.'"

"Sorry. I thought ... well, you know. Bar like this ..."

I have to admit Lennon's smile is sexy as hell. "You thought it was a fake name for a hookup? Come on, who would choose the name Lennon voluntarily? You know, apart from my parents who had absolutely no regard for how many Beatles jokes I'd get in my lifetime."

"I'm Noah." I hold my hand out for him to shake.

He holds onto it a tiny bit too long. "Wait. You gave a fake name back. That mean you want to get out of here?"

If a guy like him asked me a couple of months ago, I would've already had my tongue down his throat. And while the temptation for a revenge fuck is there, and my cock is interested, I can't do it. No way. Not because I'm still contractually needed to be Matt's boyfriend, but because I know Lennon wouldn't compare.

I may be in love with a guy who doesn't love me back, but I'm not going to get over it by getting under other guys. That would work if I was moving on from anyone else, but not Matt.

I've never, not even with Nathaniel, been so gone over a person. Since he left, everything is dull, and I didn't realize missing someone made the rest of your life suck. I've been lagging behind on the business plan for *Rainbow Beds* because I just don't care anymore. I still want it to happen, but without the person you're supposed to spend your life with, everything becomes meaningless. No matter how many homeless teens my program will take off the streets, it will never make me complete. Matt makes me a whole person. I'm not the spoiled rich guy, and I'm not the ignorant, entitled politician's son. I'm me. The real me.

Lennon's still expectantly waiting, and I finally find my words.

"Thanks, but, uh, I shouldn't. I have a boyfriend."

Lennon sits on the stool next to me. "Is he the reason you're here at eight p.m. on a Tuesday night?"

Yes. He is. Because it turns out when the love of your life doesn't love you back, it hurts like a sucker punch to the nuts. Maybe that's why this place is called Nuts and Butts.

"What's *your* reason?" I deflect.

"Wanna get laid. Is there any better reason than that?"

I chuckle. "Guess not."

"This place is dead, which means I have time if you wanna talk about it."

"I'm sure you have better things to do than listen to me whine about how my boyfriend chose his career over me."

Lennon's mouth hangs agape for a beat too long. "That deserves a drink." He motions for the bartender to give us another round, and that's how I end up drinking with a Beatle.

Lennon puts in extra effort to cheer me up and is a great distraction when he tells me about all the times his name has given him issues, and I know his misery shouldn't be funny, but with the self-deprecating way he tells it, there's no option but to laugh.

A strong hand lands on my shoulder. "What are you doing?" Damon barks.

"Talking to Ringo Starr. Seriously, the guy's name is hilarious."

"Making me love my name even more, Noah," Lennon says.

"Did you forget your name is This Ass Belongs to Someone Else?" Damon asks.

"Hmm, that doesn't sound quite right," I say.

"Is this the boyfriend?" There's something suspicious or surprising in Lennon's tone that I can't work out.

"Oh, good," Damon says. "You haven't totally forgotten about the guy who offered you the world and you rejected it. You can't be pissed about that."

I stand so fast, my barstool skids across the floor. "Well, ain't that some more bullshit right there." Ain't? I'm talking like Matt now? I shake it off. "*I* rejected *him*? He's the one who was offered a contract in New York and didn't tell me. He's the one who moved to Chicago when he could've stayed. *He's* the one who chose football over me."

"If you believe that, then clearly you're not as smart as you think you are. Why do you think he wouldn't take a contract worth ten times more money than his contract in Chicago? Forget for a second it was in New York. Say Seattle offered him the same contract, what would make him say no to a shit ton of more money?"

"He said he wanted the ring. That's more important to him than anything. Including me."

"The Warriors haven't won a Super Bowl in decades. Yeah,

they have a chance this year, but New York has just as much a shot. He was willing to give it all up. *For you.* You said no, so he took the Chicago contract."

"He wanted me to ask him to stay. That's different to giving it all up for me. That's me forcing him to give it up. He wanted the decision taken out of his hands so that when he regretted leaving football, he could blame me for his misery."

Damon takes a few steps back, and his scrutinizing stare burns into me. "You truly believe that, don't you?"

"Well, what am I supposed to believe? Enlighten me because I'm obviously missing something."

"He's an idiot for not telling you in the first place, but it's also not my thing to tell. He asked me to keep quiet, and if he wasn't my client, I wouldn't listen, but I'm going to keep my word. He rejected millions of dollars. *For you.*"

"*Why?*"

Damon's lips form into a thin line. "Does the name Rick Douglas mean anything to you?"

"No idea who that is," I say.

"He's the owner of the New York Cougars," Lennon says behind me.

We both spin to face him. "How do you know that?" I ask.

Damon narrows his eyes. "You were at the press conference."

Shit. Fucking shit. I've messed up big time. "You're a journo?"

Lennon at least has the decency to look guilty when he nods.

I charge toward him, but Damon pulls me back as Lennon throws up his arms in surrender. I try to think if I've said anything that could be misconstrued or taken out of context, but all I can remember talking about so far is his stupid name. Shit, and the fact my boyfriend doesn't love me. "You followed me here for a story?"

"No, I didn't follow you. Me being here was a coincidence, but I saw you, wasn't one hundred percent sure it was *you*, but maybe, I thought I might've been able to get a story if I got you drunk enough."

I lunge for him again, but Damon still holds me.

Lennon seems unfazed at my advance. "Then I realized your story's the same as every other football wife out there. Trust me, you don't have anything anyone wants to read. No one cares about the hardships of missing family while being paid millions. First world problems and all that."

"Did you just call me a football wife?" I ask.

"You know what I mean. You're the only gay couple—"

"*Out same-sex* couple," Damon corrects like it makes a difference. "Let's go, Noah, before you say anything else he'll use to make your life harder than it already is."

"So because I'm a reporter, I'm automatically the enemy?" Lennon asks. "Bitter much, Damon King, an almost-MLB player from years ago, who got stung by a shoulder injury?"

Damon pales.

Lennon stands. "Look, I'll make a deal. I'll pretend I didn't hear Rick Douglas's name or look into why Matt Jackson turned down a giant contract with the Cougars. I work for *Sporting Health Magazine*. We're not a tabloid. We want real stories. And all it'll take is an exclusive interview with a gay ex-athlete turned sports agent, and I won't mention anything other than what was given to us at the press conference today. You disappeared from the sports world, and now suddenly you're back as a hotshot agent representing the most controversial client in the sport, and you came out of nowhere. And now you've signed an up-and-coming hockey player. I want your story."

Damon sighs. "Deal."

"You don't have to do this," I say quietly, hoping Lennon doesn't hear. There's a reason Damon never did the interview thing after his injury. He was a mess for a year afterward, and it's still a touchy subject.

Damon turns to me. "Go to the team's hotel. Matt's in room twenty-five oh seven." He takes out a hotel keycard and hands it over. *"Talk to him.* I'll keep this guy at bay."

I hesitate, because what if what Matt has to say is something I don't want to hear? Of course, it's not what I want to hear. If it was, he would've told me before he moved to Chicago.

"Trust me," Damon says.

"You know, whenever anyone says that, it makes me trust them less."

Damon practically shoves me toward the door. "Go."

I get one block in the direction of Matt's hotel before I pause. The name Rick Douglas appears in my subconscious. While I continue to walk, I Google his name. I have to scroll past a whole heap of football shit to find what I'm looking for. Other than owning the Cougars, he's a businessman who owns a whole range of different corporations in different industries. A lot like ...

"Oh, fuck no." I don't have to search his companies to know he has to be involved with my father in some capacity.

My feet move faster, the anger in me growing. Where I've been dreading to hear what Matt has to say, now I have an urgency for it. It has me running through the hilly streets of Milwaukee trying to get to him. And almost dying in the process. Holy shit. Need air. Stat.

I make it to the hotel, only to be stopped by security. My chest heaves, because *screw running*, and I put my hands on my knees as I try to catch my breath.

"Hotel ... guest," I pant and pull out the room key Damon gave me. "In ... rush."

The guy steps aside, and I'm back to running again. From across the lobby, I can see the doors to the elevator shutting, and I push my legs harder. The dude in the elevator sees me coming and doesn't do anything to hold the doors open. Asshole.

It takes two years for the next one to arrive, and by the time I get to Matt's door, the adrenaline pumping through me is far from gone. I don't even bother with knocking and use the key.

All six foot three of him, with tight drawn muscles and that sexy as fuck ass, paces the small area between two queen beds, but he freezes when he sees me in the doorway. "Noah."

My heart stutters, and I'm stuck in a riptide that's determined to pull me toward Matt. The only noise to fill the room is the loud click of the door shutting behind me. All the anger, hate, and suspicion morph into lust, want, and need. If I didn't so desperately need to know what my father did, I'd jump Matt now and ask questions later.

"What did he do?" I ask.

Matt's brow scrunches. "Who? Damon?"

"My father," I say through gritted teeth.

Matt goes from confused to surprised as his eyebrows shoot up to his hairline. He turns his head and refuses to look at me. "Oh. Umm, that. Damon said he—"

I continue to struggle to breathe, and my chest rises and falls hard. "The only name Damon gave me was Rick Douglas. I connected the dots."

"It doesn't matter what your father did or didn't do. All you need to know is staying in New York wasn't an option. If it was, there would've been no contest. If you'd have asked me to stay, again, no contest." He tries to take steps toward me, but I step back until I hit the door.

"I need to know," I say.

"Why? All it's going to do is piss you off."

"You turned down millions of dollars for me."

Matt shrugs. "You're an idiot for thinking I even contemplated taking it. What I feel for you is worth so much more than that."

"Why didn't you tell me?" I whisper.

"In not so many words, I was told he could make your charity go away."

All I can do is blink at him. This guy ... he's it. He's *the* guy.

He'll fight for me. Defend me. Protect me. Choose me above all else—even football if I let him. Which I won't. But that's not the point. The point is, Matt is the person I didn't think would ever exist. The person who'd love me and all my bullshit. The person who could go head to head with my father and come out on my side.

"I didn't want you to lose the only thing you've been excited about in your life," he says when I don't say anything. "When you talk about *Rainbow Beds*, you're complete. You become animated and passionate, and I know you once told me you've never had that. I didn't want to tell you what he did when you weren't going to ask me to stay. I broke our deal by falling for you—"

"No. *We* broke our deal. I think I've been in love with you since the minute we landed in New York and you pointed out how spoiled I am. It was all very romantic."

"What, no love for the guy you met on the cruise?" Matt asks.

"The angry gym rat? Not so much."

"Hey, you realize I'm still that guy ..."

I shake my head. "You're so much more."

"Can I please kiss you now?"

"Fuck yes."

We meet halfway, our mouths coming together too eagerly for either of us to pull back in time. Teeth clash, and we break into simultaneous laughter.

"Ow." Matt holds his mouth.

"Oops."

"Am I bleeding?" He moves his hand and bares his teeth.

"You're all good." I step closer. "Perfect." This time when I move in, I go slow. My hand moves into his hair as my lips press softly against his.

Matt moans and grabs my ass with his big hands.

"I'm moving to Chicago."

Matt stiffens. "W-what?" His hands remain holding me against him, but he pulls his head back.

"I don't want to live without you, and you can't give up football for me. You *are* football. You were willing to give up everything, so I'm the one who should get over myself and actually do it."

Granted, the only other time I gave up everything for someone, it backfired and I was left in New Jersey getting a poli-sci degree from a sporting college. If I hadn't been so stubborn, I would've transferred to Harvard or Yale or any other Ivy League my dad would pay to get me into, but I finished my degree at Newport to spite him.

But Matt's different than Nathaniel, and I'm not the naïve eighteen-year-old I was back then.

"What am I leaving behind?" I ask. "I love New York, but—"

"Your charity."

"Pretty sure Chicago has homeless gay teens too. It's depressing I can take my charity anywhere, but it works in our favor."

"My contract is only for a year. If you set it up here, and then they cut me—"

"*Rainbow Beds* is nowhere near ready to be launched. We're still in the planning stages. And if it stays in New York, we can work something out. I can fly back and forth when you're on the road, and your season's only five months ... less if you don't make playoffs, but I have faith."

Matt pulls back. "You know how long football season is?"

"I looked it up." Yep, I'm totally gone for this guy. *I'm scheduling shit.*

"Okay, and what about your dad? He'll cut you off if you do this."

"I'm so horribly scared about that," I say dryly. "Let him leave his fortune to my cousins who don't believe I deserve a claim to the Huntington fortune anyway."

"You'd give up millions of dollars for me?"

"Would be more impressive if I wasn't worth more than my father, but sure, let's go with that."

Matt playfully shoves me, but I grab his arm and bring him against me. I don't want to ever stop touching him. Ever. Might make football practice hard, but I'm determined I can pull it off.

"If it makes you feel any better, if I had to choose between you and my money, you'd win. Always. You're the only person who's ever understood why I'm the way I am, and I'm in love with you, you dumbass."

The smile Matt gives me makes breaking down my walls and putting my heart on the line worth it.

He touches his forehead to mine. "I'm in love with you too, idiot."

"You speak to me with such affection."

"You started it," Matt mumbles.

And I finish it by gripping his shirt and dragging him backward toward the beds. I turn and push him down, but he quickly stands again. "That one's Talon's, and I don't think he'd appreciate us fucking in his bed."

"Is that what we're doing? Now we're in a serious relationship and shit, isn't the sex meant to stop?"

"If that's what you think a relationship is, I'm out. Right now."

I bring him close and breathe him in. "I really did create a monster when I took your virginity, didn't I?"

"First, you didn't take my virginity. And second, my coaches will be able to blame you for my lack of concentration because all I'll be able to think about on the field is your end zone."

"Mmm, speak football to me. Ooh, in your Southern accent."

Matt's lips latch onto my earlobe and then trail down my neck. "Instead, how 'bout I fuck you so hard you cain't remember your bank balance and the only thing fallin' from yer lips will be mah name?"

I groan. "I know this isn't the point, but I already don't know my bank balance. Unless a lot is an official currency."

"Get on the bed," he growls.

He doesn't have to tell me twice. I'm on my back faster than a virgin on a hooker. We shed our shirts, shoes, and socks, and Matt drops his pants and boxers, while I fumble with my stupid jeans.

Never go designer jeans. Stupid buttons instead of a zipper.

"Do you have supplies?" Matt asks.

That stops me short. "No. Don't you? You're the one who moved here."

"Not in Milwaukee. Who was I going to fuck at training camp?"

"Who was I going to fuck here when we were broken up?" I throw back. "You don't even have lube for jerking off? I was tested after Aron, and I haven't been with anyone—"

"Nrgh." Matt bites his knuckles. "There is nothing I want more than to go bareback with you, but I didn't bring lube. Again, training camp. Didn't think I'd have much downtime to jerk off."

"Hotel freebie lotion?" The whine in my voice is hard to hide.

"Eww, I ain't putting that cheap shit near my junk."

"Oh, sorry, Your Highness. I didn't realize you were a connoisseur of hand lotions."

Instead of throwing me a comeback, Matt reaches for my jeans and takes them off the rest of the way. "We have our mouths. And our hands. I'll fuck you when you move in." He climbs on the end of the bed, and his head dips, his mouth so close to my aching, swollen cock, but I grip his hair and pull his head back.

"You want me to move in with you?"

"Isn't that what you meant when you said you were moving to Chicago?"

"Uh ... no. I didn't think that far ahead, only that I want to be with you. But I want to live with you. Yes, I want to move in with you."

This time when his head moves toward my cock, I don't stop him. He swallows me down with that talented mouth of his, and as much as I love it, I want more.

"Matt." I pull him up, and his body slides over me. Precum and his saliva mix, and our cocks align, grinding against each other easily. When Matt rocks his hips, my eyes roll back in my head. "Goddamn it."

He continues to move over me, frotting against me while he whispers claiming words over my skin and my new favorite three words: *I love you.*

When we both become frantic, I grab his ass and ride out my pleasure. He pushes harder to the point the headboard bangs against the hotel wall, but I don't care if Matt's team-mates are on the other side. I'm so far past gone I need to come.

As I think I can't take anymore, Matt shudders above me, and it triggers my release.

Moans and hard breaths is all I hear when Matt buries his head in my shoulder, but then a voice that doesn't belong to either of us says, "Umm ..."

"Talon." Matt scrambles off me and covers me with the sheet while he wraps the comforter around his waist.

His teammate stares blankly at us, his mouth hanging open. "Umm ..."

I wonder if that's the only thing he can say.

Matt doesn't know what to say either.

When my gaze travels over Talon and lands on a very obvious bulge in his pants, I wonder how long he was watching us and why a straight guy would get turned on by that. I don't have time to overanalyze before Talon finally regains his composure.

"I'm glad you guys got your shit together, but uh, no visitors in the rooms."

Right. "That's my cue," I say and go to get up.

"Wait," Talon says. "I'll, uh, go down to the hotel bar for a drink while you ... uh, dress. And, umm, yeah ... drink. Bar."

If I was ever curious to know what two hundred pounds of awkward looked like, I'm staring at it as Talon tries to leave. He opens the door, but it gets stuck on his big foot. That doesn't stop him from trying to walk through the half-open door. He headbutts the edge and lets out a curse.

"Shit, are you all right?" Matt asks.

Talon waves him off and rushes out the door.

"I need to go talk to him," Matt says.

"Okay. Maybe I can get a room, and—"

"It's like school camp for me right now." Matt rummages for his clothes and starts dressing. "Even if I were to sneak out of my room, this hotel is fully booked with the team. I won't be able to leave without someone knowing."

I climb out of bed. "Guess I'm keeping my scheduled flight home then."

Matt deflates. "This sucks. I don't want you to go, but—"

"I understand. This is your job, and I'm not supposed to be here. I'll go home to New York and pack and—"

"Crap. What about JJ?"

"He can stay at the house however long he needs it. Look after it for me while I'm gone."

"What if you set up your charity here and then the Warriors dump me? Maybe we should sit down and think—"

I step forward. "Babe. I'm going where you go. I don't care

how we make it work or what we have to do to make it happen. It's happening. Got it?"

Matt nods. "Got it."

"Now, go talk to your freaked-out roommate, and I'll see you in a few weeks. In *our* apartment."

"Our apartment."

CHAPTER TWENTY-SEVEN

MATT

How the hell do I play this? Casual. Calm. Apologetic? Maybe I should've got Noah to apologize. He made me launch myself at him and totally forget about the fact I have a roommate that could've come back at any moment.

I stare at Talon sitting at the hotel bar a little longer than I probably should, but he doesn't appear freaked out. He's not chugging drinks, he doesn't look pale or sickened by what he saw. He sits there sipping his scotch or bourbon—whatever the dark liquid is—with a concentration line across his forehead.

Taking a deep breath, I approach and pull the stool up next to him. "So, uh ... that happened." *Great opener, Matt.*

Talon snorts.

"I just want to say I'm sorry. I wasn't thinking. Noah agreed to move to Chicago, and I kind of jumped him. I shouldn't have done that, and I'm sorry for putting you in this weird position, and it won't happen again, and—"

"Whoa, Jackson. It's okay. Wait, do you think I'm pissed you were hooking up in our room? You think I haven't seen that type of shit before on the road?"

True. I've been kicked out of shared hotel rooms over the years, but this is different. "Not with two guys, no."

He shakes his head. "I don't care you're with a guy. I thought we already established that? I think I fucked up. I wasn't expecting it, and instead of doing what I normally do, which is back away as quietly as I can and disappear for an hour or so, I froze ... and now I feel like a creep. For, like, watching and stuff."

My eyes widen.

"Not for ages or anything. I was taken off guard and I couldn't move, and then it was all over, and I had to say something or you would've thought I'd been there the whole time, but I wasn't, and ... Oh my God, I'm digging a hole here."

I laugh. "Can we totally forget this ever happened? You're not a creep. I'll never sneak Noah into a hotel room again, and if you ask for a new roommate, I will totally understand."

"Not going to ask for a new roommate, dickhead."

"Good talk. I'm going to bed ... to, uh, sleep. Noah's gone home."

"Thanks for the heads-up. I mean, probably could've done with a heads-up about an hour ago—"

"Never discussing it again, remember?"

"Right. I'll be up soon. Just gonna finish my drink."

"Don't drink too much. Coach will kill you and make tomorrow hell for all of us."

"It's training camp. It's going to be hell no matter what."

"Especially for me," I murmur.

Talon throws back the rest of his drink and stands. "You're

not worried about getting cut, are you? We're untouchables. Coach said so at the press conference."

"And what if we're all fooling ourselves, and we get out there tomorrow, and they're all gunning for me to fail?"

"Because you like dudes? You have no faith in the world, do you?"

"Well, when your own family disowns you for it, you have no expectations when it comes to people you've never met."

He grabs my shoulder. "Go out there and do your best. You'll prove you belong on this team."

"I'm ready to make football my bitch."

Flat on my back, staring up at the clear sky, I wonder what it is about football that I love, because right now I can't think of a single reason.

Talon's laugh hits my ears before his face appears above me. "Is that making football your bitch?"

I groan as he helps me to my feet. After two weeks, I'm sore all over from being tackled over and over and over again, but I'm killing it. I know I am. I may feel like shit, but if the praise from my coaches is anything to go by, I'm impressing the hell outta them, and that's all I care about.

The only thing bringing down my training—other than exhaustion—is the strain between me and some of the guys. Surprisingly, most of the animosity is on the field. In the locker room, I'm left alone. It's promising, but I'm not getting my hopes up that it's going to last.

The days drag, and I miss Noah like crazy, but now I'm not on the ground, and the pain from my last hit is dimming, I know

I'm in the right place. Even sore and exhausted, I can't stay mad at the game for long.

We've been running scrimmages all day, but when Talon says we're running the same play that just failed and ended with me getting tackled *without* the ball in my hand, Carter doesn't settle for his usual scowl that I'm slowly getting used to. His protest now comes in the form of muttered words so quiet I don't know what he says.

I'm fully prepared to let it go, like I have every other little snip someone's had in passing, but Talon takes his helmet off and charges Carter, bumping pads and getting in his face.

"Wanna say that louder so the whole class can hear?" Talon says.

"Talon, drop it." I try to pull him back.

"Nah, if he's got a problem, we need to sort it. Speak up or forever shut your face."

The offensive coach runs in from the sidelines, and Coach Caldwell is hot on his heels. Fuck a duck. "Problem?" Coach asks.

Carter looks between Talon and me and then to the coaches. "Not at all."

"Then let's run this fucking play and get it done," Talon says.

Talon off the field is a playful, cheery guy who's a great friend. Quarterback Talon is this commanding presence who's all bossy and arrogant. It's kinda hot.

We get into the line of scrimmage, and I face off with Henderson, one of the team captains.

"Lovers' quarrel?" he taunts but then he falters. "Shit. Probably shouldn't use that line with you or I'll get in trouble."

This is what's going to end up driving me and the rest of the team crazy. They're walking on eggshells, thinking they can't joke about anything they normally would with any of the other guys. Coaches in the past have called the whole team "ladies" as a form of put-down. Now with all the PC shit, they're all going to be afraid to say anything at all. No, they shouldn't say it, but I don't want to be treated differently either.

"Say whatever you want to me, Henderson. You'll be doing it while I run circles around you."

He laughs, and the tactic works, because after the snap, I pivot and run past him. Unlike the last play, where I was tackled before I even got to the ball, I hit my mark only to be beaten out by Carter stealing my fucking pass.

Oh, hell no.

Next thing I know, I've got my hands on his jersey, and we butt helmets. "What. The. Fuck."

Carter pushes me off him. "Didn't think you'd get there in time. Some of us are here because we don't need a *gimmick* to get us a pass."

An eerie silence falls on the field. And then? I burst into laughter. I laugh so hard I can barely breathe. "Are you serious right now? You think I got my place on this team *because* I'm gay? Like I'm using that to my advantage?" I laugh some more, and by now the coaches and the rest of the team surround us.

We really are like school kids.

"Jackson, are you okay?" Coach Caldwell asks.

"Peachy. My teammates think I'm waving the rainbow flag to get special treatment and don't believe I deserve to be here, but sure, I'm fantastic. Let's see, I was outed against my will, shoved in front of the press who liked to ask personal questions about my sex life, and then I had to take a pay cut because of the stupid salary cap and no one else wanting me. Yeah, I totally did this all on purpose, Carter. Maybe I'll accuse you of only getting your wide receiver position because you're black. How would *that* go over?"

"What the fuck you just say?" Carter tries to get to me, but Miller pulls him back.

"I'm just pointing out your logic is flawed."

"You don't have to explain yourself," Coach says, "but you do, Carter. You were explicitly told—"

"No," I cut in. "This is his problem. This is everyone's problem. I have upper management fighting my battles for me." I turn to Carter. "You want to apologize now or go head to head with me? Suicides. Full gear. Keep going until one of us drops. I kick your ass, you drop the attitude and acknowledge that using my sexuality to get ahead is the most ridiculous plan anyone could ever think of, because it wouldn't work. It works against me in *everything*. Even having to prove it to you right now. You beat me, you can take all the passes you want from me."

"Dude, so not a bet you want to make," Miller says.

"He can take him." Talon says. "Fifty bucks on Jackson."

I look at the coaches, and the glimmer in their eyes lets me know they're on board even though their scowls say they shouldn't be.

"Gonna eat your words?" I ask Carter.

He lifts his chin in challenge. "You're on."

It takes less than a few minutes of suicides for me to realize what I've gotten myself into. Adrenaline is replaced with pain as my limbs ache, my chest heaves, and I'm ready to vomit, but there is no way I'm giving up. I will die before I let Carter beat me.

We're on display for the entire team, plus the coaches, but

that's a good thing. I should only have to do this once to shut them all up about deserving my spot with the Warriors.

The fact I have to do this at all is the reason why no one comes out in this sport. Maybe I shouldn't have given in and should have squashed the need to prove myself, but if this gets the assholes off my back, then I'm willing to do it.

I push distractions aside and focus on the end goal, which I can't quite remember what that is when my muscles burn with lactic acid. Still, I don't give up.

I won't. Ever.

It takes a hell of a lot longer than I expect and so many rounds of suicides I lose count of how many we're up to when Carter finally trips over his feet and falls.

"Thank fuck," I mutter and drop to my knees.

Water comes at me from somewhere, I don't know where, but I don't hesitate. I rip my helmet off and guzzle it down.

"Pissing contest over then?" Coach Caldwell asks.

"Over," I say breathlessly and refuse to look at Carter.

"So, this is done?" Coach asks.

Carter's voice comes out as a rasp, but his finality is clear. "Done."

"You two are dismissed for the rest of the day. Make sure you warm down properly, or you'll be useless to us tomorrow." Coach turns to the rest of the team. "Break over! Get back to it."

One challenge down, and I really hope there isn't more to come.

CHAPTER TWENTY-EIGHT

NOAH

The moment Matt told me he loved me, I knew I would never experience that type of high ever again, but this one is a close second.

"You're not moving to Chicago," Dad says from behind his massive desk.

"Uh, yeah, pretty sure I am." I can't stop smiling, and I think that pisses him off even more. Or maybe it's my feet resting on the precious mahogany desk that has him pissed. Either way, I don't care.

"You need to make public appearances with your mother and me, and your charity is an affiliate of this campaign. You can't be across the country."

I stand. "Oh, forgot to tell you. Spoke to the family's finance guy. He's willing to release a huge chunk of my trust so the charity is *all* mine. No longer affiliated, no longer your puppet, and no longer my father."

Dad stands too and leans over his desk. "Noah, you can't do this."

"You should've thought of that before you tried to pay off yet another one of my boyfriends. Backfired this time, didn't it? And the thing that gets me the most is you still don't see anything wrong with what you did. You, of all people—someone who married someone outside his race and class against his father's wishes—should know what you're doing won't work. I was willing to put the Nathaniel thing in a folder labeled *it should never have happened*, but then you go and do it again?"

"I thought Matt would've taken the deal. Just like I knew Nathaniel would. He didn't love you, and I was doing what was best for you."

I laugh. "Like that makes it any better? It's always either the campaign or money. It has nothing to do with me."

"That's not true."

"I want to believe you, I really do, but when Matt didn't accept your deal, you threatened to take my charity away so he'd keep his mouth shut. We broke up, thanks to you. You're done trying to dictate my life, Father. If you want me to keep playing the doting son for the press and make public appearances, you will leave me and Matt the fuck alone."

He stares at me as if I'm backing him into a corner, but he still doesn't realize he did this himself.

"I'm done here." I turn to leave but he stops me.

"Leave the charity linked to the campaign. I don't want to lose you from my life, Noah. And not because of the election. Because you're my son. Despite what you believe, I did it for you. Not me."

"Will you let Matt and I live whatever kind of life we want?" I'm probably pushing my luck, but I'm on a roll.

"As long as you're not making press headlines, I'll even invite you two home to family dinners when you're available."

"Can't wait."

It's the best outcome I could ask for, even though I'd love nothing more than to not have to deal with the man ever again. If Matt can still support his parents, I can placate my father.

Look at me being the bigger man.

I blame Matt for it. The adorably nice bastard.

My phone vibrates in my pocket. "We done now?" I ask Dad. "My boyfriend is calling me."

"Hope the move to Chicago is smooth." Dad's glare doesn't match his pleasant words.

I purposefully answer my phone loudly before stepping out of the office. "Hey, babe."

"I'm dying." His voice comes with a grunt of pain.

I laugh. He said training was grueling, and I'd never heard him complain about working out before, so it must be bad. "Dying is inconvenient for me. I'm all packed and ready to move. Told my father and everything." I continue through the reception area of Dad's offices and out onto the street, feeling lighter than I have in years when it comes to that man.

"How did that go?"

"As well as I expected it to. Why are you dying?"

"I might've pulled the macho card yesterday and challenged one of my teammates. Good news is I kicked his ass. Bad news is suicide sprints are called suicides for a reason. I'm sore all over and you're not here to massage me better."

"I will be soon. By the time you head back to Chicago, I'll be all settled in. Then I'll massage whatever you want."

He swears under his breath.

"What?"

"Now I'm turned on and I can't even lift my hand to jerk off. I'm lucky to be able to hold my phone."

"It's not right how hard they push you guys."

Even Matt's laugh is strained. "This is my own fault. But the good thing is, I think I earned my place. So now if anyone questions me, it'll purely be about something I can't change."

"No one's brought up the F word yet?"

"No. Unless we're talking about the word fuck. That comes out of someone's mouth every two seconds."

"As expected. I can't wait until you're home."

Matt sighs. "Me too. I still can't believe you're moving for me."

"I'll do anything for you. Always."

"Ditto."

The line goes quiet, and for a second, I think the call has dropped out, but then I realize this is my normal reaction to hearing any form of admission from Matt. Like part of me still doesn't believe it's happening or I heard wrong. It's hard to believe that someone like Matt could fall for someone like me, a guy who's only cared about himself for a really long time. Matt makes me a better man—someone I never thought I could be.

"What are your plans for your last night in New York?" he asks.

I clear my throat. "I'm, umm, actually going out with Aron. Well, Damon and Maddox and my other friends will be there too, but I need to apologize to Aron again. I handled that situation all wrong."

"You've already apologized countless times."

"Yeah, but they were all bullshit. I felt bad about it, but I didn't understand how much he hurt until you left me. I was an asshole to him and shutting him out cold was an even bigger asshole thing to do."

"Do what you gotta do."

"You too. Try not to challenge anyone else to a duel like some old-time cowboy." Mmm, Matt in a cowboy hat. We may have to explore that. I must make some sort of noise in the back of my throat, because Matt laughs.

"You're picturing me in a cowboy hat, aren't you?"

"Able to read my mind? We're that couple already?"

"Do you care if we are?"

I grin. "Not at all."

"I gotta go—another day of torture ahead of me—but I'll see you in a few weeks."

"I'll be waiting naked for you."

"Our new apartment doesn't have curtains."

"There's one way to introduce myself to the neighbors."

"You would too."

"Jackson," a voice barks in the background. "Just because you were all ass-kicking motherfucker yesterday, doesn't mean you can slack off today."

"I'm up, I'm up. I'll be down in five. Gotta go, babe. Love you."

The phone disconnects, and my heart does that stuttering thing again and gets stuck on the words *babe* and *love you*.

Even though he's already gone, I can't stop myself from saying, "Love you too."

Matt's still inside me when I come out of my orgasmic trance and take in my surroundings. With carpet beneath my knees, cum all over my hand and stomach, Matt panting above me, and my own breath stilted, I come to the conclusion I attacked Matt as soon as he walked in the front door.

Not my original plan for his welcome back, but it works.

"That's one way to welcome me home," Matt says and slides out of me.

He said it.

We both collapse onto the floor, side by side. My knees have carpet burn, my ass kind of hurts from not enough prep, but I can't find any fucks to give. We were in too much of a hurry.

"I don't know how I'm going to survive when you're at away games," I say.

"Only about half of them will be away games. Will be nowhere near as bad as training camp. You're lucky I don't play hockey. Their schedule is nuts."

We continue to lie in the front entrance of the apartment, breathing heavy with a comfortable silence between us.

Matt's the first one to regain composure and sit up. "Whoa. You, like, furnished and decorated in here. We have curtains."

I laugh. "It's cute you think I could pull something like this off."

"Then who?"

I bite my lip. "Aron."

"Huh?"

"So, when we went out, I pulled him aside to apologize, but before I could get any words out, he *thanked* me."

"Thanked you? For being a dick?"

"I have magical asshole matchmaking powers. Do you remember Wyatt? Short, blond, angry dude?"

"No."

I shrug. "Anyway, they hooked up as kind of a rebound thing, and then they realized they were good together. Or something. I dunno. They're dating and apparently, it's serious. They both helped me move and get the apartment ready for you to come home."

"Only you could screw someone over and still hold enough charm to have that same person do you a favor."

"I'm awesome like that." I grin.

Matt leans over and kisses my sweaty forehead. "So awesome."

"Ignoring your sarcasm. How was the rest of camp?"

"Good. After the thing with Carter, he's left me alone and even says hi in passing. The first few games were rough, but preseason doesn't count for standings, and the team looks good. We were starting to gel in the end."

"You didn't get shit from the other teams?"

"A little, but not as bad as I thought. I wasn't sure what to expect, but I was planning for the worst. It's all just smack talk. It's like their loophole. They can't do anything to me, but they can try to psyche me out. But the good thing is, I can do it back to them. Like tell them they better hope I don't like it too much when they tackle me."

I laugh. "That's brilliant."

"Yeah, still didn't stop them from hitting hard. Thought it could've been an effective offensive strategy. Give the gay guy the football because no one will want to touch him. Turns out the power of football is bigger than homophobia. Who knew?"

"That's good at least."

"The real test will be when the actual season starts next week. Especially considering our first game is against the Bulldogs."

I wince. "Is that an away game or home? Either way, I'm gonna be there."

"Home game."

"I'm gonna be at all your home games."

"Do you even like football?"

"Umm ... I could learn to like it. And even if I don't know what's going on, I get to look at a group of men in those tights. I'll be fine."

Matt bursts out laughing. "Fuck, I love you."

"Of course, you do. I'm a lovable guy. It just took you forever to see it."

He kisses me long and hard until we're left panting and breathless when he pulls away.

"What's the plan now we have everything?" I ask.

"Super Bowl ring. New contract. Launch your charity ..." He grabs my left hand and rubs over my ring finger. "Maybe a different kinda ring eventually."

"Eventually? We should lock that down asap." Okay, wasn't supposed to propose like that, but that doesn't mean I don't want it.

Matt pulls back. "Seriously?"

"I know you're the one for me. If you can face off with my dad and still want to be with me, I never want to let you go."

"I want nothing more than to marry you, but it'd be a PR nightmare right now."

"Who says we have to tell anyone? We could go to a court-house or Vegas."

I can practically see the lightbulb go off above Matt's head. "We have a bye week in week nine."

Decision made, I stand and pull Matt up off the floor. I bypass the discarded clothes, the suitcase that's toppled on its side, and the fact the whole foyer looks like a crime scene and drag Matt over to the floor to ceiling windows of the apartment that overlook Chicago.

"I better do this right." I sink to one knee and stare up at my future. "Matt, not Matthew, Jackson. Will you marry me?"

"Only if we can tell people we were wearing clothes when you proposed."

I laugh. "I'll take it." I get to my feet and kiss my fiancé for the very first time.

It definitely won't be the last.

CHAPTER TWENTY-NINE

MATT

W e've lost. We've fucking lost. I don't know whether to sink to my knees and cry or just collapse to the ground and not get back up.

"Jackson," Talon barks at me in the huddle. "Head in the game. We're not done yet."

With less than a minute on the clock, and us at the twenty-yard line, it's not impossible to pull this off, but all the fight in us is gone.

One touchdown. That's all we need. So close yet still so fucking far away.

We're this close—*this* close—to winning the whole damn show, but we're running on steam.

The bright lights no longer light us up like gods but blind us and highlight our mistakes. Our fumbles. Our missed passes. We should've had this in the bag. We almost did.

Then we choked.

Not only did they catch up to our twenty-one-point lead, they've annihilated us and have run us ragged ever since. We've caught up, but I don't know if it's enough to get us over the line.

I don't want to give up, but my head decides to show its pessimistic side in the face of getting everything I've ever wanted for my whole life.

The grass no longer smells like fresh turf but of sweat and failure.

We've fought hard, but Denver has fought harder.

The screaming crowd no longer cheers our encouragement but fills our ears with taunts to pull our heads out of our asses.

"We get the ball to Carter," Talon says. "That's all we have to do and those championship rings are *ours*."

I want to yell it's what we've been trying for two plays already and it ain't workin', but I don't. I listen to my QB, yell "Break" along with everyone else, and take my position in the line of scrimmage. My knees protest, my back tenses, but I can't think about the pain.

Third down. One minute to go. I yell at myself that we're still in this, but the pressure breathing down my neck says we're gonna choke. And once you're in that mindset, it may as well be game over.

Talon yells "Hut" and I do what I know. That's all I can do at this point. I slam into Denver's linebacker and ignore the jolt down my side as we collide.

The amount of hits I've taken tonight is no more than I normally would, but each painful twinge, every sore muscle, it reminds me what's at stake and amplifies in feeling and intensity.

Carter's taken down. *Again.*

This is it. Last down. No more chances. We don't make this play, we truly have lost.

Same plan. Same play.

Only, a single voice yells at the team. "Blue Eighteen."

Play change where I get in the line of fire to receive the ball. Holy shit.

Then Talon's voice repeats the same thing, and I realize we're more than fucked, because it's up to me. What in the hell is Talon thinking?

I don't have time to freak out though.

"Set. Hut."

Years of training. A lifetime of wishing. My prison. My escape. My love for the game all comes down to this.

My legs push faster than they ever have before. My arms grow muscles I didn't know I have. I knock everyone in my path down, cross the end zone, and land that pass like my life depends on it.

And when I realize I've done it? The world fades away, and I really do sink to my knees and cry.

I don't have long enough for it to sink in completely when strong arms reach under me and lift me to my feet, and then I'm there, staring into the eyes of the most idiotic quarterback I've ever encountered.

"What the fuck is wrong with you?" I yell. Any other game, it would've just been another play. You don't do that in the dang Super Bowl. "Why did you do that?"

"Worked, didn't it?" He throws his arms around me, and then the rest of the team is there. Yelling, shouting, the deafening screams of the crowd ...

We did it? We actually freaking did it.

The field is a blur of activity. I'm attacked from all angles from each of my teammates, and even Carter takes me in a crushing hug.

"Good catch." He grins.

By the time we're ushered into the locker rooms to shower and change, the smiles can't be wiped from our faces, and our spirits couldn't be higher.

Miller hobbles into the locker room in his civilian clothes and Warriors jacket when we're almost ready to get out of here, and Talon freezes.

"You're here," Talon says, his voice croaky.

The very second game of the season, Miller fell hard and didn't get back up. Torn hamstring. Six months recovery. It took him out for the entire season, so he's been at home with his family in New York instead of in Chicago with us.

Miller's lips quirk. "What, you think I was gonna miss this?"

Talon's mouth remains agape.

"That's how you catch flies," I say and reach over to shut his mouth.

They share a weird bro hug that I can't be bothered to decipher. All I know is Talon's been lost without Miller, but right now, I have bigger things to worry about.

I grab the ring box out of my gear bag and take a deep breath.

It's over. The season is officially done, and Noah and I made a pact. We announce it to the world tonight that we're married. Have been since week nine of the season. Damon, Maddox, and JJ were the only witnesses to the nuptials, so they know, but no one else. Until now.

"Whoa, is that what I think it is?" Talon says over my shoulder, staring at the platinum band.

I laugh. "Probably not. It's not an engagement ring." I take the ring out and slip it on. "You might want to hurry up and finish putting your suit on. You don't want to miss my statement to the press."

I leave their stunned faces and head to the locker room door where I know press will be waiting outside to talk to us. Talon and Miller chase after me, although Miller struggles to keep up with his leg.

There'll be an official press conference later about the game, and they'll want me for that, but that won't be the place to do this.

As expected, the hallway is filled with cameras and reporters, and behind them, up the corridor a bit farther, is the man himself. The one I get to come home to every day for the rest of my life.

Microphones are shoved in my face and questions are shouted at me. The one that sticks out is "How does it feel having made the winning touchdown?"

I simply smile and stare at Noah while I say, "It was the second most fulfilling moment of my life." Knowing the follow-up question will be what the first was, I answer before they ask it. "Nothing will beat the day I married my husband, but this is pretty close."

Nothing else needs to be said, so I push my way through the throng of media where I greet my husband with a kiss that will go viral on the internet within minutes.

As I stand at the bar at the *Rainbow Beds* fundraiser in New York and go to take a sip of my scotch, my eye catches on my hand, and it pauses halfway to my mouth. I'm still not used to it

—the championship ring or the wedding band—but I can't get enough of either of them.

Maddox swats my hand away before I get to take a drink. "Yeah, yeah, we get it. You won the Super Bowl. Put the ring away already."

I raise my hand to run through my hair, purposefully showing it off more. "Don't know why you're complaining. You're getting ten percent of my new contract because of the ring."

Maddox smirks. "Thanks for buying us a house, by the way."

"You're welcome." The words sound sarcastic, but I actually mean it. I stare at my drink, trying to find the courage to say what I want to say—what I've wanted to say to Maddox for a long time. "I never thanked you for turning up on my doorstep and introducing me to Damon. You saved more than my career that night." I never told anyone about how dark I went after I was outed. I don't know how far I would've gone if Maddox hadn't given me hope.

He elbows me. "I never thanked you for making me realize I might not be entirely straight. Even if it did take another four years to acknowledge it."

"Call it even?"

Maddox throws his arms around me and holds me tight.

"Hands off my husband," Noah growls beside us, appearing out of nowhere. I wonder how much he heard.

"He was mine first," Maddox says, and I playfully push him off me. "Geez, I'm kidding. I have my own man around here somewhere."

My mother-in-law approaches us with her hands on her trim waist and a perfectly shaped eyebrow raised. "Noah, you

THANK YOU!

Thank you for reading *Trick Play*.

Book three, *Deke,* features a certain hockey player and a reporter with an unfortunate name.

Talon and Miller, who weren't supposed to exist past a few lines, have wormed their way into so many hearts. Their book, Blindsided, will be coming in March, 2019, but will not contain a fake boyfriend trope. Why? Because their book was never supposed to happen, and I'm not going to force a trope on them when clearly they suck at taking directions. *Sit there and look pretty, Talon. Don't say anything.*
Talon: But I'm awesome and cool, and I want a book. It's like a movie for your brain. Gimme.

For Jet fans, I'll let you in on a little secret. He was originally plotted to take the MC role in book three, but after starting it, I realized he's just way too young right now. So even though he's not a leading man yet, he'll get a book of his own when he's ready.

To read a bonus scene from Jet's perspective about the song he wrote for Matt and Noah, join my reader group on Facebook here:

https://www.facebook.com/groups/1901150070202571/.

If you'd like to stay up to date with these characters and find out what's going on with them, when the next book is releasing, or want to get in contact with me, the Facebook reader group is the best place to do so.

Alternatively, you can join my mailing list:
http://eepurl.com/bS1OFH

BOOKS BY EDEN FINLEY

FAKE BOYFRIEND SERIES
Fake Out (M/M)
Trick Play (M/M)
Deke (M/M)
Blindsided (M/M)

STEELE BROTHERS
Unwritten Law (M/M)
Unspoken Vow (M/M)

ROYAL OBLIGATION
Unprincely (M/M/F)

ONE NIGHT SERIES
One Night with Hemsworth (M/F)
One Night with Calvin (M/F)

One Night with Fate (M/F)
One Night with Rhodes (M/M)
One Night with Him (M/F)

ACKNOWLEDGMENTS

I want to thank all of my betas: Leslie Copeland, Jill Wexler, Crystal Lacy, May Archer, Grace Kilian Delaney, and Kimberly Readnour.

Deb Nemeth for the wonderful editing and helping me make Matt more Southern and giving Noah more depth.

Thanks to Kelly from Xterraweb editing—you are always the best, even under pressure for this one!

To Lori Parks for one last read through.

And Kellie from Book Cover by Design. You are always a rockstar.

Lastly, a big thanks to Linda from Foreword PR & Marketing for helping get this book out.

Made in the USA
Monee, IL
11 August 2020